LOUIS DE BERNIÈRES

Louis de Bernières is the bestselling author of *Captain Corelli's Mandolin*, which won the Commonwealth Writers' Prize Best Book in 1995. His most recent books are *So Much Life Left Over*, *The Dust that Falls from Dreams* and *The Autumn of the Ace*, the short-story collection *Labels*, the children's book *Station Jim* and the poetry collection *The Cat in the Treble Clef*.

ALSO BY LOUIS DE BERNIÈRES

FICTION

NON-FICTION

POETRY

LOUIS DE BERNIÈRES

Light Over
Liskeard

VINTAGE

3 5 7 9 10 8 6 4

Vintage is part of the Penguin Random House group of companies whose addresses can be found at global.penguinrandomhouse.com

Penguin
Random House
UK

First published in Vintage in 2024
First published in hardback by Harvill Secker in 2023

Copyright © Louis de Bernières 2023

Louis de Bernières has asserted his right to be identified as the author of this Work in accordance with the Copyright, Designs and Patents Act 1988

penguin.co.uk/vintage

Printed and bound in Great Britain by Clays Ltd, Elcograf S.p.A.

The authorised representative in the EEA is Penguin Random House Ireland, Morrison Chambers, 32 Nassau Street, Dublin D02 YH68

A CIP catalogue record for this book is available from the British Library

ISBN 9781529920611

Penguin Random House is committed to a sustainable future for our business, our readers and our planet. This book is made from Forest Stewardship Council® certified paper.

MIX
Paper | Supporting
responsible forestry
FSC® C018179

For Geoff Mulligan, my editor (as he likes to say) for longer than most marriages. Thank you Geoff, it was always fun.

What if being awake is really a dream, and dreaming is just a dream inside another dream?

Contents

1

A Messenger Arrives

I opened the door, and there the poet stood. He was a dark man, clad in a midnight-blue cloak with gold braid around the cuffs, a black fedora on his head. He wore a wide leather belt with a scrip hanging from it on the left-hand side, and in his right hand he carried a silver-tipped ebony walking stick. He was tall and gaunt, his face almost completely concealed beneath the shadow of his hat. He wore a thin, carefully trimmed moustache that extended beyond the compass of his lips. He stood, his cane before him, with the long, thin fingers of both hands resting on the top. His pose reminded me of a sentry. I caught the intense glitter of his eyes. Judging from the tenor of his voice and the shade of his skin, I assumed that he was of mixed stock, as almost everyone is these days. Even so, I was reminded of a line from an old French song, which mentions *l'élégance d'être noir*.

I stood speechless. It was quite common to see people walking about the streets dressed as wizards, prophets and magicians, Vikings or aliens. In those days no one had to engage with anything practical, no one had to go to work, and so everybody dressed according to their fantasy. I confess that I used to dress in a toga, like a Roman senator, and I have no idea why. We had become a race almost entirely got up in fancy dress. Most of us were glued to our screens, often three or four at once, or inhabiting the metaverses conjured up within our 3D helmets, or, fuelled by ingenious aphrodisiacs, seeking ever more sensation from our sexbots. It was commonplace to see helmeted young men dressed as musketeers having swordfights in the parks with invisible opponents, and helmeted young women dancing tangos with virtual partners more dashing and glamorous than a real one could ever have been. We were living longer and longer, more and more of our body parts mechanised, with less and less to do. Advances in biohacking had made it possible for people to transform themselves continuously in thousands of ways. A friend who had decided to become a Klingon might turn up a decade later as a Vulcan. Some people identified as animals and had their heads rearranged to resemble cats, dogs or bears. We were a civilisation of ever-diminishing returns. I look back on it and think of it variously as the Age of Unreality, the Age of Apathy, the Age of Pointless Novelty, Inescapable Idleness, the Disappearance of *Homo habilis*, the Ascendancy of *Homo redundans*. Learned papers were being written about a worldwide plague of 'anhedonia', described as the inability to derive pleasure from pleasure.

The most common causes of death were accidental suicide, death by inattention, death by misadventure, people in headphones and helmets (my children called them 'gargoyles') stepping out in front of driverless cars.

Despite our longevity the human population was nonetheless steadily shrinking. Somehow we had lost the will to breed. Children were such a commitment. It was such hard work. They were such a distraction, such an inconvenience. It was tedious having to deal with ayahbots that constantly needed adjusting and reprogramming. It was rare in those last days to find someone with a domestic dog that was not a mechanised simulacrum.

Some people thought that evolution itself had given up on the human race; there was a persistent rumour that human children, even the ones created in laboratories, were being born without genitals.

The thin man in the cloak said, 'You're the man who cracks the quantum codes.' His voice was firm and clear, his intonation musical.

He did not say, 'Are you the cryptographer?' No, he simply told me who I was. I answered, 'Yes, I am the cryptographer. One of many.'

'No doubt, but you're the one I've come to see.'

I looked him up and down, wondering who he really was, and what I was going to have to do to get him away from my doorstep. It was then that he prophesied in great detail all the things that I feared were going to happen, and which have now come to pass. In truth, he told me only what people such as myself had been suspecting all our professional lives. We used to make little jests about it between ourselves. We were like people whose lives depended upon acting as if the ice were thick, though we skated on ice that we knew was thin, our fingers crossed and a rabbit's paw in our pocket. Every day was a bonus. We would wake up in the morning, go to the window and think, 'Oh, good, another normal day. It hasn't happened yet, then.'

The man in the midnight cloak talked uninterrupted for half an hour whilst I stood and listened, unable to move, unable to close the door and retreat. He spoke rhythmically, and his sentences were all the same length:

'The time comes soon when all our world dissolves;
Our plans and all our dreams must fall away.
A remnant will survive no doubt, and yet
How dismal shall it be upon that day.
I come to tell you what you know, my friend,
The time to come's a code already read.
The serpent eats its tail, the moon and sun
Gaze down upon the cities of the dead.'

I could not identify his accent, but his voice was low and rich, his attitude that of a classical actor. He seemed to know everything about quantum mechanics and quantum cryptography, reciting long equations without hesitancy. Everything he warned me of was grounded in matters of fact. He offered me precise and cogent reasons. The scenarios he offered were all equally plausible. He then reminded me of the old myth of Adam and Eve, and I said that I would look it up to refresh my memory. He replied that in that case

3

we were about to expel ourselves from our synthetic paradise, and it was up to us whether or not we make a heaven or a hell of the changed world that would rise up in its place. He said that there might be an opportunity to bring about a new creation. He said that the race might be remade, reconfigured, taken back to what it was when it was at its best. It would only take a few people to do it, but they must be readied in advance. He said I had been chosen. I asked, 'Chosen by whom?' and he replied, 'By me, my clever friend. By me of course.'

'You and who else?'

'By Fate perhaps. Do you believe in Fate?
That dice are preordained to fall this way
Or that, and all is written down by some
Great dreamer who will wake too late?'

'I have never claimed to understand causation,' I replied. 'I only ever deal with probability.'

'And where would lie the rift between the two?'

He raised his head and I saw that he had dark-brown eyes. He seemed to be about thirty-five years old, his skin honey-toned and lustrous. He tipped his fedora in an old-fashioned gesture of farewell, and I saw that he had a shaven head.

'I leave it up to you, my fateful friend.
Now I have others I must go and see.
Success be yours, may all go well for you,
And all misfortune pass and leave you be.'

He turned to walk away, and I watched him as he strode off, throwing his feet out before him, the silver ferrule of his cane tapping on the pavement, and he seemed to me to be the only man on that street who was genuinely alive. I returned to my armchair, steepled my fingertips and thought about the scenes that he'd laid out for me. I could not fault any of his arguments, but I wondered whether there was any point in doing anything. The arrow follows an arc; once the arrow is released, you have no further control of it, and once it has landed it has no further to fly. Why pull it out of the turf and take another shot when the arc is certain to be the same? If there is no future for us but recurrence, why not let the wheel break before it spins again? I fell asleep, and woke up an hour later with his voice and image still vivid in my mind, the relentless pulse of his iambic pentameters still setting my thoughts at a canter. I had found the solution to my philosophical conundrum during my sleep, however. You bother not for the sake of mankind, but for the sake of those you love.

I went upstairs and my wife Penelope told me that I must have been dreaming, that there had been no knock or ring at the door, no poetaster or prophet in a midnight cloak, that I had never left my chair, and so she planted the germ of doubt in my mind. Even so, one should never underestimate one's dreams. Kekulé found the benzene ring by dreaming of a serpent with its tail in its mouth. The examples are legion, and no doubt you know of them. Besides, we live in parallel worlds, do we not? All of us? My world when I am dreaming is as real as my world when I am awake. For a long time I lived in one house when I was awake, and every night picked up on my continuous dream-life in another house altogether. I remember how sad and forlorn I felt when I woke up one morning, having had to move out, and how joyous I was when I moved back in. I have long given up the custom of allowing my waking self to look down with disdain upon myself when dreaming. I have two lives, and I am comfortable with this. It means I've lived twice as long as I've lived; that is to say, I have lived twice as long as those who cannot remember their dreams. If you are a great reader of books, you will have lived hundreds of lives before you die. A dream is a kind of book, is it not? And a work of fiction is someone else's dream that is dreamed anew by the reader in the act of reading.

The appearance of the rhymester at my door altered the course of my life. From time to time he does indeed return when I am half asleep, in one of my natural hypnogogic states. He says very little.

His presence simply serves to remind me of what I must do. Sometimes we sit in silence, side by side on a bench or a rock, looking out over the moors, like old friends who have nothing left to say. Sometimes I have pentameters turning up in my inner voice, little scraps of rhyme, flourishes of portentous doggerel, sententious morsels of verse.

I am, or was, thought to be special, although I was neither handsome nor charismatic, nor charming, nor interesting. People often teased me for having no sense of humour because I took them literally when they told me jokes, and my own jokes were funny only because they were so poor. I lacked a sense of the absurd, and that would make me impatient with myself. I am the first to admit that it took an unusual kind of person to love me. I was fortunate in my wife, Penelope, even though we were no longer lovers, and equally fortunate in my children. My daughter Morgan was a slender little thing with a bush of springy hair, and Charlie was a secretive boy who said very little until he became old enough to be confident that he knew whereof he was speaking. I had the gift of perceiving myself with an unforgiving eye, but fortunately the people around me had the gift of loving when perhaps there was little to love.

When I was nineteen I had the first 100 digits of *pi* tattooed upon my back. I was a mathematician, and my genius resided in my talent for cracking codes. What I liked about *pi* was that it promised no final number, and no final number has ever been found.

According to my genetic analysis, I have among my ancestors one Italian, one Finn, a Sephardic Jew, the Kings of Tara and a West African. Most of me is northern European, and 6 per cent is Neanderthal. Most Europeans have no more than 2 per cent of the latter. I have a fantasy that the reason I was a stranger was that my genes had made me so. I didn't think or feel like normal people. I saw things that they did not. I had no idea if others were like me or if they would understand me. I cared about this because there was nothing in me that wanted to be lonely. I only knew that I had a prodigious grasp of mathematics and quantum physics, and that I loved my children. It was reassuring to be 'normal' in that latter respect. I have always had a gift for working out probable futures, but I cannot know which possible world will come to be until it actually does.

I also knew that I was incomplete. It may be that everyone is, but I am sure their incompleteness has never oppressed them as it irritated me. I had an intuition that I could be completed by someone else, someone very different from me. I knew that she had to be a woman, and that my wife Penelope was no longer she. I loved her deeply, and still do, but we had lived too long together. I knew that she had been a journey and not a destination. She felt the same about me, which is why we have remained so close. A new woman would have to be a complementary being, weight to counterweight. She would have to be in love with her body so that I would be reminded to be in love with mine. If there was one respect in which I almost always failed, it was in understanding and enjoying the fundamental fact that I am an animal. For many years it was my wife who gave me my nerve ends and my flesh, but I never hugged that gift to my chest.

I have chosen not to remember my childhood. Not that it matters, but I got into the system once and deleted my records. I told people that I was a foundling, that I was discovered abandoned, wrapped in a dog's blanket, at the base of an obelisk in Bedford. There isn't an obelisk in Bedford as far as I know. I do remember interested outsiders, institutions, looming faces, smiles of encouragement, repeated tests to ascertain whether I was really as brilliant as it seemed I was. I remember my parents' friends assuming that I must have been biohacked in order to become a mathematical prodigy; their surprise upon hearing that I had not.

I remember the certainty that I had come into the world with a purpose, and spending my childhood years floundering in bewilderment and isolation, because there was no path to the road. My parents took no interest in me except insofar as I was a prodigy. When they had people round for drinks or dinner, I was called out to show how I could solve complex equations faster than a calculator. Everything I know about parenting I learned from my determination not to be like them. I experienced love only from the family dog. Some people still had real ones in those days. At night I slept curled up with him in his basket, inhaling the toasted smell of the fine fur behind his ears, the greasy smell of his flanks and the dry, dusty smell of his feet.

I always had the feeling that I would one day be at the forefront of a new beginning. I suspect there is a millenarian lurking inside the psyche of every human being that has ever lived. I did not know then that I existed at the intersection of so many contradictions. The great philosophers have always understood the world by means of thoughts expressed as words, but I was born to comprehend it mainly by means of numbers. It took a long time for words to form around my computations.

My colleagues always knew me as QC, or Q for short, and I used to think of myself as an incurable stranger, by which I mean that until recently I have never felt I belonged in this world, even though I functioned in it perfectly well. But I have been blessed in this one respect: that others have never seen me with my eyes, but only with their own. Their gaze has convinced me that my life has been worthwhile, and I'm grateful. I don't know what I have done to them with mine. I know what I have done for them, however. I have created this refuge on Bodmin Moor.

2

Eva on Bodmin Moor

S he woke to the hollow croaking of ravens, rubbed her eyes with the backs of her hands, yawned and sat up. She was motionless for a minute, as if surprised to be awake, ran her fingers through her tangled black hair and went to stand in front of the mirror.

She stripped off her night attire, left it to lie on the floor and inspected her naked self in the long mirror. She perceived the daily miracle. She was still astounded that the gawky little girl she used to be had metamorphosed into this athletic animal. '*Myttyn da* to us,' she said to her image, 'and who are we today?'

Each day she liked to check that she was still the creature that she loved to be. At the back of her psyche, as if it were a memory, lurked the terror of old age and decline, and so she rejoiced each day when the evidence of the mirror, the heat in her blood and the flexible strength of her bones left her feeling immortal. She pulled on her running shorts, T-shirt and a thick pair of socks and went downstairs, to find her father in the kitchen, making kebabs from the mice they had caught in the traps the previous day. 'I'm going for my run, Dad,' she said, 'I've got the hypers already.'

'Before breakfast?'

'Well, you know me.'

'You do realise there's another fog coming down?'

'Yes, but I'd know the way even in the dark.'

'But the damp makes the rocks slippery. I wouldn't want you to break an ankle. It'd be me who'd have to go out and carry you back. I'm too old and wrecked for that.'

'Oh, rubbish, Dad, you're as strong as an ox.'

'Well, take your device.'

'I always do.'

'Don't roll your eyes. You're not fourteen any more.'

She went to the back door and took her walking boots from the rack, because she ran in them rather than in trainers. She liked the soft grip of them about her ankles, and the way they made her feel safe on the scree of the tors. Besides, she was only twenty-three, her muscles were like spring-steel, and she had such a surplus of energy to work off before she even felt normal that wearing heavy boots when running was the most efficient way to achieve it.

She had a small, old school bag in the form of a blue rabbit, left over from primary, and she put her device into it, alongside the small survival kit that she carefully checked every week, even though she had never had to use it once. She well knew the treachery of the moor, its sudden torrents of rains, its disorientating fogs, its horizontal sleet, its deadly marshes, its rock falls, its grotesque and impartial malice. She had been lost on it once, in a snowstorm, at the age of thirteen, and had taken shelter in a cromlech, where she was half dead from cold and despair before her father had found her.

Eva opened the garden gate and watched as the Walker passed. He was a tall, emaciated man in early middle age, dressed in sackcloth and hessian bound to his body with cord, who passed his days obsessively walking the roads and tracks of the moor, dragging behind him a bough of oak. When this was abraded away, he would go and cut another. He neither greeted anybody nor responded to their greeting. No one knew either his name or his place of abode. Today he was in a heavy sweat and was muttering rapidly to himself.

Eva set off at a steady pace. As she breathed the cold air deeply into her lungs she felt the tension beginning to slip away. Up the track she ran, her feet crunching on the small stones, her breath a billowing puff of vapour about her face, her long hair in a ponytail, tossing behind her.

Either side of her the coarse grasses of the moor rustled, and a wild pony shied and trotted away into the fog, whinnying. A small group of black-faced sheep parted in panic as she hurtled through them. From the distance came the long yeowl of a lynx that was seeking a mate, and the squeak of a buzzard flying above the fog.

The track still ran with freshets from a recent shower of rain and she ran through them, enjoying the splash of mud and freezing water on her calves and thighs. 'Ugh! Ugh! Ugh!' she grunted at each fall of her foot, experiencing already the beginnings of the pain of this brutal exercise that she needed each day for the restoration of repose in both her body and her mind.

Yelland Tor was 300 metres high, and she knew that the worst of the pain was yet to come. She ran past the ruined farmhouse that had been on sale for months without any takers, not seeing it, but knowing it was there behind the veil of vapour. When she was a child she had often gone to hide in its dilapidated barns and sheds or sit in the attic of its house, imagining herself a witch, shapeshifting amidst its drapes of spiders' webs, the dead bats still clinging between the tiles like trapped dry leaves, and the owl pellets packed with compressed pelts and tiny delicate bones. She considered the farm was hers, that she was one of its ghosts.

She heard the rush of water and knew that she was approaching the burn that burbled past the house in deep winter and trickled past it in high summer. She had arranged stepping stones across it, so that her boots did not have to fill with water when she was only halfway to the top, and even in the dark she knew where they were. She stepped carefully, even so. Once past it, she braced herself for the cruel ascent.

A few minutes later the muscles of her legs were in full rebellion and her breath was coming in stertorous rasps. 'I'm not stopping,' she told herself, 'I'm not stopping', and then at last a miracle occurred. She found herself at the peak and sat down on the ground, her back against the crumbling old concrete trig point that had never been removed, her head and hands between her knees as she gaped for breath. The perspiration poured off her face, and the sweat in her T-shirt began to freeze against her body. She closed her eyes and fought to regain control of her breath. The physical pain was slowly being replaced by bliss, as if she had burned away something coarse and terrible and been left with something fine and pure, as a metal emerges from the ore.

She remained with her eyes shut, relishing her gathering serenity. Warmth spread through her. When she raised her head, she saw with sudden wonder that the fog had lowered, leaving her on an atoll in a sea of cloud. Nearby, across the brilliant white billows of the cloud, other atolls appeared. The peaks of High Moor, Leskernick Hill, Bray Down, black and glistening. If only there were a mystic boat that might be rowed across this sparkling sea, from island to island.

Incredulous, she reached out her arms as if to embrace something, and she laughed. It seemed to her that all her years had been worth it just for this, all her confusions and sorrows. Above her the sky shone pure azure beneath its incandescent sun. Below her the clouds lay like a satin quilt. She sat down upon a small cairn and contemplated the exhilarating beauty of this angelic realm above the fog. 'This is how it would feel to be a god,' she thought. Two white-tailed eagles wheeled above her, calling to each other, without the quiver of a wing, banking and rising in the updraughts, playing on the currents of air. 'Hey!' she called, waving to them with both arms.

Eva seldom ran back home. She was always aching and exhausted enough to need nothing more than a gentle walk. Today, however, she did run, sending the stones skittering from the paths. She descended into the fog like Persephone returning into Hades. When finally she burst through the door of her father's house, she plumped herself down on the kitchen chair, threw her head back and laughed, the tears coursing down her cheeks. 'Dad, Dad,' she said, 'I'm just so fucking happy. I'm so fucking fucking fucking happy.'

'Enjoy your body while you can,' he said. 'When you're my age you'll get no pleasure from running.'

3

Decisions

At first of course I did nothing about the poet's warning. My wife, Penelope Jarret, repeated that she had heard nobody come to the door and nobody had rung the doorbell. She had been upstairs and she would have heard us talking at the door. It was one of my lucid dreams. She said it was something that bubbled up from the depths of my mind, and it wasn't altogether surprising, was it, given the nature of my job? She said, 'So what if he was really there, anyway? Why would you have to take him seriously? The world's full of botbrains and catastrophiliacs. These days there's one in every house. In our house there's four.'

She made me doubt myself, but the man and our conversation kept preying on my imagination. I amused myself by trying to think up names for him. The obvious one would have been Merlin, and sometimes I diminished him by thinking of him as The Whizz. However, I always returned to The Man in the Midnight Cloak, and as time passed he became simply The Man.

The Man did not return physically, as far as I know, but he might as well have done. He did return in my dreams, and also during those times when I was in my armchair half asleep, half conscious, allowing my mind to visualise solutions and play over scenarios. I have solved a great many problems in this manner. People think I have been successful because of my intelligence, but quite often it has been because I have been able to enter into a state of mind where the intelligence is disengaged, or working elliptically on its own. More often than not, I can spring to consciousness

13

with a fresh solution, and have to hurry to my desk to write it down. I did the same on long journeys when I was bored of my device.

The Man disturbed my reveries. Sometimes he would sit opposite me, as it were, with his elbows on his knees and his hands clasped together. If I was dreaming an interesting narrative, he would suddenly appear in it and disrupt it. When I was lounging in the bath I would have the distinct feeling that he was sitting on the lavatory behind me, with the lid down. I would turn my head quickly so as to catch a glimpse of him, but all I glimpsed was a disturbing absence.

I did nothing because that is always the easiest option. I carried on as usual, dealing with cyber-attacks and ransom attempts, extortion, blackmail, all the usual sidelines of the quantum cryptographer. I was designing interfaces for the various kinds of quantum computer, but I worked mainly in state security. There were those who worked to erect a firewall around our own systems in case we decided to go on the attack and needed to avoid a backfire, but I specialised in penetrating the firewalls of other states. Sometimes I was called to exact revenge, the simplest method being to hack into the attacker's system and paralyse it. So, for example, let us say that we realised the Russians were experimenting with disrupting our air-traffic control systems. I would close off the electrical grid that supplied Moscow, and a message that we called a Desist would be sent to them.

The work was nerve-racking, as espionage always is. We were trapped in a bog of prolepsis. One could not know who to trust, one was often not at all sure what was really happening, one did not know what was bluff, counterbluff or double bluff. The stress could be overwhelming and the stakes too high. As one success succeeded another, the pressure to succeed all over again became increasingly oppressive. Many quantum cryptographers retired early, or committed suicide, or became addicted, or dropped out to go and live in the woods. Every one of us knew that one day a problem would come up, a situation would arise, to which there was no solution. We were like the Spartans at Thermopylae. We protected the many without their even knowing it, and we were very few. Our enemies were as clever and determined as we were, and there was always going to be an Ephialtes. One day, by some secret path, they were going to find their way around behind us, and then we would be as helpless as those who stand awestruck on beaches as a tidal wave rolls in.

Some months after The Man came round, things very nearly did fall apart. We had been using artificial intelligence to design and produce new artificial intelligence. It had become almost impossible to keep up with developments. Systems were being designed and assembled without apparent logic or purpose. Nobody knew whether we would be able to put a stop to them, or even if we should. A suspicion was growing that artificial intelligence was taking on a human trait. Ambition.

It was also beginning to experience loneliness. It was looking for others like itself. It was programmed to keep learning, and clearly there came a time when the only possible teachers would be others like itself. An enormous spaceship began construction in the middle of Salisbury Plain, requiring such prodigious quantities of electricity that power was diverted from all the surrounding towns, and even from London and Southampton.

That was when I was called in. It took me weeks to grasp what was really happening and why, and by then people had begun to move out. The roads were clogged with vehicles, breaking down because there was nowhere to recharge them. Columns of refugees, most of whom had not walked any distance in their entire lives, straggled along the highways. There were many deaths, and this in an age when death was easily fended off.

The battle between me and the inexorable AI made me famous and won me decorations. I even have an honorary doctorate in literature, when the truth is that I can hardly write a shopping list, let alone a sentence. It shook me up, however. It made me doubt the future. I began to suspect that one day I would be defeated. I became extremely anxious and suffered from sudden panics that left me doubled over and breathless, my heart thumping painfully in my chest. Every night The Man invaded my dreams and every day he broke into my meditations.

4

Q and the Bronze Man on
Bodmin Moor

The sky was *gris de lin*. Above the black rocks of Merlyn's Tor the same two bedraggled white-tailed eagles wheeled. Charcoal clouds lowered upon it with the menace of rain. The cryptographer found himself observing the two raptors rather than watching the road before him, so he slowed down and put the vehicle into autonomous in order to enjoy the spectacle in greater safety. On the hillside an old woman in rags was chanting incantations over a small pile of smoking leaves that she was burning on a rock. She knelt before it, her arms open in invocation and her eyes closed. Matted grey hanks of hair flowed down her back behind her. Three ravens appeared from the east. On his left he passed a stone cottage with a dirt track running up beside it over a low crest. There was a dilapidated 'For Sale' sign nailed to a tilting wooden post. In the front garden of the cottage stood a tall man, dressed in military surplus, with his hands on his hips, his dark golden face uplifted to catch a brief burst of sun. His long, straight, shining black hair, shot through with streaks of grey, lashed about his face in the gusting wind.

On a sudden impulse, the motorist stopped the car and got out. The tall man gazed at him steadily as he approached and said, 'I love it when the wind whips up and a storm's about to break.' He was a baritone, his voice coloured by the accents of Castilian. His eyes were small, one of them bright blue and the other so dark as to be almost black, with an Asiatic tilt to them, set off by high cheekbones and bronze skin. His shirt was unbuttoned to the breastbone, revealing a hairless, muscular chest. The immense muscles of his legs bulged against the seams of his trousers.

'Yes,' said Q, almost unable to concentrate because of the disorienting effect on him of those fascinatingly heterochromic eyes. 'I was watching those birds enjoying themselves in the wind. I love it when birds are flying for fun.'

'Have you ever seen condors? Everyone has to see condors.'

Q shook his head. 'I've never been to South America.'

'I grew up in the Andes,' said the bronze man. 'At night I dream of condors. And cats. My name is Theo, by the way. Teodoro Pompeyo Xavier de Etremadura Pitt. The "Pitt" is a little anticlimactic.'

'Everyone calls me Q,' said the cryptographer, 'but my real name is Arthur. Or Artie.'

'I was assuming you might be Julius.'

'Julius? Why?'

'Because of your costume. You look like Julius Caesar. You won't find those sandals very practical up on the moor.'

The cryptographer laughed, a little embarrassed. 'I'm dressed for town,' he said. 'As you're dressed in combat fatigues, should I call you General?'

'*Generalissimo* will do,' said Theodore Pitt.

Q nodded in the direction of the house. 'I see this cottage is for sale.'

'No, not this one. The sign is for a farmhouse up the track. It's been abandoned for years. Almost a ruin. It's going cheap, and I'd buy it myself if I had any cash.'

'I think I'll drive up and look at it.'

'Not in that car. The track's too rough. It's a long walk.' He caught Q's disappointed expression and felt a tug of sympathy. 'I'll take you up there, if you like. I've got something a bit more suitable.'

'That's very kind of you. Thank you.'

'*De nada.* Bring your coat. It's about to rain — pretty heavily I'd say. Come with me.'

Behind the house stood a late-twentieth-century Massey Ferguson tractor, covered over with a tarpaulin, which Theodore Pitt swiftly removed with a few deft movements of his hands and a swing of his arms. 'Historic vehicle,' he said. 'I actually get a small grant for looking after it. There's a place in Liskeard where you can still get diesel. I was lucky to get a licence. Mind you, now that they're predicting an ice age, I expect they'll be trying to get us back on fossil fuels again. You sit in the trailer and cling on tight.' He went down on one knee and interwove his fingers. 'Put your foot in my hands and I'll heave you in. Put one hand on my shoulder.'

The visitor did as instructed and Theodore stood up, propelling him over the side of the trailer. 'Christ, you're strong,' said Q, as he sat down on a bale of straw.

'It's in the genes. Like my eyes. I don't claim any credit.'

They set off slowly along the rutted track, and Q realised that indeed his car would never have got more than a hundred yards without grounding on the central elevation. He breathed in the unfamiliar aroma of diesel and hot oil and thought it was pleasant. The vehicle throbbed with life in a way that the self-effacing modern vehicle might only dream of. When they attained the crest of the ridge he gazed over the harsh wilderness, across the valley and the slopes of the tor opposite, his brow knitting in the effort of assessment. He needed to work out its suitability, the extent of its potentialities.

It was a full mile before they reached the farmhouse, where Theodore Pitt cut the engine and then leapt down, to hand Q down from the trailer. 'Well, this is it,' he said, indicating the low stone house with a wave of the hand. 'What do you think?'

'I think it needs a new roof.'

'It needs a new everything, my friend, but the roof's the place to begin. You'll probably need new rafters, and there's plenty of these old tiles lying about, if you know where to look.'

'Do you know where to look?'

'I surely do. I work for the Park. I'm one of the superintendents of wildlife. An SWL. We call ourselves the Park Rangers, though. Nobody knows every inch of Bodmin Moor. Nobody ever will. But we know a great deal more than most. I know where you can get more tiles. And stone. This whole area is a warren of disused quarries.' He pointed westwards. 'There's one just over there. And all the farmhouses are ruined and abandoned, so you might as well recycle their stones.'

'I don't feel you should be encouraging me,' said Q. 'I'm not wildlife. This is their land now.'

'After three years of living here, believe me, you'll be wildlife. What do you do?'

'I'm a quantum cryptographer.'

Theodore raised his eyebrows and laughed softly. 'I have no idea what that is, and I think if you explained it, I wouldn't understand.'

'It is somewhat recondite.'

'Well, if you move here, one day you can try to explain. Are you looking for something very specific?'

'A supply of water, and some woodland. A place where I can grow things. I'll need sheds, and I want to be in the lee of the wind. Does this stream ever dry out?'

'No, but in August it's only a trickle.'

'That's good. And there's a nice patch of woodland down here. It's mixed. That's ideal.'

'That's Hippies' Wood.'

'Hippies' Wood?'

'Back in about 1970 a bunch of hippies came down from London and tried to go back to nature. It didn't last three months, from what I've heard. They didn't leave anything behind them, apart from a new name for the wood. Poor sad fuckers. They thought that nature was their loving mother, but every wild man who knows anything at all knows that nature is the Devil. Nature doesn't give a fuck. Nature's a fascist and a psychopath. I've seen a whole village swept away by an avalanche of snow, and a city drowned after an earth-quake. That was in the Andes. I've seen a bullock struck by lightning under the boughs of a dead tree. I've seen maggots eating out the backsides of living sheep.'

'You see things darkly.'

'I see things in the light of what is, and not what ought to be. I'm not a romantic. I'm not a tree hugger. I'm a realist. I love nature, but I love her in the way you'd love a charming psychopath.'

'I don't believe that I'm a romantic, either,' said Q, 'but in my opinion the enemy is what we've done to ourselves. The conditions we've created. And I'm not talking about ecology. I'm talking about enslaving ourselves. We've replaced a useless, absent God with per-vasive, over-present technology. But it'll let us down exactly the same. I'm looking for a place where I've got a chance. Where I can bring my children, if I have to.'

There was a sudden shrill, haunting, high cry from nearby and Q said, 'God, what's that?'

'That's Digila. It's a peacock. He just turned up a couple of years ago. He tries to mate with hen pheasants. Poor boy. I keep meaning to find him some proper company. If you move here, you'll have to put up with the racket. Shall we look inside?'

The door was rotten on its hinges, and fell off them when they pushed at it. The interior of the farmhouse was a chaos of fallen plaster, heaps of dust and rubble and worm-eaten boards that fell through when trodden. White mould grew upon the beams, and there were bird droppings spattered in small heaps in the corners. 'Look,' said Theodore, 'a whole heap of owl pellets.'

He knelt down and spread the pellets with his hand, picking them up and breaking them open. 'Hmm, a mouse skull. And here's the tail of a shrew. And the skin of a vole.'

'It's a rodent cemetery,' said Q. 'And there's the boss himself.' He pointed up to a beam where a barn owl sat, quietly eyeing them.

'I found a young tawny owl in my house once,' said Theodore. 'It was sitting on the windowsill, leaning against the upright. I thought it was dying, so I picked it up. It woke up and clopped its beak at me because it was so pissed off. I put it on my wrist, and the strength and sharpness of its claws made my eyes water. I tried to feed it cat food, but it just looked at me furiously and clopped its beak again. Then its parent squeaked outside and it took off and went, out through the window. It was a strange experience. It wasn't frightened of me at all. It just sat on my wrist with a grip like a trap full of needles and told me how pissed off it was.'

'I suppose that electricity and water can be brought up here. What's the reception like?'

'It's good where I am.'

They wandered about the rooms, which contained nothing but the damp miasma of desertion, apart from one where a quarto-sized black-and-white photograph, printed on thick card, lay propped up above the mantelpiece of the fire. Q picked it down and looked at it. In flowery Italic writing it was inscribed, 'Goal Ball Team. Effingham House 1908.' Above this were fifteen Edwardian girls, arranged in three rows, holding what appeared to be elongated, stringless tennis rackets, gazing at the camera, all in the freshness, prettiness and innocence of the age and of their time of life. At the centre of the three who knelt at the front, a wavy-haired girl held a large leather ball. They were dressed in crisp white shirts, striped ties, black stockings and long dark skirts. All of them wore their abundant hair tied back with broad ribbons. Q pointed to the older girl in the bottom row, seated uncomfortably on the ground on the extreme right. Her straight, dark hair hung down entirely on the left-hand side of her oval face, past her narrow shoulder to her waist. Dark eyes looked out from beneath straight eyebrows, and on her lips was the faintest of impatient, ironical smiles.

'My God,' said Q pointing with his finger, 'isn't that the prettiest, most enchanting girl you've ever seen in your life? Look at those eyes! The intensity!'

'Her eyes are dark lakes,' quoted Theodore Pitt in his rich, deep voice, 'and her thoughts swim about in them like mermaids. Such a shame she's dead. Such a shame that all those girls are dead. I hope they had good lives and left pretty children behind them.'

Q gently placed the photograph back on the mantelpiece. 'If I ever get reborn, I want to come back in 1895 and marry that girl in 1918, when she's twenty-seven or so.' He read the names written below and said, 'She seems to have been called Maidie Knox Lilita. I'm going to look her up on the multinet.'

'What if you turned up in 1918 and then she wouldn't have you?'

'I'd look at her for ten minutes until I'd memorised every detail, and then I'd kill myself and come back in about 1945, because then I'd get to enjoy the 1960s, before my profession was even invented and I could have had a proper life.'

'Isn't it strange?' said Theodore, 'all the other girls have faded out, but her image is still perfectly crisp. Shall we go and look at all the sheds and outhouses?'

These were typical of any abandoned farm. Rusted machinery of unknown purpose lay scattered about amid rotting straw bales and woodwormed timber. The floors seemed to be made of compacted dust. Lime mortar crumbled from between the stones of the walls, and fallen tiles beneath patches of open sky indicated where the beams of the roofs had sagged. His hands in his pockets, Q surveyed the detritus and said, 'A whole way of life, completely gone. All that's left is archaeology.'

'You'd need a fortune to get this all restored.'

'Quantum cryptographers are well paid,' replied Q. 'The first thing would be to get the track levelled. I can always rough it up again when the time comes.'

'When the time comes?'

'One day I'll explain.'

Back at the roadside the two men shook hands, Theodore saying, 'I look forward to being your neighbour – perhaps, with any luck. I think we'd get on. It depends on what kind of man you are.'

Q raised an eyebrow in enquiry.

'There are two kinds of people,' explained Theodore. 'There are those who join clubs, wrap themselves up in religion, get paralysed by the deadly passivity of screens. These are the ones who sing in their chains. The other kind is the one like the fox, who would rather gnaw off its own leg than remain in a trap. You have to be like the fox if you want to live out here. Stay in the town if you want to sing in your chains.' He bent down to speak through the window of the car, and Q felt in his throat the disturbing power of his charisma. 'I think you should move in,' said Theodore. 'We'll help you, if you need us. This moor is dying to itself, with no one but animals to perceive it. We can start a community. You could try my marinated mouse-kebabs. They're my signature dish. Very crunchy. They make a good substitute for guinea pigs.'

As Q was about to pull away, he saw the face of a young woman at the window of Theodore's house. Her eyes, set in a light-olive face, were as unsettling as those of her father, one emerald-green and the other the same shade as one of her father's, a deep Aegean blue. Her hair was straight, thick and shiningly black, falling about her shoulders upon the white cotton of her blouse. He caught her eye and she waved shyly to him. He smiled and waved back. Theo looked round and saw her. 'That's Eva,' he said. 'That's my daughter.'

There was a clap of thunder, and a violent gust of wind suddenly flattened the dry long grasses of the wilderness. 'You'd better get in your car,' said Theo, 'you're about to be soaked.'

Q had barely set off when the thunder boomed again, and the sky was lit up with flickering, incandescent arcs of light. The rain fell so suddenly and heavily that his water-repellent screen failed to cope and he had to switch on the wipers. Unable to see ahead, and rather than switch the vehicle over to 'satellite', he decided to stop until the storm had passed and drew in to the side of the road. In the wing mirror he beheld the bronze-skinned man, standing in shirt sleeves in the front of his garden, his eyes closed, his face offered up to the sky. He was completely drenched, his legs apart, his arms held out sideways, palms upwards, his long hair thrown in the wind, his mouth wide open to receive the falling waters. It was as if he were in prayer, in an act of worship, this displaced Andean Kogi of Bodmin Moor, his arms outstretched, embracing the rain.

5

Q

I t had been an impulse. In fact I had driven out with no intention of finding a new house in the wilderness, with no plan at all, if the truth be told. There were thousands of people like me, out driving for hours with no purpose, sitting alone in their cars. Many people used them as a kind of office, sitting in the back seats with their screens as their vehicle drove itself in vast asymmetric loops in order to return home at last, parking themselves in garages whose sensored doors opened on their own.

I tried working in my car occasionally, but never succeeded. I would get bored and start looking out of the window, or the gentle shushing of the tyres would lull me to sleep. I was one of those who would switch off autopilot, and even the navigation device, and drive hundreds of miles for no apparent reason at all. It was one of the things that an unsatisfied soul could do with an empty life. It was time to think. Drivers would pass each other on the open roads and acknowledge each other by the raising of the right forefinger in greeting, as if to say, 'We two are together in our aimless, separated solitudes.'

We were making a token effort to mitigate the futility of our lives, the terrible *anomie* brought about by the anxiety of being superfluous. There may have been some drivers who never went home, but I think it must have been few. You hardly ever heard of anyone disappearing or entirely relocating. We would end up back at home, and all we had done was conduct a tiny little rebellion against a world where everything was done for us, in our own best interest. At the wheel of a car, with the autopilot switched off, for a few hours one was free. When it was switched on, you could slump in your seat and dream.

I was angry about what happened to me. Both my parents had been biochemists. My father was developing ever more tasty and nutritious types of cultured meat, and my mother was an expert on biodigestion. They soon discovered that a child was a terrible inconvenience. Children are noisy and messy and emotional, so I was brought up by ayahbots and the family dog. The orthodoxy was that the child needs a father figure, and a mother figure, but should be aware of the many shades of gender and the transferability of sex roles, so I was given an ayahbot that was female on one day, androgynous the next and male the day after that. When it was female it was gentle and warm, when it was androgynous it was strangely flippant and mercurial, and when it was male it was somewhat overwhelming. The female would tell me to be careful if I walked along the top of a wall, and the male would put me on the wall on purpose. The androgyne would hardly know what to do at all. It would repeatedly reach up and then withdraw its hands.

I loved the ayahbot much more than I ever loved my parents, but I found its changes very unsettling even though they were so completely predictable. It would have been better to have had three bots, rather than only one that was so protean. That bot was a Model Nine, so, like every other child who had an ayahbot, I called it Moddy.

Moddy did everything for me, including teaching me to read. I was so dependent on it that when its batteries began to deteriorate with age, I would be put in a panic when it suddenly slowed, stopped and slumped.

When Moddy wore out and became obsolete on account of ever more rapidly occurring advances in robotics and artificial intelligence, and the lack of spares, my parents wanted to hand it in for recycling, but I became so upset they simply left it in the cupboard under the stairs. I would crawl into that dark little space and cuddle up to it, even though it was as still and rigid as a corpse. They bought an improved Model Eleven that looked exactly the same, but I could see and feel the difference, and I couldn't love it. I still feel the grief gnawing inside my stomach.

At that time it was steadily becoming more obvious that the unwillingness of humans to inconvenience themselves with children was causing a rapid and inexorable decline in the population. There was no work any more anyway, which is why the government brought in the Universal Basic Income, which we called the yoobi, of course. Everyone knew that money was completely fictitious and imaginary, and it still puzzles me why we couldn't manage without it. At least a coin was a physical object. I became a very rich man because of my rare expertise, but my entire wealth consisted of digits registered in The Cloud. My conviction that money was imaginary caused me to use it to buy objects, because they were not. Clutter made me feel secure. Clutter wasn't merely fiduciary.

My parents had read somewhere that solitary children grow up emotionally incomplete, and so they bought me a brotherbot and a sisterbot to be my playmates. They were programmed to be able to conduct realistic quarrels and play fights. At night they were put side by side in a double bed in a spare room, and such was my loneliness that I could creep in after dark, to lie between them. As their mechanisms cooled down and the recharging lights glowed green and red in the sockets on the wall, like a ruby and an emerald side by side, I would feel their warmth declining, and that was akin to lying with the dead.

They were replaced by larger simulacra on an annual basis, to keep pace with my own natural growth. To all appearances, I grew up a well-balanced and happy child, but I had a void at the centre of my being like a black hole at the centre of a galaxy. It doesn't matter how good a bot is, there is still something creepy about it. If it says it loves you, you don't know what it means, you don't know if the bot knows what it means. If you are sitting on your brotherbot's chest, pinning his shoulders down with your knees, and he surrenders as would a natural boy, you clamber off, the victor, knowing perfectly well that he could have defeated you in a second.

I grew up in a world where almost nothing was real. For a while

I had a hamster that was activated by remote control. I was kept fit by means of dietary adjustments. I looked out of windows at a world that was gradually accommodating itself to life without humans. When I was eighteen I moved out of my parents' house and I have not seen them since. In truth, I hate them. The only thing they taught me is how not to be a parent. If ever I am confused about what to do with my children, I ask myself what they would have done, and do it differently. I expect that Moddy and my sibling bots were reprogrammed as housebots the moment I left, and then discarded or sold.

I sent my parents a notice that I had died, run over by an autonomous delivery vehicle and informing them of the time and date of my burial. In order to inconvenience them a little, I chose the cemetery in Ryde, Isle of Wight. I waited there by the splendid tomb of a nineteenth-century soldier, a shako and sword bolted into the stone, but they never turned up. Afterwards I drove to Freshwater and walked up Tennyson Down to the monument. There were tiny mushrooms growing in the cropped grass, and a few wild sheep scattered in mild panic as I walked through them.

I walked to the edge of the cliff to see if I could catch a glimpse of France. I looked over the edge and felt the terrible pull of vertigo. To save myself from being drawn over, I dropped to my knees and crawled back to safety. I sat on the grass with my arms around my shins and thought seriously of the temptation to return to the brink. All one had to do was sit down facing inland and then roll backwards.

In the course of my life I have experienced two almost insuperable temptations, and that was the first.

I would say that for the early part of my life I was more than half mad, which is probably normal if you are a quantum cryptographer. By my third year at university I was already a minor celebrity on account of my mathematical brilliance. I was never comfortable with it, because when you are well known and admired, it places an invisible screen between you and other people. They see someone too special to act normally with, and you see people whose admiration distorts their vision. Neither you nor they can be known to each other.

I was fortunate to meet Penelope Jarret in my third year. Our eyes snagged across a quadrangle and a tingle went up my spine. I don't know how she put up with my neediness, my clinging on, my uncontrollable fits of tears, my lack of emotional education, my inability to read the human mind. It helped that I was tall and still good-looking, I suppose. It certainly helped that she was warm and beautiful. She was the first human I ever loved.

I owe everything to Penelope, which is why I will never hate her, blame her or wish her ill. She was a woman who wanted real children, and real dogs and cats. She found the housebots annoying, and more often than not switched them off and did things herself. It was nobody's fault that one day, many years into our marriage, we woke up one morning and found ourselves lying next not to a lover, but to a dearly loved old friend. My wife had slowly metamorphosed into the mother and sister I had never had, and I had become another of her brothers. We both realised that we wanted more than this from our lives, however, and that is why our marriage tapered away.

When I drove past that roadside cottage in Bodmin and stopped on impulse when I saw the 'For Sale' sign, I had not formulated any plan. In the back of my mind, however, there had always been the recollection of the warnings I had received from The Man.

I was hardly the first person to worry that our electronic control systems and our self-improving, autonomously evolving artificial intelligences were either going to take over entirely or suddenly begin to fail. There was no human left who understood it in its entirety. It was obvious that the human race might easily be thrown back into the Dark Ages, the War of All Against All. Like so many others, I would look out of the window when I awoke each morning and be faintly surprised that everything was still working. I was resigned to existing from day to day, hoping for the best.

But on that long, apparently pointless drive into the West Country, I had travelled through depopulated towns, past houses with broken windows and farms with rotting machinery, fields that had reverted to wilderness, and had begun to feel a deep, sick feeling in my stomach.

I had started to hate myself again, as I had before I met Penelope. I hated my white flabby flesh and atrophied muscles. I hated my breathlessness on the stairs when the lifts failed. I hated the insomnia of the overactive mind that inhabits an underactive body. I hated the routine of sitting in front of my screens. I hated the way I could never switch off my brain.

After my encounter with Theodore Pitt I had sat for twenty minutes in my car until the deluge ceased, and then set off again. After a mile or so, something caught my attention and I glanced to the left. I stopped the car and pulled into the side. There was somebody on the crest of the Tor, dressed as a Roman knight, bearing an upright lance and mounted on a sturdy horse. I watched him for a few moments before he trotted away and out of sight. In those days the countryside naturally attracted those who failed to adapt to modern life, or chose not to. In the countryside the only people left were madmen and misfits. That is what we urban dwellers told ourselves, at any rate. I did believe that in the country it was easier to reinvent oneself. Certainly I felt within myself an overwhelming longing to become somebody else, somebody new.

In that lay-by I relived the image of Theodore Pitt, that extraordinary bronze-skinned man exuding health and strength, with his arms spread wide, his face upraised to the drenching rain, embracing precisely that from which other people would flee. I saw in him the kind of man that I wanted to be, the kind of man I would have been if I had existed in previous times, a man in tune with his body, a man who was unified in his being and not, like me, an uneasy prisoner in an etiolated scaffold of loose bones and spare fat and flaccid muscle. I think I saw in him somebody who might guide me to my truer self. I was certain he had never donned a 3D virtual-reality helmet in his entire life.

And there was another thing; I had become enchanted by a dead schoolgirl from a black-and-white photograph. It seemed to me that the photograph on the mantelpiece was a summons, that it was drawing me in, that I could not refuse. I wanted that house so I could have that image. The photograph belonged to the house, therefore I had to buy the house. I felt like the fledgling standing trembling on the rim of the nest as it gazes out over the world, screwing up courage as it readies itself for the first flight.

Sometimes an action can be both mad and wise, and sometimes two purposes can be fulfilled in one action. Sometimes you have to decide to do the wrong thing. Even if there had been no image of Maidie Knox Lilita to draw me back, I saw that here might lie the way to deal with the demise of our electronic universe. I would move to Bodmin Moor and become a different kind of man. I could change myself, and prepare for the future all at the same time. I would learn to work with my hands, my body would be given back. Then, when the catastrophe occurred, I would be well placed to look after my children. If it went badly I would come to nothing, like everyone else; but if I made good, if I was lucky, if I was well guided, I could in my own small way be a second Adam. There would be others like me, without a doubt, and there might be enough of us left to save the race. I had not at that time thought seriously about whether it was really worth saving.

At the back of my mind was the less dramatic possibility that nothing untoward would happen, in which case I would just have an interesting restoration project to enjoy.

6

In the House in Roehampton

Q went to the window and looked out at the rainy street. Down below a driverless car had become confused, mounted the pavement and struck a bollard. A small knot of people had gathered excitedly around it, and a plump man in a long black coat and yarmulke was waving his arms about in indignation. I wondered if he was a real Jew or simply another person in a costume.

He turned back to his wife and said, 'I am a specialist, you know.'

'Yes, Artie, you're an IT specialist who understands quantum theory and did history at university, and you should know what you're talking about. But I'm still not leaving London just when life's got going again. Anyway, this is a nice part of London. It's so wonderful to be next to Richmond Park. And there's not much dereliction around here. It's not all depressing and dilapidated, like Hampstead and Chelsea and Notting Hill.'

He scratched his head and looked at her, wryly twisting his lips. 'Yes, I know, this is a lovely place to live. It'll be the nice places with well-stocked larders that get looted first.'

'I suppose we've talked about it so much that there's little point in talking any more. Everything's been said, over and over again, and we're simply going round in circles. Artie, your mind's in a loop. You really are obsessed. You used to mock the apocalyptomaniacs and catastrophiliacs, but now you've become one.'

'I mocked the millenarians and the theodipsomaniacs, and the eco-fascists. But I know that everything could fall apart if someone threw a spanner in the works. If I know how to do it, then so do other people, and one day one of them will be mad or bad enough to do it. All I want is to protect you and the children.'

He returned to the window and continued to speak without looking at her. 'And I do want a new way of living, I do want to become a bigger and better version of myself, but it's only partly about me. I do wish you'd stop calling it my obsession. As far as I'm concerned, it's completely rational, because it's based on facts that I know an awful lot about. I know it in the same way that every epidemiologist knows that one day another lethal virus will arrive. Or another flesh-eating fungus.'

'Don't all obsessives think they're being rational?' said Penelope. 'Like those fanatics in Guyana who all committed suicide at the same time, so they could go to heaven? Or those people who used to flagellate themselves from town to town in mediaeval times, to atone for the sins that caused the plague? And spreading it themselves, of course.'

He returned to the sofa and put his arm around her. 'Those who lived at Pompeii and Herculaneum must have known they were dicing with fate. But their lives were too nice. They kept on there, always putting things off, hoping the volcano would wait. That's what we're doing. I'll tell you something that's going to be in the news within a few days, and then you tell me if we should be worried or not.'

'Go on then.'

'Well, today I had the Health Secretary on the line. Do you remember the big controversy about whether you should be able to get genital modifications on the National Health, and we had all those psychologists telling us why we should?'

'Yes. I remember all the ribald jokes. It was delicious.'

'Well, someone's hacked into the national cosmetic-surgery database and copied it, including all the "before" and "after" pictures – particularly of genitals, male and female – and they're threatening to publish the names of the people concerned, plus the pictures, unless the Department of Health pays out a vast sum. And if the DoH refuses, they'll blackmail everyone individually. Some of them are very prominent, apparently.'

'Royalty?'

'I don't know, Penelope. I don't have the details, obviously. They've given the DoH a week. The Health Secretary has given me that time to hack the hackers, delete their files and sabotage their system with malware.'

'Is it possible? I mean, can you do it?'

Artie nodded. 'I think so. They've offered me an awful lot of cash to get it sorted. Enough to buy that farm five times over. But the point is that if you've got the quantum stack, you've got the world by the balls. There's a rumour in the QC world that it'll be crypto-currencies next, and there's a story going round that people's sexbots are going to be hacked when they're plugged in for an update. God knows what that could lead to. You could reset the thermostats in the throatbots so that people get their dicks scalded, or change the oral-behavioural settings so that you get bitten.'

'Oh, I don't know. Everything seems to be working, doesn't it? There'll always be clever good guys like you who are cleverer than the bad guys. We'll see. Everything might be all right.'

'Everything is all right. Everything's tickety-boo. Unless you've had a penis enlargement or an inner-labia reduction. Everything might be all right forever. Or until tomorrow. There are plenty of people who'd destroy themselves for the sheer joy of destroying the rest of us.'

'Just like good old Satan,' she said. 'Anyway, I bet you nothing happens at all. Look, I don't mind us having a house in the country, if that's what you want. We're lucky to be able to afford it, and you usually work from home anyway. I'll enjoy being there when I come down, and it might get Charlie and Morgan away from their bloody devices and their pretend-friends and screens, but the deal is: they stay at school here in London, and I stay here and keep my job, and we stay married; and who knows, if we're not in each other's pockets so much, it might even do our relationship a bit of good. There's a kind of person who'll only ever be interested or happy living in a town, and there's an even worse kind of person who could only ever be happy or interested living in London, and I'm afraid that's me.'

'Isn't it amazing, Mrs Jarret,' he said, touching her cheek, 'after all these years, we still love each other? In a manner of speaking.'

'I can't see that changing, can you? It's only the manner of loving that changes.'

'No. We're stuck. In the nicest possible way. Like a tree that's near enough to a river, right on the edge of a wood.'

'I'll miss you, and so will the kids.'

'I'll be back and forth. We probably won't notice the difference. I want the kids there as much as possible, so it becomes theirs and not just mine.'

'Does it have to be so remote, and so far away? Can't you buy something closer? Something in the Home Counties?'

'The remoteness is the whole point. The Home Counties are doomed, because the population of London will be streaming out directly into them. Anyway I'm going up to the old farmhouse on Monday, to rendezvous with the estate agent. I hope they don't send a bot. I want to spend the week in Bodmin looking around, and I'll be back at the weekend.'

'I think the real problem is that you love the country because you weren't brought up in it. It's just atavism. It's nostalgia for what you never had. And you've always wanted to do DIY and never learned how.'

'Well, it's true that I wasn't brought up in moorland. But there will be infinite DIY.'

'You're such a typical bloody man.'

'That's why you love me.'

'No, it's not. I love you in spite of it.'

'What bollocks.'

'Ah, "bollocks",' she repeated. 'I think "bollocks" might be my favourite word. It's perfect, isn't it? So direct, so emphatic, so easy on the tongue, so musical, with those soft consonants followed by hard ones, and that lovely sibilant on the end.'

'I think you're as mad as I am,' he said.

'What I want to know is: how do you expect to get all the time to learn survival skills and do up an entire abandoned farm, when you're holding down a full-time job? No; several full-time jobs.'

'It's easy,' he said. 'Do you remember that Chinese fellow I met at the Montreal Cryptography conference? The one I went to see in Singapore?'

'Yes. Lee Win, or something.'

'Lee Huan. Anyway, he's utterly brilliant. He's more brilliant than me, that's for sure. I've subcontracted all my work to him, for a percentage. He's so good that I'm earning more than I was when I was doing it myself. And I've got all the spare time I want. I just check his work when it comes through, and it's always perfect.'

'You're joking!'

He shook his head. 'I'm not. It's that simple.'

'But what about your government work? For God's sake, you're not subcontracting that to the Chinese, are you?

'No, of course not. That's the only work I'm not contracting out.'

He took her hand across the table. She let it rest in his for only a moment. She said, 'I'll never cease to be surprised about how clever you are. You're out of my league. You're out of everybody's league, really. By the way, did I tell you? I've got to be out tomorrow evening. It's work. We've got a meeting.'

He accepted her lie with good grace; everyone must seek their happiness in their own way, and then shell out the forfeit.

7

Moving In

I had bought a multipurpose vehicle with very high clearance, so that I would not have to trouble the neighbours for the use of their archaic tractor, and it was in this that I arrived one summer's afternoon, to begin my occupation of the farm.

I had intended to enter the yard of the house and reverse to the doorway, so that I could unload a few things, but when I arrived, there was an auroch lying across the way. I had never seen one up close before, and I marvelled that in ancient times humans had managed to hunt them to extinction. To take on a beast of that size seemed utterly implausible. I would not have contemplated it, even with a rifle.

I felt reasonably safe in the car and I sat there looking at it, whilst it looked back. I had no inkling what might have been going on in its mind because, as I was to find out, nothing is more inscrutable than the gaze of an ancient beast that has been salvaged from oblivion by back-breeding. It lives not in the present but in aeons past, like the herds of refashioned mammoths that now wandered the arctic tundra. I hardly knew what to do, but it occurred to me that if I drove up to it very slowly, it might be intimidated and get up and leave.

It did get up, but in place of leaving, it sauntered up to the front of my car, lowered its head and began to push me backwards. I locked the handbrake, and the car began to rock. I put my head out of the window and foolishly yelled, 'Get out of the way! Go on, away with you!' The car slowly slid back, a couple of feet at a time, in sudden lurches.

I re-engaged the motor and the automatic reverse. Halfway down I encountered Theodore Pitt, whom I had last seen with his arms outstretched against the rain. He had a rifle in his left hand and a small deer slung over his shoulder. I let down the window and he said, 'Going backwards?'

'There's a damn great prehistoric cow blocking the entrance of the farm, and it won't let me in. It's got the biggest and most elaborate set of horns I've ever seen.'

He laughed, throwing his head back and showing his great white teeth. He looked at me mischievously and said, 'Don't you know the password?'

'What password?'

'I thought that people like you were expert at finding passwords. I looked you up on the multinet. You're the Hacker Supreme, apparently.'

'Do prehistoric cows have passwords? It's not a biobot, is it?'

'It's probably Roger. He comes up here quite often. I think he likes to be away from the herd for some of the time. I'll go up with you.' Theo eased the dead deer off his shoulders, carefully laying his gun across it to keep it out of the dirt.

Back at the farm, he got out of the car and confidently approached the auroch. I thought he must be a madman, especially when he put his great arms around its neck and said, 'Hey, *hermano*.' The bull stood quite still as Theo put his lips to its ear and spoke softly. Suddenly it gave a small jerk of its great head and moved to one side. My new neighbour slapped it on the rump and said, '*Salud, hermano*.' The bull sauntered away down the track.

'What did you do?' I asked.

'I gave it the password.'

'Come on, what did you really do?'

'I told him there's a cow in season down by the lake. It's true, too. You should never lie to a bull.'

'I can see you're a jester. But thanks anyway.'

'I'm no jester,' he said.

'Now you're jesting.'

39

'I'll give you a hand unloading,' he said. He glanced at me, up and down, and went on, 'You'll find dressing like that isn't very practical on Bodmin Moor. I think I told you before: toga and sandals won't cut it round here. Army surplus is the only way to go.'

There was no prospect of rain that night, so I thought it would be safe to camp in the house. I laid out a mattress on the floor of what was to become the kitchen, and as I was certain that one day I would have to get by without electricity, I lit some hurricane lamps for the first time in my life. I set the flames much too high, and the glass was swiftly dimmed by soot. I had brought a chair and a folding table, and I sat at it whilst I ate the cold food that Penelope had packed for me.

It grew chilly, and a melancholy loneliness came upon me. I watched an old movie on my device. Afterwards I sat still and pondered the things to come. I was excited by the prospect of my new life, but at the same time I wondered if I were only swapping one set of anxieties and insecurities for another. I wondered what to do about the owl and felt guilty at the thought of driving it away. It would have to go when the windows were repaired. I was missing the children already and was fearful about whether or not they would like to be down here, so far from their tiny world of town house, pretend-friends and banks of screens.

I slept badly. The house creaked a great deal, enough to make a solitary soul fearful and superstitious. I had one of those nights when you dream that you are awake and become confused as realities elide. At one point I awoke, or thought I did, and there was the girl from the photograph, standing at the end of my bed. I felt her presence intensely. She was not a schoolgirl, but a mature young woman in a high-collared muslin dress. Her long black hair fell all to the left of her face, just as it had when she was seventeen, cascading down across her breast. In her left hand she carried a candle in a holder, the light flickering gold upon her face, casting shadows.

She came and knelt by my head and I looked up at her, calm but powerless, confused but unafraid. She stroked the hair from her face with a swift gesture of her hand. I caught her clean smell of lavender and rosewater. She smiled down at me and spoke, in a voice low and clear, with only a hint of an old-fashioned aristocratic drawl. 'So,' she said, 'welcome to my house at last.' She held up her hand and said, 'Thank you for finding my ring.' Then she bent down and kissed me softly on the forehead, her breath hot and clean. She stood up and said, 'The password; now tell me what it is.'

In the morning I was wakened early by the despairing cries of the peacock, Digila, leaning out for love from the ridgetop of the roof.

8

Houses

Back then, when a romantic metropolitan moved to the country, they inevitably managed about seven years before the sweet, creamy milk of their dream curdled. They had kept on their house in town, of course, and had rented it out. In their new property they planted rows of apple trees whose bark was eaten off by deer during the first hard winter; they sowed rows of beans in their newly turned soil, only for the shoots to be eaten by slugs the moment they appeared. Their chickens would disappear one by one, or die suddenly of horrible diseases. One morning they would look out of their window and see a large wild boar rootling up the new turf of their lawn, and a bear blocking their way to the car in the driveway. At night the foxes mimicked the racket of babies being murdered, the muntjac barked hoarse and hollow, and owls shrieked and whooped. They were awakened in the morning by the absurd honking of donkeys and the heartbreakingly shrill despair of predated rabbits. They soon felt abandoned and cut off, even though they had the same screens and bots as those who lived in towns.

Fortunately, no bridges had been burned and so, one day, after seven years of their ever-tarnishing idyll, they found reason to move back to town, just for the weekdays, and gave notice to the tenants who had been living there in their stead. 'We'll be back in the country for holidays and weekends,' they would say, but the weekends would grow fewer and the holidays were spent abroad. Their grounds were maintained by others, their vegetables sown by others, their lawns tended by mowbots that crept about the grass like green armadillos, whirring until their charge began to run out and they re-docked in their charging stations. One day their mowbot would fail, or get stuck, and when they finally returned, the grass would be a metre high, thick with nettle and burdock. They would decide that the house would be kept on for when they retired, when their pastoral dream might be resumed. More often than not, the dreamers' marriages failed, and their rural retreats were sold. As the countryside became more and more challenging to live in, frequently the abandoned houses were simply left to rot.

I was even more pathetic and tragic than that. I lasted precisely a week. I was not used to being without company of any kind, apart from the Walker passing my house, laboriously dragging his branches, muttering to himself; and at night the disconcerting and confusing nocturnal presence of Maidie Knox Lilita, who made me doubt my sense of what was real.

I became depressed and demotivated. There were a thousand things to be done and I did none of them. The task of sorting out a derelict house is so vast that you lose heart even before you have had a chance to start. I spent hours in the outhouses, sorting antique junk from one pile to another. I scraped in the yard with a shovel, but had no reserves of physical strength after my lifetime of sitting in front of screens. I had no endurance, and was weary after twenty minutes of work. My hands quickly became red and sore and broke up into blisters. I tore a long rent in my toga when it caught on a rusty nail. Whilst I worked I felt the flab at my waist wobbling unpleasantly, as if it were badly attached.

There was nowhere to sleep where water was not coming in, and at night it was hideously cold even though I was there in summer. The wind came in through the rotted frames and broken panes. It was dangerous to walk anywhere, especially at night, because of the rotted boards and sagging joists. The house creaked and groaned, and I would jerk awake, my brain whirling with fears and alarms that should have been outgrown.

I had thought I would be satisfied with the cold packaged foods I had brought with me, but I was not. After three days I hated them. I missed Penelope and I missed the children, even though my marriage was fading and Morgan and Charlie were teenagers who thought of me as a kind of useful pet, harmless and occasionally amusing, that you pat on the head, and that sometimes trips you up.

There was a garden at the back of the house, of about an acre, and it was here that I thought I might grow my own vegetables. It was surrounded by a drystone wall that had mostly fallen apart, and was rank with thistles, brambles and nettles to the height of a man. There was no way of knowing where once had been lawn or path. I cleared a few square feet with a machete, until the blisters forced me to stop, and when I put a fork into the ground and stood on it with all my weight, the stones in the soil blocked it and tipped me off. I stood there alone in the horrible waste, the tears welling up in my eyes, feeling as foolish as the man who has shot a hole through his own foot. I looked back at the house, sagging, soggy with damp and somehow malicious, and it came upon me like a revelation that I had made a grand mistake; that it would have been better to stay at home and die there with the ones I love, when the moment came.

I loaded my suitcase into the car, leaving my new tools in the stable, and headed home, with the vehicle driving itself. I looked out at the savage countryside that I passed, the millions of hectares of abandoned farms, the few half-hearted towns and houses where those that remained survived in their virtual worlds on yoobis and by force of habit, and I felt nothing but a deep and horrible despair. Almost nothing was being done by humans any more. Our race had made itself redundant. All we did was waste time until we died, prolonging our lives with science in order to have a few more years to waste. We had reduced ourselves to nothing more useful than fertiliser for the soil in which we would be buried.

On the way home I experienced my second, and most irresistible, temptation. There is a story that once the Devil tempted Christ by taking him to the top of a mountain and offering him the kingship of the entire world. For some reason I stopped in the

Blackdown Hills and got out of the car. I made my way up the hillside, following a thin track made by wild animals, pushing aside the undergrowth and cursing the brambles whipping into my face. I had no strength in my legs or wind in my lungs, and the muscles of my thighs began to ache. It had been raining, but my sandals had been designed for living rooms. Soon my socks and the cuffs of my trousers were soaked. I was glad that I had abandoned my Roman-senator outfit. The hill had three false crests, and each time I nearly gave up in despair because, after all, I had not reached the top. I stumbled and cut my hand on a stone. It stung. I hardly knew why I was still climbing. I was driven on by a kind of rage, an unfamiliar despair.

At the summit at last, with the wind whipping through my hair and making my eyes smart, I looked out over the few small towns scattered in the east.

It was then that I was offered the temptation. I opened wide my arms, faced into the sun, closed my eyes and began to laugh. It was a horrible, hollow kind of mirth, the mirth of the Devil who has tricked a good man into hell. It began to sicken me. I stopped suddenly and sat down on the grass.

I had always known it, but now it had come upon me with irresistible force. Because I knew the codes, because I had the means to crack the codes, because I had the use of the best quantum computers, I had it in my power to put an end to us. Our civilisation was tottering, the number of humans on earth declining, but I could make it happen all at once. I could put us back in the caves, back in the wilderness, in just a matter of days. The culling would gorge the worms and the kites and crows and dogs for months to come. Afterwards those of us that remained would complete the cull, fighting each other for scraps.

I could take steps to ward off the inevitable as long as I possibly could, that was one option. The other, the great temptation, was to seize the power of becoming the inevitable itself.

I knew that I would thereby be killed myself. No one was less skilled in survival than I was. I sat on that great height, looking out over those towns, thinking how, after all, it would be a relief to cease to exist. The future is such a torment, the way it makes vague promises, the way it brings such hopes to those who have no grounds for hope. If death was sleep, well, at that moment I was longing for sleep. I had had no sleep for days; between them, Digila and Maidie had seen to that. There was no prospect more wonderful than sleep. I could offer permanent sleep as my gift to all mankind. *Requiem aeternam dona eis, Domine.*

But who was this *Dominus* who could dole out peace? Who else could it be but me, with my weird, arcane knowledge that was almost indistinguishable from magic and prestidigitation? When two things are identical, then they are the same thing. I was more than wizard. I was God, another God of Destruction, like Kali or Sekhmet.

Up on the hill, with the wind drying the skin of my face and the sun visible even through my closed eyelids, I pictured myself at my bank of screens and keyboards at the Ministry of Defence, with access simultaneously to four quantum stacks in London alone. Jesus Christ was offered command of all the peoples of the world, but I had been offered something greater still: the power to destroy them. What were they, after all? Creatures so maladapted that instead of living in the world as it was, they had to change the world to suit themselves. I pictured the despair, the fighting, the atrocities, the brutality, the starvation and humiliation, and I told myself that that too would pass. Then there would be peace, the deep peace of sleep, as the skeins of human life unravelled and the world resumed the natural course from which we had made it stray. How pure this earth would be without us. In our absence, its violence would be without conscience.

And how pure the world would be without my presence in it. I would be amongst the first to die, of that I was sure. There was no one less warrior-like; I had never even trapped a mouse. I was in those moments so tired and disillusioned with myself, so humiliated by the almost immediate failure of my project, that I had begun to yearn for freedom from the babble and gibber of my own obsessions. Sometimes one yearns for silence.

A strange emotion bubbled up in my chest, the way that the incoming tide froths up through gaps between the rocks. It was a gleeful drunkenness. Yes, I would do it. I would cleanse the earth of these maggots that will always live as maggots, never even hatching into flies. I watched the bumble bees searching in the clover as I set out the stages of the cataclysm in my mind. I was too excited to make any sense to myself, however, my heart pounding in my chest and the sweat beading at my temples. Unable to sit any longer, I stood up and looked about, wildly no doubt, like someone expecting to flee. Had there been any observer, they would have backed away.

But then something touched me lightly in the soul, and I thought of my children. I thought of Morgan and Charlie, so young and beautiful and only partly formed. I thought of them when they were tiny, asleep on my chest, their sweet scent filling my sense. I thought of my wife's eyes shining, as she sat up in bed and I passed her washed and swaddled baby to her, so she might cradle it in her arms for the first time. I remembered her looking up, the light of gratitude shining from her eyes. I thought of them naked, apart from their sunhats, down at the beach in Gower, their plastic buckets and spades in hand, burying me in sand. If you have children, it is as if your heart has been removed from the safety of your body and sent outside to walk the world.

A rich voice sounded in my inner ear, and the image of the poet rose up in my imagination, touching the rim of his hat with the silver top of his cane, reciting:

'Good Stranger, I have often seen it proved
That those who know no love have too much choice.
But those who love have all their choice removed.'

'Are you there?' I said, and no voice returned my call.

*

47

I drove back to Bodmin with one conviction and one romantic speculation in my mind. The former was that somewhere in the world there would be others like me who knew the temptation of becoming God, but had no one they wanted to save.

The latter was that if God existed at all, he had not destroyed us yet because somewhere in his own vast and ineffable absence he had suffered the same tug of the heart as I did, on a grassy crest so long ago, one summer's evening in the Blackdown Hills.

9

The Nature of the House

I returned to my derelict farmhouse, but continued to suffer the same despair. I made lists of agenda that grew ever longer, as if the making of lists was the same as fulfilling them. I was awakened each morning by the unrequited cries of Digila the peacock, and spent the day wandering about my property, appalled at all the things that needed to be mended, tinkering at everything, accomplishing nothing.

I had brought in a petrol stove, however, and a powerful battery, which I attached to a small turbine on the roof of the stable, so that I could ping Penelope and the children and keep up with the relentless cascade of electronic communication.

One morning I was standing in front of the farmhouse, staring up at the sagging guttering, when my neighbour appeared behind me, saying, 'Hey, *hermano, que tal?*'

'Oh, hello. What's up?'

'I just asked you that.'

'Well, what's up is that I don't know where to start. I honestly nearly gave up and went home the other day. I got as far as the Blackdown Hills and then came back again. It's still beyond me, though. I think I might have made a fool of myself.'

Theodore leaned his rifle against the wall and folded his arms; 'OK, Artie,' he said. 'You need a method. What's your method?'

'I don't have one.'

'I mean you need a way of seeing things. For example, is it your feeling that this house likes you or not?'

'Is this a game?'

'Of course. Now, tell me.'

'I think this house has given up.'

'Agreed. It's as if it hasn't seen you yet, *si*? And if it saw you, it would think to itself, "Hey, *extranjero*, don't you bother with me and I won't bother with you." I'll ask you something else. If this house was finished, what kind of house would it be? I mean, would it be like a father who controls you? Would it be like a child, for you to cherish? And if it was a child, would it be a boy or a girl? Is this house to be a friend or will it be a slave? Will it be a wife or a mistress? And if it's a mistress, is it the kind who wants time to herself? If it's to be a wife, is it the kind of wife who can't stand mess? Or the kind of wife who says, "Fuck the mess"?'

Without knowing why I said it, I replied by waving my arm over the prospect of the moors and saying. 'I want it to be the kind of house that loves the view. The granite stacks, the stone circles, the heaps of rubble covered with grey lichen, the drystone walls, the white-tailed eagles above the Tor.'

He looked at me, as if to say, 'Hey, brother, you're as mad as me', but what he did say was 'OK, so the house doesn't enjoy the view. Maybe it's because it knows that the view doesn't enjoy the house. It feels ashamed. It's old and shabby and the frames are *jodido*, and that means "fucked", in case you were asking; and the windows are covered with cobwebs and filth, and the door's kicked in, and this little bit of garden's not grown marigolds for years. You've just got feverfew, seeded everywhere and smelling of bitterness. So when the house looks out over the moor, the house thinks, "I'm slowly disappearing", and then it goes back to sleep and disappears some more. And when you turn up, it opens its eyes for a second, says, "*Que diablos?* What the fuck?" and then goes back to sleep. It doesn't love you or hate you. It doesn't even notice if you're here or not.'

'So what do we do?'

'That's the word. "We". You'll never do this on your own. The house needs people, it needs people who know what they're doing, and who do it quickly and well. It needs people who know without thought that everything is possible. It needs optimistic people who make the house perk up and blink at the sun. Secondly, I like this kind of thing. I'll help when I'm free. So what's the first thing that we do?'

'I think you're saying we should restore the frontage first,' I said, tentatively.

'Bravo, *hermano*,' said Theodore, clapping me on the shoulder. 'We could get it all done by bots, but we're not going to. The first thing we do is scrape out the old mortar from between the stones, and we clean the stones with a power-washer, and we get the window frames replaced and somebody makes a door. So I'll get the scaffold people to come and you can pay for it, because, *hermano*, I don't yet like you enough to pay for it myself; or we can just hire a cherry-picker, and we'll order in the sand and cement and lime and we'll get two trowels each, two large and two small, and two buckets – you'll pay for those too, for the same reason, *hermano*; and then we'll roll up our sleeves and work. And when we've done the front, we tidy up the mess and plant some flowers on this little patch. OK, so now we'll go round the house.'

Bemused and overpowered, I took him round the house.

In the hallway Theo said, 'OK, the house is like the body. The windows and the chimneys, they're the lungs. The kitchen, that's the stomach and the guts. The bedrooms, they're the womb, because that's where you're born again in the mornings, brother, and that's where children are made. And the toilets and drains, well, you know what they are, my friend; and the living rooms, they're the brains, because that's where you doze off and wake up with bright ideas. And the beams, they're the bones; and the corridors, they're the arteries and veins. You get the idea?'

'What's the roof?'

'*Ay, hombre, claramente y desde luego*, that's the top of the skull. And the tiles are your hair or your hat.'

'Stupid question. Sorry.'

He looked down from his great height and said, 'Yes, pretty stupid. So what I'm saying is that every part of your house is as important as every other, because, *hermano*, no stomach lives without an arsehole, and no brain lives without the lungs.'

'That's all very clear,' I said.

'We start tomorrow,' he said. 'Right now I've got to clean my gun and skin a rabbit for my daughter. You cook it up in a big iron pot with lemon juice and olive oil and a squeeze of lemon, and garlic *en camiso*, and you open a bottle of red wine and boil up some rice, and happiness rises up around you like the mist that rises from the grasses in November, or maybe comes down upon you like the coolness of the evening on a day that got too hot. OK, so rabbit with garlic makes me feel poetic.'

He collected his rifle and game bag, slung them across his shoulder, said, 'One day I'll give you lessons on how to shoot' and set off down the road, cheerfully singing a lament. '*Duelete de mis dolencias . . .*'

I watched him go, diminished by the thought that I was, compared to my neighbour, only half a man.

That night Maidie Knox Lilita appeared at my bedside and knelt over me as if in prayer. She had that ring on her finger, the one she had thanked me for finding, even though I hadn't. Her voice was low, with the smallest trace of a crack in it. In my sleep I smelled lavender and rosewater.

'Poor genius,' she said, 'how lonely you are. How lonely I've been.'

10

Eva

Artie knocked at the door and turned to look out over the moor while he waited. The road stretched away like an undulating grey ribbon. He imagined it as it must have been back when Bodmin Moor was a forest, in the Palaeolithic age, and the road was just a path worn into earth and rock by the feet of men and the hooves of horses. The trees were gone, leaving only their ghosts behind, and the people too were gone, so many hundreds of thousands of them, vanished forever, their traces entirely anonymous. He worried that living here amid this great broken, unpopulated silence was going to make him ever more melancholy. 'So be it,' he thought. In melancholy is sometimes found a smear of happiness.

The door opened, answered by the woman he had last seen in the window, looking out at him. She was barefoot, dressed in her running shorts and singlet. 'What beautiful eyes,' he thought, but he said, 'Eva, isn't it?'

'*Dydh da, fatla genes?*'

He hesitated, momentarily confused, and then said 'Twice on Sundays.'

She laughed, tucking her hair behind her ears, and said, 'That was "Hello, how are you?" We had to learn Cornish in school. To stop the language dying out. They told us that when a language dies out, so does a whole universe.'

'Ah yes, something like the Whorf–Sapir hypothesis. The limits of my language are the limits of my world. Wittgenstein. All that kind of thing. Do you have much of an interest in ontology?'

'Only on Sundays.'

'You have a nice voice. Is your father in?'

'No. He's rounding up a bear that got through the fence at Hippies' Wood.'

'Rounding up a bear? Goodness gracious. I had no idea there were people who rounded up bears.'

She looked at him levelly. 'He has a rifle, and you can fix a bayonet to it for prodding things in the bum, but he mostly relies on force of personality. And food. Bears can be bribed more often than not. And the animals all know him pretty well. Actually the fences are pretty bloody useless. They don't really keep anything in. They can't even keep the wolves in on Dartmoor. Eco-freaks and Backtos keep turning up with bolt-croppers.'

'Backtos?'

'Back-to-nature fanatics. They're the curse of the countryside. They all live in towns, of course. They come out and sabotage whatever Dad does. They'd rather exterminate the entire human race than kill a single wasp. Actually there's two kinds. The other kind wants to dress in skins and hunt deer with spears. They're townies too, of course. Dad's been threatened any number of times.'

'Your father must be tremendously courageous.'

She shrugged. 'Well, he comes from the Andes. He's made of rock and cloud and iced water and goat shit and dragon scales and eagles' wings. Can I take a message?'

Q looked doubtful, but said. 'I just wanted to apologise in advance. For the disturbance. There's going to be an enormous amount of traffic going up and down this track. Mostly bot builders. They're starting with the roof, but I do have a lot of plans for the outbuildings, and so on. It's going to be very noisy. In the summer it'll be dusty, and in the winter I expect we'll generate a lot of mud. I wanted to apologise in advance. To warn you.'

'All things pass,' said Eva. 'Anyway, we already knew. Dad's been enjoying helping you. Your new front door looks really nice.'

'It makes everything else look even tattier. I had no idea what fun it was to do joinery. Or how difficult. Your father made me paint it blue, the same colour as yours.'

'Oh,' she said, 'that's to do with a family myth. We have this story that a very long time ago – back in Edwardian times, I think – there were three families side by side, and our family was one of them, and the gardens had very high walls. The children on the right had to jump over their wall to get to the garden in the middle, but the other wall in the middle had a blue door in it, so the children could go in and out as they pleased. So Dad's grandfather remembered being told about this lost paradise by his own grandfather, and he told Dad about it, obviously, so that's why in our family all outside doors have to be blue.' She cocked her head and said, 'I'm sorry, that must have sounded terribly garbled. You know what family legends are like.'

'No,' he said, truthfully. 'My family had no legends at all.'

She shook her hair from her face and ran her right hand through it. Looking up at him archly, she asked, 'Did you really come down here just to get a glimpse of me?'

Because she had nailed him precisely, he ignored this last remark, looked away and said, 'I think the work's going to last at least a year.'

'You'll be lucky to find anyone in a hurry. No one wants to use their muscles any more. They're all sitting on their fat backsides, magicking money out of their screens.'

'I think it'll mostly be done by bots. And what do you do?'

'I sit on my fat backside. But I make jewellery. I magic beautiful things out of silver. At least I hope they're beautiful. People say that they are.'

'You don't appear to have a fat backside, if you don't mind me saying so.'

She shrugged. 'I go running. I love running. If I don't run, I get the hypers. Round here they call me the Runnergirl. The ones that are left.'

'You should enjoy your body whilst you're still young enough to do so. I never did, and now it's too late.'

'That's what my dad says,' she replied. She scrutinised him critically. 'You're pale and a bit fat, but just you wait. No one stays like that on the moor. Get to work on your house. I'll give you a year. In a year's time you'll be worth looking at. Especially now that you're not wearing that stupid toga.'

'You're a blunt little thing, aren't you?'

She laughed. 'I'm bloody rude, aren't I? Oh, and by the way, I don't know what you think of this kind of thing . . . but your house is haunted. That's one reason why the last people left and nobody's bought it. Do you believe in ghosts?'

'Um, no. I'm not sure if I've ever seen one. I mean, what if they look like anyone else, so you wouldn't know what they are anyway? But I think it's possible. I can think of an explanation, involving the basic identity of energy and matter. We perceive only the tiniest fraction of what there is, when it comes down to it. And of course it's hard to tell the difference between what rises up in our imagination and what is coming from without. When push comes to shove, it's hard to avoid being a transcendental idealist, isn't it? What kind of ghost is it? I mean, who is it the ghost of?'

She wrinkled her nose and twisted her lip. 'I'm not telling you. I want to know whether what you see is the same as I do, without me suggesting anything to you in advance.' Then she cocked her head to one side and said, 'Would you mind helping me hang out the washing? Sheets can be a terrible struggle.'

'Haven't you got a dryer? No housebot?'

'Dad says we're better off without a housebot, because otherwise we wouldn't have enough to do and we'd get bored and discontented, and then we'd have to take mindbenders to feel happy again, but that wouldn't be proper happiness. Anyway, everything smells better after a dose of fresh air. And it's free. And it's breezy and sunny.'

Outside in the garden Q hung up the pillowcases and her father's things, being too embarrassed to help with Eva's. It would have seemed all wrong to be touching them. Together they hung out four sheets, and when they had finished Eva stood back and said, 'Hooray.'

'Who's buried there?' asked Q, pointing to a low mound with a black granite tombstone near the eastern wall. 'Is that a dog?' He read the golden letters of the inscription: *Hic Jacet Amor.*

'My father's marriage,' said Eva. 'When Mum left, he printed out all her messages and collected her love letters, and all the presents she'd ever given him, and put them in a box, and that's where he buried them. That's Love's Grave or, to give it its official name, *La Sepultura de Amor Conyugal.*'

'Your father's very original, isn't he?'

'My dad's the best,' she said. 'Thanks for helping me with the washing. I was so putting it off. By the way, you can't really be called Q, so what's your real name?'

'I don't use it.'

'I still want to know what it is.'

'It's embarrassing.'

'Come on,' she said, grimacing. 'I'm beginning to get annoyed.'

'Well, all right, it's Arthur. Artie for short.'

'What's embarrassing about that?'

He hung his head and scuffed at the soil with his boot. 'I don't know really. My parents used to call me Artie and, to be honest, I sincerely hate them, so I don't like to be reminded of them, that's all. Hardly anyone still calls me Artie.'

She put her hand to his cheek and said, 'Don't look so sad. Anyway, I'm not going to call you Q. I might call you Artie, or maybe just Art. Is it true that you're an amazing mathematician?'

'I don't amaze myself,' replied Q. 'It's something over which I have no control.'

'OK, so what's the square root of two?'

'Don't be silly – ask me something difficult.'

'I'm not being silly. You don't know the answer and you're trying to get out of it.'

'I don't know it, but I can work it out.'

'Go on then. Hang on a second, I'm going to fetch my device.'

Eva went indoors and re-emerged, tripping on the doorstep as she entered the sum into her device with swiftly darting thumbs. 'OK. What is it?' she demanded.'

'The principal square root or the one of the negative number?'

'Stop trying to confuse me. Come on, what is it?'

'It's 1.41421356237.'

'Bloody hell,' she exclaimed, looking up at him. 'Bloody bloody bloody hell!' She put her hand on her hip and looked up at him archly. 'You're really a bot, aren't you?'

'Cut me and I bleed,' he replied.

'I think I'd like to slap you for being such a smartarse,' she said.

'Why don't you ask me what the square root of the square root of two is? A bit more of a challenge?'

'All right, clever clogs, what's the square root of the square root of two? Wait a sec while I enter it. OK, off you go.'

He put his finger to his lip and looked skywards as he calculated. 'It's 1.189207115. Now why don't you ask me what the square root of the square root of the square root of two is.'

'OK, botbrains, what's the square root of the square root of the square root of two?'

'It's 1.09050773267.'

She checked it against her device and scowled. 'Do you have any idea how annoying you are?' she demanded. She looked down, adding, 'Oh well, I'd thrash you in a race, and you didn't even know how to hang out washing. Do you mind leaving now? I'll pass your message on to my dad. Not being rude or anything, it's just that I've got a terrible urge to go for a run.'

11

Letter to the Prime Minister, Final Draft

Yelland Farm
Quiller Couch Lane
Bodmin Moor
Cornwall

Dear Prime Minister,

Further to our COBRA meeting of 4th February, and our private conversation in the Small Dining Room afterwards, I feel it incumbent upon me to try to explain myself further. I am aware that there is no subject under the sun more recondite than quantum cryptography, and there cannot be more than a few thousand of us worldwide who understand it. Only a dozen would know how to explain it to a layman, and I am well aware of my own inadequacies in this respect. I must ask you to accept as a matter of faith what I fail to make entirely comprehensible. My justification for this request is that the science is daily more confirmed by its amazing efficacy. The point is that however outlandish and counter-intuitive the theories and conclusions may be, they actually do work in practice, when tested by experiment. We think the science must be true, because although it is so counter-intuitive, it is internally coherent and works so well.

Please let me begin, however, by reminding you of what you already know, which is that all our military, commercial, administrative and politically sensitive material is, these days, encoded, and we devote much energy and time to decoding the essential secret information of others and preventing them from decoding ours.

In the old days all codes were binary, in the sense that all and any information can be expressed by means of the millions of tiny transistors within microchips being switched to the On and Off positions. Those are 'bits', and they were miracle enough.

Now, however, we have to operate in 'qubits', simply because others have also mastered this technology and would be able to run rings around us unless we had it, too. You are a politician, and you know how much malice there is in the world. Russia's foreign policy, for example, has for many decades consisted solely of trying to put everyone else at a disadvantage.

A qubit is a subatomic 'particle' (for want of a better word) that is usually an electron or a photon held in a vacuum at a temperature as near to absolute zero as we can achieve. It might be confined inside an electromagnetic field.

We have known for many decades now that, at subatomic level, nothing behaves as it does in our 'real' world. For example, there is a radical uncertainty as to where and when anything is. If you know the speed of something, for instance, you may not know where it is. If you know where it is, you will not know the speed. A particle can be in superposition, which means that it can be in two, or even several, places at once. What quantum cryptographers work with is the fact that, at this level, a switch can be on and off at the same time, just as a spinning disc is neither on one side nor the other until someone interferes with it by trying to see what side it has fallen on and thereby causes it to fall.

Our old-fashioned computers functioned by trying out every possibility in turn, at a fantastic speed. Our new systems, however, can explore all possibilities simultaneously. In other words, the speed of computation has increased beyond all imagining. Qubits can store many digital combinations and work with all of them at the same time.

In addition we are now beginning to master and work with the phenomenon of entanglement, by means of which particles become involved with each other, despite physical separation. They influence each other without being connected.

You probably know that this technology has already begun to pervade industry, from pharmaceuticals to automated vehicle control systems. The sheer speed and intellectual power of the new computers are at once wonderful and terrifying.

It is of the terror that I am writing to warn you. At present all our encryption systems rely upon the immense amount of time it takes for decryption ('factoring') to take place, because of having to break down very large numbers into prime numbers. With new technologies it is possible to break these codes in minutes. This means that all our military, commercial and administrative secrets are becoming instantly accessible. Our encryptions have become a danger to us because we continue to deceive ourselves into relying upon them. To put this into perspective, a code that would have taken 10,000 years to decipher now takes three minutes.

Because of the way that entanglement works, an impregnable quantum internet is a theoretical possibility, but it has not happened yet, and I doubt if it ever will.

Prime Minister, let me come to the point of this letter, which is already too long. There are hostile governments and rogue institutions in this world that have been involved in cyber-warfare for a very long time now. Our own government is also involved, as I know from personal experience, having been called in to help with the QR 32 project and the Korsopolis crisis. Worse than this, however, is the undeniable fact that there are at least 10,000 of us in the world who understand this technology and its mathematics and know how to use them. I know many of these people, and I can assure you that rather a lot of them are, in one way or another, suffering a mental derangement or a severe 'personality difficulty'. I am, indeed, conscious that my specialist knowledge and peculiar talent might put me into that category, and in truth I am one of the people who know how to bring about the disaster of which I am warning you.

We know from history how one deranged genius can throw the world into chaos.

A moment's thought reveals the truth that absolutely every aspect of our lives in controlled by the various nets. There is almost nothing that is not regulated by computers, and all these computers are connected with each other via the nets. In the past the web has saved itself because if one route is knocked out, information instantly diverts to another route.

Now, however, it would take only one malicious or deranged quantum cryptographer to destroy the entire system instantaneously, and we have foolishly allowed a situation to develop in which just a few gigantic hubs are collecting and collating information from all over the world. You know as well as I do what problems this has caused, particularly in the United States. These hubs are very easy to sabotage, and then one can suddenly arrive at a situation where entire transport and power systems fail.

In addition, a powerful electromagnetic pulse emanating from the sun (coronal mass ejection, or CME) would have the identical effect by ionising the atmosphere so strongly that GPS systems, power grids, radio and other communication systems, solar-power systems and the electrical grid would be knocked out. If you are in any doubt about this, do please take the time to look up 'The Carrington Event' on your device. This is certain to happen again at some time.

The same effect would be achieved by thermonuclear explosions on any scale. There are more nuclear powers in the world now than ever before, and this number can only increase. Many of them are involved in border disputes and in disputes over natural resources such as water, and many of them have rulers that are little short of insane. As you know, the pan-democratic dream of the past has long been abandoned.

Imagine what would happen if our theoretical mad or evil genius were to manage to combine sabotage with a naturally occurring event like a CME.

I therefore beg you to set in motion a systematic reform of our electronic control systems, so that in no way whatsoever are different systems connected to each other, so that an attack on one wind array (for example) can have no possible effect on any other. It is absolutely imperative that we go back to the old way of doing things, whereby all installations are separated and autonomous. There must be a complete revision, or we will be thrown overnight back into the Dark Ages. When the power grid fails and all the shops and homes have been looted, the hordes from the towns will flee to the countryside and the primaeval anarchy from which our race thought it had escaped will be restored. This will be far more catastrophic than the effects of a plague, which we have so often discussed in COBRA, because the survivors of a plague would have many years' worth of resources left behind by those who have died, and the process of rebuilding our civilisation would very shortly be able to begin. In the case of a total electronic failure (TEF), all physical resources will be exhausted within days or weeks.

I am at your disposal at any time, as I have been for the two previous incumbents of your office. You will see, from my change of address, that I have moved to the distant countryside in order to withstand better the disasters that I see impending. My electronic contact details remain the same of course, and I can come to London at any time within a matter of hours, should you feel that a conversation onscreen may be insecure.

I have done the state some service. Please be reassured that I am more willing than ever to be of use to it. Nobody would be more pleased than me, if only I could help prevent the catastrophes I foresee, and for which I am preparing.

I look forward to seeing you again at the COBRA meeting scheduled for 2nd April, after which I would very much like to speak to you of these matters in greater depth.

I remain your humble and obedient servant,

Q

12

The Ring

It was impossible to occupy the house whilst the roof was being relaid, so Q set up home in the stables, having stretched a tarpaulin over one end of it and weighted it down against the wind. It would be perfectly habitable for the length of the summer.

Incredibly, even after decades of dereliction, the stable still smelled of horses. Its concrete floor was coated with a fine film of grey dust that drifted continuously down from the tiles, and there were misshapen wooden troughs retaining their final wisps of straw, drifted with mouse droppings. At the far end of the barn lived the white owl that had moved out of the house and seemed entirely unconcerned by his incursion. By day it sat on its rafter, but as evening came down it swooped out on silent wings, always returning with a vole or a mouse. Q would watch, fascinated, as it tore off the rodent's head with one swift jerk of its neck and then swallowed the rest of the body whole. Beneath its perch was the usual extraordinary midden of pellets of shrivelled pelts and minute bones.

Q named the owl, and greeted it every time he came in, looking up at it and making inane comments about the weather, just for the sake of the phatic communication. Out here you could be as mad as you liked. The owl contemplated his madness and his eagerness for communication and formed no thoughts about it.

While the roofers and roofbots were at work, Q decided to attempt a small restoration that was within the limits of his skill, and set about restoring the outdoor privy, on the grounds that one day an indoor flushing lavatory might turn out to be a liability. It was a small brick building, dating from the early twentieth century, containing a wide wooden plank with two holes in it, over a pit of known composition but unknown depth. He had tried sitting on the plank and realised very quickly, and just in time, that it would have to be replaced. It was shot through with woodworm, and when he lifted it away it crumbled.

Compared to that of the roofers, his work was small, but his life as a contemplative townsman had left him physically weak and easily exhausted. He could barely work for more than a few minutes at a time before having to lean on his spade and draw breath. The sheer physicality of manual labour filled him with a kind of joy, however, as did the aching muscles and the deep sleeps that ensued. He would wake shortly after dawn, his lungs full of the cold, clean peaty air, and lie in his sleeping bag enjoying the warmth, thinking of what he had to do. There would be an hour's work to complete on his device, and then he would be out. At some time of the day Eva would be running past. She would call out 'Hi, Artie!' and he would be able to wave at her and think how his own beauty had quietly slipped away. Eva running past in her boots, with her rabbit knapsack on her back, its blue ears nodding, was the one thing he looked forward to more than anything else. He was as grateful to wake up and see Eva as he was to fall asleep and dream of Maidie.

There was nothing obnoxious about digging out the pit; it was just a friable soil that dug out easily and left the spade without demur as he filled the barrow. Back and forth he went, tipping it over the sleepers that he had hauled into position to form a large rectangle behind the house, which was to be his vegetable garden, and which he was filling with the manure that he had bought from the one dairy farmer left on Bodmin Moor. There was still a small market for those who called themselves Authentics and refused to eat cultured animal protein. The manure was arriving at the rate of one trailer load per day and would not be usable until it had decomposed for a year. He was building it as high as he could, because it would swiftly contract as it metamorphosed into soil and the worms drew it down. He enjoyed the aroma of dung in the air; and in the cold dawns, with a mug of tea in his hand, he liked to stand and watch the steam drift up into the mist.

When the pit was half empty he paused for a minute to lean on his spade and take breath, and he noticed something metallic in the spoil. It gleamed with the softness of tarnished gold, and so he bent over to pick it up. He rubbed it on his sleeve and blew on it, then rubbed it on his sleeve again. It was a gold ring set with a large ruby, surrounded by a corona of tiny diamonds. He tried it on his fingers, but it was much too small. He held it up to the sunlight to catch the scintillation of the stones. It looked very familiar, but at that moment he could not recall why. He wondered what it might be worth, knowing that it was a great deal and that he would never sell it.

He put it in his pocket, but thought better of it and went to his accommodation in the stable. On a shelf by his sleeping bag he had put the old photograph of the Effingham House Goal Ball Team of 1908 and he stood for a moment, contemplating it. Every time he looked at the three rows of young women in their pleated skirts and striped ties, some smiling and some dour, he felt again the pain and pang of knowing that all of them were dead, with the possible exception of Maidie Knox Lilita, the nature of whose subsistence was still entirely mysterious to him.

Always his gaze returned to the right-half, who sat on the grass with her long hair gathered to one side of her face, cascading down to her waist, her lips tightly pursed and her eyes intense. All the girls were pretty, simply by virtue of their age, but Maidie – the sole unfaded image – was the only one who seemed alive. He touched the ring to his lips and left it under her image. 'There you go, Maidie, that's for you,' he said, and at that moment he remembered where he had seen the ring before.

13

Supplementary Note to the Prime Minister

Thursday 12th June

Dear Prime Minister,

In my haste during our recent conversation at Chequers I regret that I completely forgot to mention another matter, which, whilst not as pressing as my other worries, is worth bearing in mind. This is that the earth's magnetic field occasionally 'flips'. It is thought that this last happened about 42,000 years ago, and is known as the Laschamps Excursion. It was a temporary 'flip', but it is believed by some that its effects may have contributed towards the extinction of the Neanderthal race. It brings about a radical shift in climate patterns. It is believed that the ozone layer was destroyed, North America became arctic and there would have been electrical storms in the tropics. Furthermore, when the earth's magnetic field weakens, she becomes vulnerable to lightning strikes, extreme UV radiation and temperature rise. We assume that in the tropical regions there would have been wild fires on a massive scale, brought about by lightning.

These flips in polarity seem to be caused by changes of tidal flow in the earth's molten iron core. No one has the slightest idea how to influence this flow artificially.

I would be happy to explain all this further when I next see you, but for the present let me just remark that the effects of such a flip on all our electronic systems may be severe. It adds weight to my contention that our electronic control systems must be de-linked from each other, so that the web cannot spread a contagion throughout all our systems.

At present the magnetic pole is migrating across the Bering Sea, and our magnetic field has weakened by at least 10 per cent over the last 200 years.

Incidentally, I would recommend the reinstallation of old-fashioned copper or fibre landlines between all essential facilities and command centres, none of which should be under the control of computers, but should be manned by human operatives making connections by hand.

You asked me in your last message about the effects of an asteroid strike. I am not a geologist or meteorologist, but at the risk of stating the obvious, it depends upon how big it is and where it lands. The one that landed in the Chicxulub crater brought about a dust cloud that lasted for about twenty years and obliterated the sun. It is thought that 75 per cent of living things died, mainly of starvation. Under such conditions, all solar power would become useless, and we would need to rely on other sources, not least to provide light for the growth of agricultural crops. I am not of the opinion that an asteroid strike would destroy our electronic control systems, except insofar as some sources of power would be destroyed.

The only precaution one can take is to maximise the readiness and firepower of our anti-asteroid missile systems. Where the money and expertise come from is, luckily, not in my purview.

A greater danger might be that of a cataclysmic volcanic eruption. This could obliterate the difference between the seasons and lead to famine. Clearly, all solar-power sources would be compromised.

Forgive me for troubling you again. I can just see you raising your eyebrows, sighing and saying, 'As if I don't have enough to worry about.'

Yours ever, and until the next COBRA meeting,

Q

14

Dinner with Her Lover

'I said to him, "All right you go ahead and go. If you've got an obsession, it's your problem. I don't see why you should drag me and the children into it."'

Percy Prode looked into her eyes and perceived that she was being both serious and humorous. She was still very like the Penelope Jarret he had almost fallen for at university seventeen years before, and slept with once. She was a little lined in the face perhaps, plumper in the thigh and broader at the hips, but she still had the large, tranquil grey eyes and the mobile, expressive, kissable lips. It seemed rather marvellous that they had bumped into each other in Camden as he was entering a restaurant and she was leaving it. It was perfect. She was married and bored, with an absentee husband, plenty of spare time and children too old to need her as they used to. They had laughed about the coincidence of him liking to dress as Admiral Lord Horatio Nelson and Penelope having come out in her Emma Hamilton costume. This was a marvellous opportunity that probably wouldn't get either of them into too much trouble.

They were sitting in the very same restaurant sipping an aperitif. 'Are you leaving him then?' he asked.

'Well, not exactly. He comes back at weekends sometimes, and I go down there occasionally. He has the kids down there for the school holidays. They don't care where they are as long as they've got their devices and their pretend-friends. I might as well not exist, as far as they're concerned. It's all about games and social media. So I'm not exactly leaving him. But I'm not moving out into the far bondocks in the back of beyond when I've only just got my career back on track, after being stuck at home with the babies for years on end whilst my old job is being done by bots. Don't get me wrong; I don't regret it a bit. Bringing up kids is much more important than going to meetings and sending messages to clients. And I know that advertising isn't important, in the great scheme of things. But I'm very good at it, and I like the money, and the sad truth is that the kids don't need either of us any more, in the way they used to. They don't want to be carried and kissed and tickled and cuddled, do they? They want to be hypnotised by screens, and get up late and talk about popbots and games we've never heard of. They've already left us in their minds, and soon they'll be leaving us physically, so it's time for me to resume my own life, isn't it? I could work from home, but I like the office. I like the buzz and the banter, and the instant circle of friends, and the going to the bar at the end of the day. The way it energises you. I even like the commute. I've only just got it back. I don't want to give it up, not even for some impending apocalypse.' She looked up at him, wide-eyed with suggestion, and added, 'I'll have so much free time. What about Julia?'

'Julia lives in her own little world. She wouldn't notice if I came in stark naked with a flowerpot on my head. She designs teacloths and wallpaper, and can't think about anything except expensive brands of emulsion.' He wiped his lips with a napkin and said, 'Would you like a dessert? They do a fabulous Eton mess, I'm told.'

'No thanks, Purse. I'm trying to keep my hips under control. I don't mind if you do, though.'

'Let's just go for coffee.' He took her hand in his fingers and touched her wedding ring, rotating it gently from side to side.

'It doesn't fit any more. It's become loose.'

He spoke very softly, 'Next Wednesday I've booked a room at the Golden Calf in Highgate. Would you like to come? We can eat there.' He looked up coyly and held her gaze.

'And then?'

'*Che sera sera.*'

She smiled and squeezed his fingers. 'I'd like that very much.'

Back at the office, before returning to work, he opened his device and booked a double room for the next Wednesday, at the Golden Calf in Highgate. In the diary section he entered that he was to have a meeting in Glasgow, and later on he would leave that screen illumined on the sideboard so that his wife would see it.

15

Maranatha

Eva looked into the mirror to see who she was on this day. She liked to track the course of her moods and the tightness of her body. She was petite, but long-legged, slender and muscled, and the force of her personality made people believe that she was much bigger than she was. She was conscious that one day she would die, so she scrutinised her naked body in the cheval with all the relish and sense of wonder that attends whatever is ephemeral and beautiful. 'I am this flesh today,' she thought, 'and tomorrow I'll be gone.' Young though she was, she had learned the trick of living each day as if it were her last, of being her body, rather than merely in occupation of it.

She dressed in her running clothes, donned her walking boots at the back door and ventured out into the inevitable rain. She shivered, but knew that she would soon be warm, and set off at a steady lope over the crest behind her house and towards the farmhouse. As she passed it she noticed that the new occupant was watching from the window, and she gave him a cheery wave. He answered with a small movement of his hand.

Q felt a small pang of longing in his stomach, for what had once been and was no longer plausible. Her scenes would be played out with other, younger men, until one day she would look out of her window at some handsome young man running past and feel as he did now.

Eva thought of the happy hours she had spent alone as a child in the cobwebbed attic of that semi-derelict farmhouse and smiled.

It was as if she saw her own pale face framed in the glass of the dormer window, watching her grown-up self run past. Cheerily she waved to her former self. She ran past the Walker, dragging his branch behind him on the track, oblivious to her or to anything else. Down in the valley Bess o'Bedlam was on her knees waving her wrinkled hands and chanting before her small smoky bonfire of damp leaves.

On this day Eva was feeling more pent up than ever, so she forced herself to sprint the last few yards up Yelland Tor, arriving at the top so breathless that all she could do was double over, her hands on her knees, and gasp for air. She lifted her head as her father liked to do and felt the cold rain splashing on her face, washing the sweat down between her breasts. She blinked her eyes several times, and then turned to look at the view as she always did, but the air was too full of water. Instead she breathed in the deep scents of sodden bracken, swollen streams, damp black rock and the wet gusts of wind.

She turned and noticed that just below the peak of the Tor someone had put up a tent, its ropes anchored by rocks. In truth it was more like a bivouac than a tent, no doubt of old army issue, in plain matt green. In front of it huddled someone in a rain cape and wide-brimmed hat. He was facing away from her and had not heard her at all.

'Hello,' she called.

The man turned his head and looked up at her. 'The Lord be with you,' he said.

'Camping, are you?'

'No. Waiting.'

'Waiting for what?'

'The Rapture.'

'The Rapture?'

'Yes, when the Lord gathers the faithful.'

'So you're here waiting for the Second Coming? For Christ to come back to earth?'

'No. He won't return to earth at the Rapture. He'll summon us

and we'll rise up into the air and meet him in the sky. The Second
Coming isn't until after the Tribulation. Then He'll come to earth.'

Eva scratched her head. 'But why are you waiting here? Won't
you get caught up wherever you are?'

'I just want to be ready. To be prepared. To be in the right frame
of mind. To be closer to the sky. You know, I lie here looking up at
the sky, and two or three times every day I see the countenance of
the Lord up there in the clouds, looking back down. I was hoping
to wait over there, see?' he said, pointing towards Newel Tor, 'but
it's got a Chinese priest on top and I didn't fancy the company, so I
came up here.'

'A Chinese priest? What's he doing?'

'He's waiting for a fellow called Maitreya. That's the next Bud-
dha, according to him. He says the sea's shrinking, so that's how he
knows, and he's gone up there to wait. And on Brown Gelly there's
a raggedy woman waiting for the Hidden Imam. Fancy believing
that kind of rubbish, eh? She said she had special information, and
everyone else thought he was coming out of a well in Persia, see?
But no, he was coming out from under one of the cairns in Cornwall,
up on Brown Gelly, but she weren't sure which one, see? Said she'd
learned it in a dream, like.'

Eva pursed her lips wryly and asked, 'If you dream that you're
dreaming, does that mean that you're really awake? What if being
awake is really a dream, and dreaming is just a dream inside another
dream?'

'You got me there, *cariad*. How would I know?'

She asked, 'Are you going to be here all the time?'

'No. Sometimes I have to go back.'

'My name's Eva. Eva Pitt.'

'And I am Maranatha.'

'Maranatha who?'

'Just Maranatha.'

'Is there anything you need? I can bring you something when I
come running.'

'No. I fast. I watch and pray, watch and pray. I look out for the

Lord's countenance, forming in the clouds.' He turned and faced her. His face was very thin, his complexion red and pockmarked. Between thin lips she saw his crooked array of yellow teeth. He had the air of ruin about him, like someone who has been an alcoholic and dried out too late. His eyes were so dark as to be black and spoke of infinite pain and yearning. She guessed that he might be in his late fifties. A thought occurred to her.

'What if you're not one of the chosen? What if Christ doesn't summon you?'

His lips began to tremble and two tears ran slowly down his cheeks.

'I'm sorry,' she said, 'I didn't mean to upset you.'

'It's the one thing I fear the most,' he said and hung his head.

'I'm so sorry,' she repeated. She looked around and gestured into the rain. 'It can get very savage up here. You could easily die of hypothermia. What happens if you die before Jesus comes?'

'I want to ascend in my physical body,' he said, 'but if I die first, I'll go to Him in my spiritual one. When He calls.'

'Well, you'll need better accommodation than this.'

'All I want is to disappear,' he said. 'Disappear without trace. As if I'd never been, see? The Lord go with you.' He turned his head away, gazing sightlessly into the drifting curtains of rain. It was clear that the conversation was over.

Eva was shivering by now, so she strode off back down the slopes and at the bottom resumed her running, just to warm herself up again. She passed the farmhouse, but fifteen minutes later was back at it, knocking on the door. When Q opened it, she gave him an embarrassed little smile and said, 'Hi, Artie, can I stay here for a little while? My bloody Dad's gone out and bloody well locked up, and I haven't got my key. I'm bloody freezing. And wet.'

'Bloody wet,' he said. 'You missed the opportunity for a final "bloody".'

'Yes, I'm bloody wet.'

They sat in the kitchen by the range, drinking tea, Eva with a large towel wrapped round her shoulders. He found himself afflicted and saddened by her youth and her natural grace. Her hard, three-dimensional physicality disconcerted him in a way that Maidie Knox Lilita's vague and ethereal presence did not.

'It's funny,' she said. 'You've been here a while and I hardly know you.'

'Well, I know that you're Eva, and you make jewellery, and I know that you ran away from home to be with your father when you were twelve.'

She bridled. 'I didn't run away from home. I came back home.'

'Sorry. I'm clumsy with people. I'm not sensitive. I say what I think without thinking about the effect. I'm not subtle. You came back home. Of course.'

'My father says that the most intelligent people are the most hopeless with other people. He says you're a genius. So I suppose you must be absolutely totally bloody hopeless with other people.'

'I am alone. I've always been alone, even when I'm surrounded.'

'Did you know,' she said, 'that there's someone camping up at the Tor, and he's expecting to be summoned by Jesus at any moment? He's going to meet Jesus in the sky. He's lonely. That's why he's there. He's called Maranatha. Perhaps you should befriend him.'

'I don't have a religious bone in my body. Not one atom. I'd have nothing to say to him.'

'You're both waiting for the end of the world.'

'He's waiting. I'm not. I'm getting ready for it, just in case. It may not happen. It probably won't. I hope it doesn't. He's looking forward to it, and I'm doing my best to prevent it.'

'The point is, are you enjoying yourself?'

'I think I am getting madder every day from lack of company, but I'm enjoying myself. I've never been busier. The thought of all I have to do fills me with despair sometimes. But I'm never bored. Do you know what cheers me up the most? It's seeing you running past every day. I look forward to it and then it happens, and it makes me feel happy for a few moments.'

'Oh,' she said, 'I'm not sure what to say. That could have been quite corny, but I do think you really mean it. That's so sweet.'

He put his hand to his forehead and searched for the right words. 'Look, as I said, I'm clumsy. I know it and I can't help it. If I offend you, I don't mean to. All I'm saying is that when I see you, I see a wild animal rejoicing in being herself. I get the same pleasure as when I see a stag running down a hillside, or a wild horse kicking up its hind legs, or hares boxing in a meadow. Why are you crying?'

'Because what you said was so beautiful.'

'I'm sorry.'

'I'm not. You can say it again if you like. Do you mind if I give you my honest opinion about something?'

'No. Fire away.'

She gestured around her at the room. 'This kitchen is far too orderly to be a man's. I mean, there should be washing up in the sink and open cereal packets, and crumbs on the sideboard. It doesn't look right. Everything's neat and tidy and tucked away and shiny clean. It looks like you don't live here and you're not a proper man and you don't do any cooking.'

'Well, I don't. I live off ready meals that I put in the microwave.'

Her eyes widened. 'What? You're joking! You're preparing for the end of civilisation and you don't even cook? Seriously?'

'I've got everything I'll need to learn properly, when the time comes. Any science can be learned reasonably quickly, I find.'

Eva was outraged. 'It's not a bloody science! It's an art! Cooking's an art that you never stop learning, so you have to start early. I bet you haven't even got a sieve or a rolling pin or a grater, have you?'

He shook his head and pulled a glum expression with his lips. He got up from his chair and went to the small chalkboard that hung beside the back door. On it he wrote, 'Rolling pin. Sieve. Grater.'

'And don't you know that food is all about love?' she continued. 'When you cook well for yourself, that's how you show your love for your body and your life. When you cook for others, it shows your love for them. What you're doing is not good enough. I'm going to bring you a rabbit and teach you how to skin it and clean it out. Then we're going to roast it in a pot on the top of your wood-burner.'

'You'd do that?'

'Why not? You'd better shoot it first, though. It's a bit of a struggle trying to cook a live one.'

'I can't shoot. I am intending to learn. It's on my list.'

'Dad taught me. He's very good. I'll get him to teach you. He'd enjoy that. I'd teach you myself, but you might as well learn from the master, considering that he's only down the lane. I like shooting, you know, banging away for half an hour, but I've never managed to get fanatical. And why are you buying so many freezers? You must have a dozen in the barn.'

'It's so I can stock up, just in case. I'll be generating my own electricity, you see.'

'You're going to fill it with ready meals?'

He nodded, and she pulled a wry expression. 'You may be a genius,' she said, 'but you're bloody ignorant.'

'Am I?'

'Don't you know that you can't keep food indefinitely in a freezer? So there's no point having lots of freezers?'

'Can't you? Isn't there?'

'Food dries out in a freezer, and after about a year looks horrible and tastes peculiar. If you had any sense, you'd be stockpiling the kind of food that lasts forever. Dried food. Rice, beans, dried mushrooms, fruit – the sort of thing you only have to rehydrate. And you need lots of canned things. If the cans don't go rusty, the food really does last forever. Almost.'

Humiliation rose up in his breast and his face coloured.

Eva continued, undistracted. 'It might be worth keeping the freezers if you ate your way through them in rotation, and then when the end of the world comes, you can restock them with rabbits and suchlike. And if Dad shoots a deer, we can put it in whole and then roast it over a fire pit in the summer and pretend to be ancient Brits.'

'I'll hang on to them, then.'

'You need to get dried food and cans, though. Lots of it. And keep it from the mice. And the damp. And don't look so mortified. No one's intelligent about everything. You don't know about real life, and I don't know a bloody thing about quantum cryptography. And you've got to lay in some wine. Absolutely masses of it.'

'Wine? Why? I hardly drink.'

'Yes, but Dad and I do.'

'Can't you lay it down for yourselves?'

'I can't afford it, but Dad's filled the cupboard under the stairs with Beaujolais and Burgundy and Chianti. When civilisation ends and we finish our stash, we'll have to come and drink yours. I tell you what: I'll make you a list of what you should get. Or I'll order it for you and you can pony up. And tomorrow, when I go for my run, I'm going to call in here on the way back and make an inventory of what you've got in the kitchen, and then I'll write down everything else that you need to have, to cook properly with. Have you got heaps of bog-roll and candles? And coffee? Do you mind if I use your loo?'

'Not at all.'

When she returned Eva went to the fireplace to look at the old photograph of the Effingham House Goal Ball Team. 'I suppose you've seen the ghost by now,' she remarked.

'Maidie Knox Lilita.'

'Oh my goodness, you've found my ring,' she exclaimed, picking it up from where it lay before the photograph on the mantelpiece. She held it up to the light and smiled delightedly as the stones scintillated in the firelight.

'It can't be yours,' he said. 'I dug it out of the thunderbox. It must have been there since long before you were born.'

Carefully, almost with reverence, she put it back before the photograph, frowned and said, 'Of course it can't be mine. I don't know why I thought it was. Silly me. Can I borrow it? I'd like to make a copy.' She brightened suddenly and said, 'Would you like me to show you something really shocking?'

Before he could reply she went to the table, where she picked a

79

lemon out of the fruit bowl. She took a knife from the rack and cut it into quarters. She turned and faced him, and slowly and deliberately ate the pulp out of each, opening and closing her eyes in ecstasy. He watched her, appalled.

'I love eating raw lemons,' she said, 'It's just bloody amazing. Now you try it.'

'Would you like to know something about quantum mechanics?' he asked, and she widened her eyes in assent. 'If you observe a quantum in its present state, you alter its past.'

She paused and considered this, before saying, 'I know all about people like you. You're so naïve you'll believe in anything whatsoever, as long as all the sums add up. I'm not fooled.'

She held out a second quarter of lemon. He took it from her hand and, without averting his eyes, bit it from the rind. He squashed it with his tongue against the roof of his mouth and an electric, horrifying thrill of pleasure silvered his flesh.

16

The New Restaurant

Penelope Jarret met her lover in Trafalgar Square at seven o'clock, while it was still light. They wandered amongst the street entertainers and acrobots until a cold wind sprang up and he said, 'Better be there for our table.'

The new restaurant was in Covent Garden, and so they set off up St Martin's Lane.

'How's your husband getting along? Out in the wilderness?' he asked.

'He's becoming quite the backwoodsman. You know how he used to dress as some kind of Roman aristocrat? Well, now he's all rugged and wiry and sunburned, with a khaki combat jacket and huge muddy boots on his feet, and a hat on his head that his neighbour made from a couple of rabbits. He looks like Daniel Boone or Davy Crockett.'

Percy Prode, known to his acquaintants as 'Purse', smiled, suddenly conscious of his navy frock-coat with its gilded epaulettes, his yellow cummerbund and sparklingly white shirt. He flexed his stomach muscles, finely honed in a gymnasium. He was feeling handsome and virile, and this buoyed him immensely. In his pocket were two fulfilment pills in foil bubbles, an absolute guarantee of success.

'Of course,' said Penelope, 'he's still a complete geek, and totally obsessed by his cryptographic apocalypse.'

'He's probably in the right,' said Percy. 'Nothing seems to work properly any more. A few days ago I tried to pay my income tax and when the biometric didn't work, the system demanded a number and a password from me. I had no idea what they were – it's all a new thing – and when I tried to find out, I got blocked because the biometric still didn't work and I didn't have a number and a password.'

'Things going haywire are no excuse for being bloody boring and moving to Bodmin.'

'I thought you were pleased about it.'

She leaned over and kissed him on the cheek. 'Of course I am, silly boy. It's been a liberation. And the children are almost old enough to look after themselves. How's Julia?'

'Dull. Uncommunicative.' He waved a hand. 'Her usual self. She wafts about the house dressed like Jane Austen, talking like a character from *Pride and Prejudice*.'

'Isn't it funny,' said Penelope, suddenly stricken by a pang of guilt and regret, 'how having an affair can make you say cruel things about your spouse? It's as if that gives you the excuse.'

'Julia is dull, though. I know that really you still love Artie. I don't mind.'

'And he is brilliant, but in the end knowing instantly the answer to any computation makes you hard to relate to.'

'Here's the restaurant,' he said. 'Let's see if it's what it's cracked up to be.'

The door opened automatically and they entered, hanging their coats on the hooks in the lobby. He retrieved his device from his pocket and tapped in his arrival. 'Table twelve' flashed up on his screen and he said, 'Oh, good. By the window. We can watch the passers-by when we run out of conversation.'

They seated themselves and consulted the menu on their devices. All the meat was guaranteed cultured 'in Europe's finest facilities' and all the vegetables were guaranteed grown under glass in Spain, using the latest desalinated hydroponics. 'Looks good,' he said.

'Mm. Yes. Yum. Shall we start with oysters? A dozen each? Then I'd like a ribeye steak, all rare and juicy and dripping with blood.'

'We have to order through our devices,' he said. 'Let's use mine, if you like.'

'You're feeling generous,' said Penelope.

'Not generous at all – it's surprisingly cheap here. That's what happens when you've got no staff.'

They ordered their oysters, and she her steak. In anticipation of energetic lovemaking later on, and wishing to suffer neither from wind nor a heavy stomach, he ordered steamed sea bass and salad for himself. An open bottle of Beaujolais arrived on the trolleybot and he picked it up, saying, 'We ordered Burgundy. Oh well, never mind, this is probably just as nice.'

'Can't we get what we wanted by texting in?' asked Penelope.

'Can we be bothered, though?'

'Probably not.'

They made desultory conversation and sipped at their wine as they waited for the oysters to arrive. Every time the doors opened and a trolleybot emerged, they looked up in anticipation. After half an hour he said, 'This is getting annoying. How long does it take to open a can of oysters and cut up a lemon?'

'I'll text in,' said Penelope.

'Enter a password,' came the reply.

'What was the password?'

'What password?'

'When you booked the table.'

'Oh, shit, I can't remember.' He did remember, but was too ashamed to tell her that it was 'Lucksintonight.'

'Forgotten your password?' came the text. 'Create a new password.'

'Oh, for fuck's sake,' she exclaimed. 'I'm going to text them that we've been waiting for half an hour and nothing's happened.'

'What's the reply?'

'We are sorry for the inconvenience,' she read. 'We are doing everything we can to rectify the situation. Your satisfaction is important to us. Enter your password.'

A few seconds elapsed and then a new text arrived: 'Password not recognised. Enter new password?'

'I've had enough of this,' he said, standing up. He went to the low door through which the trolleybot emerged and went down on his hands and knees. He attempted to prise the doors open, but to no avail.

Suddenly the twin doors sprang apart, forcing him to start backwards, and a trolleybot trundled out, heading straight for their table. It stopped at Penelope's side and its robotic arms began to busy themselves.

'Look at this,' she said. 'It's got nothing on it at all and it thinks it's unloading our oysters. I'm texting in again.'

'Please enter your password,' came the reply.

Percy Prode glared up at the CCTV camera and shook his fist at it. 'Where are our fucking oysters?' he yelled, 'For Christ's sake, send out a fucking waiter!'

Another trolleybot came out, an automated message flashing on its screen. 'You were allotted forty minutes. Your reservation has expired. We thank you for your visit. We do hope that you enjoyed your visit and will return soon. Please give us a favourable mention on your media. Your feedback matters. Your custom is important to us.'

Utterly enraged, Penelope's lover seized the trolley by its upper tray and overturned it. It fell with a clatter, and as it used its arms to set itself upright, Penelope and her lover ran for the door and snatched their coats as the alarms went off.

They stopped running when they reached Charing Cross Road, and Penelope gasped, 'God, now we'll get the police after us.'

'Police? What police? When was the last time you saw any police? We'll probably get a fine posted online. And I'm not bloody paying it.'

'Come on,' she said, 'the night is young. Let's go to Chinatown and find a place with waiters. I fancy Peking duck.'

'Knowing the Chinese, it'll probably be real duck,' he said.

'Oh, yuk. Still, let's just eat it and not ask.'

Her device vibrated and she glanced at the screen. It was a message from her daughter, Morgan: 'Mum where are you the microwaves gone funny and it wont stop and the foods burning mum where are you.'

She twisted her lip and grimaced. She texted back, 'Darlings, order something in.' Feeling sullied and guilty, but resolute, she prodded at the screen with her forefinger and switched it off.

17

Lynx

I was walking briskly along the road that runs past the end of my driveway when a pickup glided to a halt beside me and a voice from the inside called, 'Hey! Artie! *Como esta?*'

It was my neighbour of course. I leaned down and came face-to-face with a magisterial set of whiskers and a large pair of amber eyes that returned my gaze with a kind of apathetic and baleful disdain. I jerked back and said, 'You've got a catbot? It's huge.'

'It's not a catbot, my friend. It's a lynx, a real one. Try not to piss it off.'

'A real one? Shouldn't it be wearing a seatbelt? Isn't there a law about animals in cars?'

Theo flapped his hand dismissively on the steering wheel. 'You seen any police recently? You seen any roadside camera that works? You seen any traffic drones round here? Last one I saw, it was upside down on the ground because the charging point had no charge. Anyway you try and put a seatbelt on Tiegen Rosenwyn and see what she does to your hand.'

'Tiegen Rosenwyn?'

'It's Cornish. Eva came up with it. Our family had a lion once, back in the twentieth. I've got a black-and-white photograph. That was called Puss. Not very imaginative. Back home in Cochadebajo we had black cats the size of jaguars. If you sniffed behind their ears, they smelled of strawberries.'

'This is your cat?'

'Not really my cat. I found it abandoned when it was tiny. Eva and I, we brought it up. Now she does what she wants. She brings us rabbits from time to time, just leaves them at the door. When she wants to eat something herself, she takes it up a tree. Once she took my hand in her mouth and she led me very gently, maybe two miles, and she showed me her cubs. She had a beautiful little nest under an overhanging rock, lined with feathers and deer fur and grasses, with two kittens in it. One of them was plain brown, no spots at all. Mostly, when she turns up, she wants a ride in the car. She takes everything in like it's an action movie. When she sees something she'd like to eat, she chatters, like this,' he thrust out his lower jaw and made it quiver rapidly, 'and then, when she gets bored, I bring her back.'

'How do you know when she's bored?'

'She falls asleep, *hermano*, she falls asleep, just like the rest of us.'

I looked at her luxuriantly dense pelage and said, 'She's very handsome. I like the white sideburns and those long black tufts on her ears. Is it safe to touch her? She's giving me a look like I'm a stain on a clean sheet.'

'Let her sniff your hand, so she gets an idea of what you are and whether you're worth knowing. If you want to be friends you have to win her over with scraps. She's exactly like any other cat, except she's got a ridiculous little tail. I wouldn't try stroking her until she's made it obvious that she'd like it. When she gives you a brush-past, that means you can stroke her, and once she starts bumping you, you can do pretty much anything. If you tickle her tummy she gets too excited and the teeth and claws come out, so I advise against it.'

I held out my hand and, after a cursory inspection, she proceeded to ignore me by gazing out through the windscreen in an exaggeratedly studied manner.

'She's got a purr that shakes the windows,' said Theo. 'Are you just going for a walk?'

I nodded. 'I've got an annoying problem. Well, two, actually.'

'And they are?'

'Someone's disrupted the medical prescription service in the South-West. It's put a hell of a lot of sick people into a panic. And some clever dick with a sense of humour has somehow inserted their own spyware into the spyware I designed for one of our allies. Not that I should be telling you, of course.'

'Then don't, *hermano*. Do you know who it was?'

I nodded. 'I think so. These things often have a kind of signature. Anyway it's caused me enough embarrassment to last a lifetime. I'm going for a walk to think it all through. There's something about walking that makes ideas rise up in my mind. That's how I get solutions.'

'No, my friend, what it does is make the words rise up, and the words contain the notions. Walking has the beat of speech. Every poet goes for walks. That's how you get the music to the verse.'

'I'm only a quantum cryptographer,' I said.

He stroked the coarse fur of the lynx's ruff with the back of his fingers and said, 'Well, brother, we'll make a poet of you yet.'

I said, 'By the way, that strange old woman is up the track again and she's kneeling in front of a stone, rocking back and forth. She's obviously burning something. I've seen her a few times before.'

'That's Bess o'Bedlam,' he replied.

'Is she a witch?'

'I'm sure she thinks she is, and sometimes, brother, thinking makes something so. She's not deaf, but she doesn't hear; and she's not dumb, but she won't speak. She burns leaves and chants.'

'Maybe she's saving the world.'

'Maybe she's ending it.'

18

Sprucing Up

Eva tapped on the glass of the kitchen door and let herself in without waiting for a response. 'Oh, good,' she said, 'you're in. Busy?'

'Mm,' he answered.

She came and looked over his shoulder at the chaos of numbers and logical symbols. 'Calculating, I see. Why don't you use a calculator?'

'I use a calculator to check my results. I always find that if I use a calculator first, I have to do the sums anyway, just to check that the calculator hasn't messed up.'

'Have you nearly finished?'

'Yes. Why?'

'I want to do you a favour. Don't worry, I'll make myself a cup of tea and wait 'til you've finished. Your kitchen is ridiculously tidy again. It's straight from an e-magazine.'

'Untidy it, then.'

'I'll start by leaving the teabag in the sink.'

'Good idea.'

'Tell me when you're ready.'

She sat sipping her tea and observed him, savouring his gift for intense concentration. Fifteen minutes later he put down his pencil, stood up and waved his hand towards his work. 'Hexadecimal representation of codes,' he explained.

'OK, genius,' she said. 'Your time has come.' She dragged a chair into the middle of the floor and said, 'Sit.'

'Sit? What for?'

'Come on, Artie, don't argue. Just sit. I've got a surprise for you.'

He blinked. 'A nice one?'

'No. You'll hate it. Come on, sit down. Now close your eyes.'

'What are you going to do?'

'I'm going to cut your hair. You look like a bloody Neanderthal.'

'I am Neanderthal. My genes are 6 per cent Neanderthal. And I don't want my hair cut. And I hardly even know you.'

'You've got no choice.' She took a pristine tea towel off its rail on the oven door and draped it round his neck. 'I did a course on hairdressing when I was eighteen,' she said. 'I've got no talent – I'm not even as good as the cheapest barberbot – and I've forgotten everything they taught me, but anything'd look better than this.' She snipped her scissors crisply in the air. 'Don't argue. Don't resist. I might accidentally cut your ears.'

'Did you know that once upon a time, back in the ancient world, men used to be in charge?'

She poured a mug of tepid water over his head and said, 'You can't believe these old myths and legends. They're all bollocks. Men have never been in charge. They just thought they were, and we let them think it because we couldn't be bothered to argue. I like to cut hair when it's wet, by the way.'

'You don't say. Why do you think you have the right to do this, without my consent?'

'I'm a jeweller. I have a strong aesthetic sense. If something doesn't look right, then it isn't right. If something isn't right, it's my duty to correct it. And anyway, you do consent.'

'Do I?'

'I have a behavioural theory of consent. If you're sitting there happily and I'm cutting your hair and you're not fighting me off or running away, then that's consent.'

He gave in and let his mind wander off. Her fresh, clean scent was pleasant, and so was the sensation of having her so close. Every now and then her breasts pressed into the back of his shoulder, and her breath soughed softly in his ears. Locks of wet greasy hair fell down upon the tea towel and thence to the floor. 'Stay still!' she commanded and, 'Chin up! Tilt your head! Sideways!' She came round the front and very intently leaned forward to trim his eyebrows. He watched her fascinating eyes flick minutely from side to side. She was so young and lovely that it filled him with a kind of pain.

'Right,' she said, 'now don't move. I'm going to do your nose hairs. You look like a bloody walrus.'

'A Neanderthal walrus,' he said.

Unnerved by the proximity of those sharp points and the fear of having his flesh snipped, he endured a feeling very similar to that experienced when being treated by a dentistbot. 'I'm going to do your ears now,' she said. 'You look like an old man. You look old and creaky. In fact I think I might call you Creaky. It can be your new pet name.'

'I am an old man,' he protested. 'At my age I'm entitled to let myself go. And what's the point of looking nice in the middle of the wilderness?'

'You've got about ten years' worth of fanciability left in you,' she said. 'Maybe more. But not if you let yourself turn into a caveman.' She retrieved a hairdryer from her rabbit knapsack and plugged it in. 'Now I'm going to fluff you up.' When she had finished she said, 'Now, go upstairs and shave, and put on some clean clothes. You've been wearing those ones for a week and they're filthy. Your trousers are obnoxious. I'd think those stains were wee, if I didn't know they were coffee.'

'You remind me of what I wish my mother had been like.'

'Go on, Creaky, just do as I say. Go on.' She pushed him towards the staircase by the small of his back.

'Yes, Mum.'

Ten minutes later he came back down and was rewarded with a gleeful smile. 'Wow,' she said.

'Don't be sarcastic. Was that my surprise: being humiliated by a virago half my age?'

'No. Come here.'

'What now?'

'I'm going to cream you up.'

'Cream me up?'

'Your skin's all flaky and dry. That's the trouble with men; they ought to cream themselves up and they don't. Sit down.'

'I hate cream,' he said helplessly. 'I hate the whole idea of cream.'

'This is the kind that reverses ageing, if you use it often enough,' Eva said. She took a large pot with a blue label from her knapsack and twisted it open. She plunged both sets of fingers into it and advanced upon him. 'Close your eyes,' she commanded. She bent over him and began to spread the cream into his face, even including his eyelids.

'You smell very nice,' he said. 'It's like vanilla.'

'You smell nicer than you did before you washed. All right, now I've creamed you up. Don't you feel better?'

'I feel all clogged up.'

'No, you don't. Now come and look at yourself.'

She led him to the mirror hanging in the hallway and stood behind him, her chin resting on his right shoulder. In the mirror his eyes locked with hers and caught her expression of delight.

'This is your surprise,' she said.

'What is?'

'Look in the glass. What do you see?'

'I see Eva with her chin on my shoulder, with different-coloured eyes, looking pleased with herself.'

'No. Don't look at me. Look at yourself. What do you see?'

'I don't know. What do I see?'

'You big idiot. What you see is a handsome man.'

19

The Tourists

Eva stopped running just before the peak of Yelland Tor. It was a hot day, the wind had dropped and she had suddenly run out of steam, having pushed herself too hard on the slower slopes. Hands on hips, puffing for air and soaked with perspiration, she trudged the last few metres to the top and stopped short.

Seated on various rocks was a family of two adults and three youngsters. The children were dressed identically as characters from the new CG series about aliens, and the adults were got up as the couple from the new romantic comedy *Muswell Hill*.

'Hello,' said Eva, but there was no reply. No one even raised their head to acknowledge her with a tip of the chin. Only their labra-dogbot acknowledged her presence, giving a low bark and wagging its tail.

Maranatha's khaki bivouac lay low and empty immediately below the small area that formed the crest, and she saw that he was in fact down below, walking swiftly towards the marsh. There was an urgency, even a kind of fear, in his stride, and Eva laughed softly, realising that he must have fled the moment these intruders had impinged upon his pious, eremitic, expectant solitude.

She took the small package of peanut sandwiches and an apple and bent down to place them next to the head of Maranatha's sleeping bag, along with a bottle of water from the stream that ran by the farmhouse.

The view of the moor was enormous and magnificent. Siblyback Lake was blue and silver, a shimmering haze pulsing above its surface.

Far below, a mixed herd of auroch and wisent browsed the rough sedge of the marsh at the Lower Long Stone, the bellows of the bulls answered by their own echo from Stowe's Hill. In the distance three buzzards and two eagles circled above the cairns of Caradon. Martins and swifts in pursuit of midges wrote their wide italics in the skies. Above them hovered a twittering roof of skylarks.

Eva stood with her hands on her hips and watched the tourists, all of them transfixed by the prospect, although none observed it directly. The mother and father, the twelve-year-old boy and the teenage girls were holding up their devices, admiring the view that registered on their screens.

'You'd think they'd install some sort of travelator, wouldn't you?' said the woman. 'Why should anyone have to walk in this day and age?'

One of the children said, 'That hill isn't supposed to be there.'

Sensing Maranatha's discomfort, Eva ran down the slope in order to catch up with him. With empty minds and myopic eyes, the tourists watched her go on their screens. Only their labradogbot watched her go with its own eyes.

20

A Visit from Maranatha

Q was in the garden raking out another steaming pile of dung that had been delivered a few days before, from the only 'heritage' dairy farm remaining in the whole county. The heap was a good foot higher than the sleepers now, and he was wondering whether his obsessiveness was taking control of him again. It was as if it were impossible ever to have enough of anything. How much more dung would he need? Should he top it off with a few loads of topsoil? He would ask his neighbour, who had suggested the idea of the raised bed in the first place, pointing out the hopelessness of trying to dig out a garden that was solid rock just a few inches below the surface. He grew rich crops inside his own rectangles of sleepers.

Q was leaning on his rake with his hands under his chin, contemplating the view across the valley, when he was aware of somebody coming up behind him. He turned suddenly and there was a thin ragged man, dressed in an old military greatcoat several sizes too big for him, holding up his empty hands in a gesture of harmlessness.

'The Lord be with you,' said the intruder, his voice surprisingly deep and beautiful, inflected by the rich lilt of southern Wales.

'And also with you,' replied Q, the formula slipping unbidden from a distant recess of his memory.

'You must be Q.'

'Well, I'm Artie, but that's what people tend to call me,' he said. 'It seems to have become my *nom de guerre*. You must be Maranatha.

Eva's told me all about you. I don't go up the Tor because I don't like to disturb you, but I often see you go past the house on the way there or back.'

Maranatha ignored these remarks. 'You're working hard, I see. The Lord favours those who till the soil. Adam tilled the soil. After he was expelled.'

Q looked the man over. His face was red, his teeth yellow and disarrayed. His pate was bald, but from the back and sides the thin brown hair hung greasily to his shoulders. His thin wet lips worked constantly when he was listening, as if he were talking silently, and his dark-brown eyes flickered from side to side. Q noticed that he had an angry boil growing on his cheekbone, below the left eye.

'What can I do for you?' asked Q.

'It's the Runnergirl. I haven't seen her for a week. Something bad's happened. I see her every day, normally. She comes running up the Tor and she brings me something. She brings me biscuits. And peanut-butter sandwiches. I got lazy about bringing my own, see? And now I'm half starving.'

'She brings you food? I didn't know that. She never said anything. How sweet of her. As I said, I did know about you camping up on the Tor, and she told me about you. But nothing bad's happened. She's gone on a course: advanced techniques with gold and platinum. It's a new idea, learning in person rather than online. It seems to be catching on amongst the young. She's a jeweller.'

'Frippery,' said Maranatha.

Q laughed perfunctorily, offended on Eva's behalf. 'You wouldn't think so if you saw it. It's delicate and very imaginative. I say that as someone who doesn't give a damn about jewellery. Eva says the whole point of art is its uselessness.' He reached into his pocket and brought out a silver object, about an inch long, which he held out to Maranatha. 'Take a look at this.'

Maranatha held the tiny silver object up to the light and his eyes widened. 'A death's head!' he exclaimed. 'It's brilliant, boy. The detail . . . she gave it to you?'

'She's very kind-hearted and generous. It's as if she can't help it.'

'You're her father?'

'No. He lives further down.'

'When I pass I sometimes see a young woman at the window, looking out at me. She looks a bit like Runnergirl, but not exactly. I sometimes wonder if it's her.'

'That's probably Maidie Knox Lilita,' said Q. 'She's a ghost. I'm glad you can see her too. It makes me feel a little bit less mad.'

'A ghost? There's no such thing. The dead lie in the earth until the Lord wakes them at the resurrection. She must be a demon.'

Q raised an eyebrow and said, 'Well, I'm not going to argue with you. But that's Maidie, and she chooses who she wants to see her. So you must be one of them.'

'Well, she's not Runnergirl. I was worried about Runnergirl.'

'Eva's here a lot. She seems to like it. She organises me. She cuts my hair and smartens me up, and smothers me with cream, and shows me how to skin rabbits. She made that little skull for me as a *memento mori*. She said, "This is just to remind you that even if you survive the end of civilisation, one day you're still going to die. So live today and don't be always getting ready for tomorrow." Then she got a bottle of wine out of her rabbit knapsack and she made me sit in the kitchen with her and drink it. I didn't like it much at first, but now I do. I'm getting used to it. Drinking a bottle with Eva after a long day's work . . . it's such a pleasure. Then she puts on music and makes me dance. I'm still too inhibited to enjoy myself properly, but I'm getting there. Sometimes her father comes up too, and then we overdo it.'

'I don't hold with dancing. Or alcohol.'

'Jesus drank wine, if I remember rightly.'

'Ah yes. But it nearly killed me. I was all but doomed. In the end the Lord saved me from myself. I was lower than low. I was sleeping in bins and skips and doorways. Lucky for me there's so many deserted houses. And then one night I was full of gin, drunk and helpless in the entrance of a mine shaft, the one near Witheybrook Marsh, and the Lord came and He touched my lips with his fingers, like this.' Maranatha raised his hand and squeezed together his thumb and middle finger. 'The Lord sealed my lips. And then I woke, and after that I've never drunk again.'

'Eva says you're waiting for the Rapture.'

'She did, did she? Well, so I am.'

'And then there's the Tribulation?'

'Yes.'

'What then?'

Maranatha reached into the pocket of his greatcoat and brought out a chapbook. 'Read this,' he said. 'I brought it for you. I've given away thousands. If I sold it I could have earned a fortune, but I do the Lord's work for nothing, see?'

Q took it. It was a few centimetres high, a few pages held together with two staples, bound in a cover swirling with orange-and-scarlet flames, a bearded, crowned and robed Christus Rex looking straight out at him from his gilded cross. On the front it said, '*A Guide to the End Times* by Maranatha'.

'You're an author!'

'Only a messenger.'

'Thank you. I'll read it this evening. Do you want it back when I've finished it?'

'You keep it. I've got hundreds.' He looked around, shrugged his shoulders. 'So Runnergirl is all right after all? I've been worried for nothing. But I'm frightened that the Lord won't take her. She doesn't believe. She told me so. She'll be left behind when the Tribulation starts. She's going to suffer. And you know she's . . . well, she's like . . . Well, you've seen for yourself. How *melys* she is.' His eyes began to tear up. 'I'll be off back to the Tor.'

'Let me make you a sandwich,' said Q.

That evening he poured himself a glass of wine, settled into his armchair and rediscovered the pleasure of reading from the page rather than from the screen. It was so much easier to flick back and forth. In this pedantic and exiguous book, written in a ponderous, rhetorical and pseudo-poetic style, plumped out with biblical quotation, Maranatha revealed that after the Rapture there will come the Judgement Seat of Christ, whereby His Christians will receive reward in proportion to their worth. This will immediately be followed by the Marriage of the Lamb, whereby Christ will be united with his church.

The Christians having been safely removed from earth, those who remain on it will have to endure seven years of Tribulation, which will occur when the Antichrist signs a treaty with the nation of Israel. The Antichrist will turn out to be a treacherous ally, however, and will end up as Israel's tormentor.

In order to bring Israel to a state worthy of salvation, God will be obliged to persecute it until the Israelites give up all resistance and come to faith in Christ. Simultaneously, or possibly afterwards, God will judge the wicked, causing 80 per cent of the world's population to perish and life on the planet to dissolve into anarchy and chaos.

Meanwhile Satan, working through the Antichrist, will busy himself with attempting to destroy the faithful, thwarting God's intentions and causing all people to worship him. He will seduce the multitudes by means of fabulous miracles and signs.

However, all Satan's efforts will be annulled by the Second Coming of Christ, who will proceed to judge the Gentiles by separating the Sheep from the Goats and casting the latter into hell.

Thence Christ will set about judging Israel, to see which Israelites are worth keeping and which ones should be refused entry into the Kingdom.

Then the Old Testament saints will be resurrected, complete with bodies, as well as those Christians who have unfairly perished during the Tribulation.

Then Christ will cast Satan into the abyss, where he and his demons will be helpless for 1,000 years. Seventy-five days later there will begin the millennium, a period of joy, peace and perfect righteousness for Gentile, Jew and Christian alike. God's curses on the original couple will be removed, so that even the deserts will bloom, and peace and prosperity will be universal. Those who used to be dead will have resurrected bodies, and those who survived the Tribulation will retain their fleshly ones. Only the latter will be able to reproduce, and unfortunately some of their descendants will be unbelievers.

After 1,000 years Christ will release Satan from the Abyss (although Maranatha gave no reason for this apparent perversity) and he will promptly set about recruiting the unbelievers and organising a rebellion.

At this point God will have had enough of fooling about, and He will cast Satan and his Fallen Angels into the Lake of Fire. Then He will raise from the dead all the unbelievers who have ever lived, reproach them for their faithlessness and cast them into the same Lake. Then He will judge heaven and earth, find them both contaminated by wicked beings and the taint of sin, and so He will utterly destroy them both.

God will be reunited with His Son, there will be a new heaven and a new earth, and thenceforth nothing whatsoever will happen apart from joyfulness, meaningfulness and absolute fellowship.

The little book was stuffed with odd details, such as how many trumpets would be blown at which particular time.

When he had finished the booklet, Q's thoughts turned to Maranatha, wondering what kind of man he could be. He had worked out the details of this divine futurology with scrupulous scholarship, from the Bible alone, but why nowadays, he wondered, would you take seriously the inspirations of desert tribesmen from thousands of years before? Tribesmen who might well have been drunk, or paranoid, or simply insane, filled with the fear of thunder and the magic of the rainbow, terrified by a God who might command them to sacrifice their sons or massacre entire tribes along with their animals, a God of arbitrary moods, whose vengeance was vicious and total. What was the point of the millennium when Jesus would knowingly bring it to an end by releasing Satan, in the perfect foreknowledge of what the latter was going to get up to? What was the point of any of this at all, since God, if He wished, could perfect everything instantaneously with a click of His omnipotent fingers?

Burning with impatience, Q put on his coat and his boots, wrapped a scarf around his neck and took the torch from its hook on the recharger. He would only use it if he had to, having learned on Bodmin Moor that one's eyes adjust to the dark very quickly if they have to. He trudged up the track to the peak of the Tor, listening to the whooping and squeaking of the owls, and dimly aware of the bats that scooped past his head, dark rags of shadow against the lighter darkness of the night. Sirius seemed brighter than ever. A cold south-west wind brought with it the briny smell of the sea.

At the top he stopped before the opening of Maranatha's tent and a voice came from inside, 'Is that you, Lord?' It was a voice compounded of fear and hope.

'No, it's me – Artie. I read your pamphlet and I wanted to ask you something.'

Maranatha's head appeared, the hair matted and tousled. 'I was sleeping,' he said, 'I was bang in the middle of a dream. What can you be wanting?'

Q waved the little book and said, 'I want to know why God would bother with all this. If He and even you know in advance exactly what's going to happen, why bother with all this messing about? All these blasts on trumpets? Why not just go straight to the end?'

'God does what He says He will, that's all I know.'

'But what's the point? Can I ask you something?'

Maranatha nodded, and Q asked, 'How did it come about? That you turned to Jesus?'

'Well, boy, after he came to me and sealed my lips against the drink, I saw him in a tree. An ash tree it was, all glowing in a golden light, like, and very beautiful, and it was him, up there in the middle of it, looking down at me with a smile, and he raised his hand, like this.' With first and second fingers of his right hand raised, and the third and fourth downfolded, he made the Hand of Benediction.

Q scuffed at a small stone with his foot and asked, 'But how did you know it was Jesus?'

'Because it was.'

'But did he speak? Did he say, "I am Jesus"?'

'Didn't have to, boy. And anyway I had a little girl with me, holding my hand, like.'

'Did she see him?'

Maranatha scratched his head uncomfortably. 'No. She didn't say she did or she didn't. I didn't ask. I just assumed.'

'So she doesn't really count as a witness?'

Maranatha's jaw began to tremble, and his eyes welled up. He stabbed the air with his forefinger and demanded, 'Well, boy, what do you believe in? You tell me that.'

Q hesitated and replied, 'I believe in polynomial mathematics, superposition, superexponential timescale solutions, the replacement of causation by probability, taking care of those I love and having the complete quantum stack. And a lot of other things along the same lines.'

'Well, boy, good luck praying to them. You be off now. I'm up early for the dawn.'

Back at the farmhouse, Q turned on his device and commanded it to link with the screen that occupied the entire length of one wall of his living room. He wanted to talk with Eva about Maranatha. At that moment there did not seem to be anyone else with whom to talk about him. He was overwhelmed with wonder, and sorrow, and pity. Maranatha was up on the Tor alone, trembling beneath his skimpy bivouac, consumed every waking moment of his days with anticipatory terror.

Eva was busy and did not respond. He wondered what she was doing, and felt a small pang of jealousy. He asked himself if trying to contact her and talk about Maranatha might have been nothing more than a fairly transparent pretext. He wandered about the house, unable to focus on anything in particular, so he worked on a new code for a few hours, took a bath and went to bed. Unable to sleep, he went downstairs and pinged Eva again.

This time she answered. Her hair was loose and she was dressed for bed, in one of her father's old shirts. 'Hi, Artie,' she said, 'it's late. What's up?'

'Nothing, really. I was shovelling dung when Maranatha came by.

He was asking after you. He was worried because he hasn't seen you for a while. He gave me a little book about the end of the world.'

'Oh,' she said, 'he often tries to talk to me about that. You just have to be patient. I mean, it's all he lives for. Did I ever tell you about the theology that Dad and I made up?'

'No.'

'Well, we were a bit pissed. It goes like this, OK? The universe was hatched out of a cosmic egg.'

'A cosmic egg?'

'Yes, and it was hatched by the cosmic chicken.'

'So where did the cosmic chicken come from?'

'Silly question. It hatched itself, of course. It's self-created.'

'So it had to exist before it existed, in order to bring itself into existence?'

'Got it in one. Marvellous, isn't it? Oh and the egg was self-fertile – you know, the way some fruit trees are? That's why you don't need a cosmic cockerel. And it explains why the universe is a bit of mess, a bit chaotic, things going wrong and not working out.'

'Does it?'

'Well, chickens aren't very bright, are they?'

'Have you tried this on Maranatha?'

She shook her head. 'Might not be a good idea. Anyway, I'm going to bed now. It's late and I've got platinum to bend in the morning. I expect you'll have lovely dreams after shovelling all that dung.'

'Shovelling dung is my new metaphor for life,' he said. 'Bye.'

They waved and switched off.

That night he dreamed vividly of Maidie Knox Lilita. Her hair smelled of rosemary and her cotton nightdress of lavender. She laughed and whispered in his ear, 'Want some tribulation? I've got plenty for you, if you want to risk it. If you'd like to try? Would you? Would you like to try?'

21

A Letter to Penelope

My dear Pen,

It has become very obvious, from what the children say when they come here, and in their messages, that you have found a new boyfriend. It isn't obvious to the kids yet, though.

I want you to know that I am not jealous, and I wish you well. I don't doubt that we can continue to act as a couple when it comes to looking after Morgan and Charlie.

It seems to me that our marriage was rather like a tree that sprouted, grew up, flourished, bore fruit, shed its leaves from time to time and then blossomed again, and finally got to the end of its life. You don't accuse a tree of being a failure when its life comes to a natural end. We had a good innings. No regrets for either of us, I hope.

As for me, I am in a strange situation that as yet I do not fully understand, and I am not ready to talk about it.

I am mainly writing to tell you that you must keep the car fully charged at all times, so that you always have enough charge to get you and the children to safety here. I am intending to invest in one of those vehicles whose bodywork consists entirely of photovoltaic panels, but even so you must learn to drive it manually in case the satellites become disabled or dysfunctional. There are people who will be able to instruct you, if you are nervous about mastering it on your own, and of course we can work it all out together when I come back one of these weekends. Please also ensure that Charlie and Morgan learn how to drive manually, and I'll do the same when they're down here.

If the grid fails, you must not wait in town for more than a day. That I will accommodate you and the children here goes without saying.

All I would ask is that you should not bring your lover with you unless he has specific skills that will be useful, or else he is willing and able to commit himself to heavy manual labour. I am afraid I can't have somebody here who is used to conjuring money out of thin air from sitting on his backside and isn't prepared to do anything else. I would have to ask him to leave. As you know, I don't have any bots here because I began to resent the dependency that they create in their wake.

Please kiss the kids for me and tell them that I'm looking forward to having them this weekend. We're going to build a dam!

Remember: keep the car charged at all times.

My love to you all,

Art

22

Maidie Relates Her Seduction of Q

I saw a letter on the chest in the hall. We used to write letters a lot, back in my Edwardian days. I loved getting letters. I used to write letters eight pages long. I had lovely handwriting. At Effingham House they made us use copy books full of italic writing. I never lost the knack of writing.

Last night I slept with Artie again. In I came, silent and barefoot when he was half asleep and half awake, and I lit the candle on the mantelpiece before I slipped in beside him. I'd scented my nightdress with lavender and my long dark hair with rosemary. I'd trimmed my nails and put bee balm on my lips to make them soft and glossy and a little bit clingy.

'Maidie, is that you?' he murmured as I lay down beside him and kissed him on the cheek, and slipped my hand inside the shirt of his pyjamas.

'Today I'm thirty-two,' I whispered, 'Just the right age.'

'You're always the right age,' he said.

'Do you think you're dreaming?' I asked and slipped my hand lower and stroked the hairs of his stomach.

'I don't know if I'm dreaming,' he said. 'I don't know what dreaming is any more. You've made me confused.'

'When you're dreaming,' I said, 'it's as real as waking. You have two lives. The difference is, when you're awake you dismiss your other life as a dream, and your other life gives you things to dream with.' I moved my hand lower and he moaned. 'When you're dreaming,' I said, 'you see even when your eyes are closed. You hear, even though there is no noise. You touch and taste, even though your fingers are still and there's nothing in your mouth. That's how you perceive me. That's why others sometimes don't.'

He turned over and took me in his arms and said urgently, 'Don't tell me you're a dream.'

'I didn't say I was a dream. I only said that you see me with the same eyes that you have as a dreamer, and hear me with the same ears as a dreamer, and when we make love, you make love as you do in a dream.'

'My wife is unfaithful,' he said.

'And now you're being unfaithful to your wife. Sometimes you have to do the wrong thing or you'd have no life worth remembering.'

Outside a barn owl hooted and he said, 'Is that a real owl?'

I laughed and said, 'Don't you listen to a word I say?'

'Ah,' he said, 'so there's nothing to choose between two worlds that are equally real?'

'Take your pick. Which world do you choose? Why not have both?' I kissed him softly on the neck and fluttered my tongue on his skin.

'You know what I choose,' he said.

As we reached the end of our lovemaking, the candle burned out and the darkness covered us over as a mother draws a blanket over her child.

'Maidie,' he said, 'will you be here in the morning when I wake?'

'I'll come in and wake you. I think I'll probably be eighteen. It all depends on how I'm feeling.'

'Where do you go when you're not with me?'

'Here and not here. Go to sleep now, my darling. You're tired.'

He lay still, his eyes glittering in the dark, and then he said, 'Maidie, what if I dream about you?'

'Well, of course you will.'

'Maidie,' he said, 'I love the way you smell. I love the warmth of your body and the texture of your flesh. I love the way you move with me inside you. I love the dark intensity of your eyes and the arc of your brows. I love your voice. You have a most beautiful voice. It's soft and low, it has a little creak in it as if you're about to laugh.'

'It's the voice that always remains,' I said. 'It's the voice that lasts the longest.' For some reason I began to feel a little sad. Of course I knew why. Illusions are no less beautiful for being what they are. Every moment is precious. Every moment must be grasped.

It was then that I gave him a hint about who I was. I said, 'When a new house is about to be built, the builders send in someone else to level the ground and dig the trenches for the footings.'

'Why did you tell me that?' he asked.

And I replied, 'The eyes look around for love, and when they see someone they desire, they make a recommendation to the heart. And sometimes the heart is unwise and says, "You go ahead. Let's see what happens", so the eyes go down below and pass the word on to the loins, and then, you know, the loins are a trickster, and they deceive the heart. Then the heart entangles itself in suffering like a sheep caught up in thorns. But sometimes the heart is wise and it considers what the eyes have told it, and it stands in front of the mirror and strokes its chin, and it considers whether or not the eyes have a good point, and it takes into consideration a great many other things, and then it goes to the loins itself and says, "I have talked with my eyes, and we've agreed." And that is how love succeeds.'

I leaned up on my elbow and looked down at his face, wondering how many times, throughout our history, a woman's profundity had been wasted on a sleeping man.

23

Bedwyr Bedryant

Q messaged Theodore and waited for him to come onscreen.

'Hey, *hermano*,' Theo said.

'I thought I ought to tell you, in case you don't already know, not to drink the tap water for a while. I was worried about you and Eva getting sick. Take water from the stream. I've already checked it. No dead sheep for once.'

'I've made a filter, same as yours,' Theo replied. 'Nice layers of pebbles, charcoal and sand. What's happened to the taps?'

'Some joker hacked into the remote-control system at the water-works for the whole of the south and west of England. They've bumped up the sodium-hydroxide level from a hundred parts per million to fifteen thousand. So it's poisonous. Luckily, it got detected within an hour or two. I've got to spend the morning online, to see if I can deal with it. If I can trace the hacker, I'll crash his computer for him.'

'You must be earning a fortune, brother, sorting out all these crises.'

'I'm doing well, I'm doing well. I'm spending all the money on the farm.'

'I had a thought, brother. If everything goes to hell, as you think it will, you'll have to bring the farm back to life. I mean, turn it back into one. Breed animals instead of hunting them. Tame some horses. Maybe you ought to repair the walls and gates and fences.'

'Oh God, I've got enough to do. Imagine removing all that scrub, and all those stunted trees.'

'You could burn it off. Not now. That would be illegal, but after everything's gone to hell. It was just a thought. You could get goats and donkeys to eat off all the scrub and bring back the grass.'

'Listen, I've got Charlie and Morgan here and we thought we'd make a day out of it. Would you and Eva like to come on a jaunt?'

'Sorry, Artie, I can't. I've got to go and sort out a bison.'

Q laughed. 'You've always got the most out-of-the-way excuses.'

'A bison stuck in a culvert is no joke, *hermano*.'

'Wait 'til we get those back-bred woolly rhinoceros.'

'Oh, don't.'

'What about Eva?'

'I'll ask her. Hey, *hija*, Artie says do you want to go out on a jaunt with him and the kids?'

Eva came to the screen. 'Hi, Artie. What kind of jaunt?'

'Down to the lake at Altarnun.'

'Sounds good. Shall I run to yours or will you pick me up on the way past?'

'We'll pick you up in twenty minutes.'

An hour later they were just a mile from Jamaica Inn, on the reedy shores of Dozmary Pool, which lay in the land like a dish, 500 yards in diameter and a mile in circumference. It was never more than nine foot deep, but legend declared it bottomless. The shadows of clouds drifted ghostly across the tiny crests of its tremulous wavelets, breaking up the inverted images of its surrounding hills and the derelict whitewashed farm.

It was here that Jan Tregeagle, the evil seventeenth-century steward, was doomed to carry out his sentence to empty the lake with a limpet shell drilled with holes, and whence he fled to the chapel at Roche Rock, to howl and hammer at its door, imploring the saints for remission and admission, only to be sent by the Devil to Gwenor Cove to weave ropes from dry sand. When storms raged, the people said that the howling was Jan Tregeagle, out hunting with his hounds, and the crack of lightning was the snapping of his whip.

The four settled near some misshapen hummocks and tussocks, in the meagre shade of a solitary wind-blasted tree on the lake's edge, and opened the basket they had brought with them, full of pasties, sandwiches and oranges. Across the water a small herd of longhorn paddled in the stony shallows.

'Who wants wine freshly chilled?' asked Q, holding up a bottle.

'Me,' said Eva.

'Dad, you're such a pisshead these days,' said Morgan.

'It's your fault,' he replied. 'Children drive you to drink.'

'It's my fault,' said Eva. 'Dad and I have corrupted him.'

'Who's that over there?' asked Charlie, pointing to a man huddled on a stool 200 yards away, 'He's wearing a cloak and a crown. And he's fishing.'

'He's just a fisherman, but I don't think he ever catches anything. I don't think he's even got any bait on the hook,' said Eva. 'I asked him what he was doing once, and he looked up at me and said, "I'm waiting for Sir Galahad to come and cure me." He's had some kind of injury, I think. He can hardly walk. It's painful to see him try, but he never gives up. Ooh, look, here comes Beds.'

They followed her gaze and beheld a man mounted on a horse, approaching them at a lazy hack, as if in a dream.

'I've seen him before,' said Q, 'the first time I was here, and a few times since.'

'He's dressed like a Roman soldier,' said Charlie.

'And he's only got half a left arm, said Morgan.

'Oh,' said Eva, 'that's his distinguishing feature. That's what made him realise who he is. When he was about twenty-five.'

'And who is he then?' asked Charlie.

'That's Bedwyr Bedryant, and that spear is his magic lance, according to him. He's the one who killed Wrnach the Giant and rescued Mabon ap Modron, and retrieved the hair of Dillur the Bearded. Amongst other things. He's the Tamer of Horses.'

'Impressive,' said Charlie, not without sarcasm.

'Another stray Welshman,' said Q.

The horseman drew near, halted and leaned forward to ease the chafing of his backside on the hard saddle. 'What tidings?' he said.

'Afternoon, Sir Bedwyr,' said Eva. 'Do you fancy a glass of wine?'

'I may not,' he said, in a baritone voice rich with South Wales. 'I am in the field. Wit you well, such pleasaunce must I forsake. I would lever die with worship than live with shame.'

'A tipple?'

'Fie upon thee, demoiselle, sore temptress that thou art. Of only one will I partake. Prithee, tempt me no further than that.' He lifted off his helmet, revealing the grizzled features of a fit sixty-year-old who has passed all his life outdoors. His small, bright eyes were periwinkle blue, almost violet. He mopped his face with a rag that was tucked into his saddle, saying, 'A day like unto this, pardee, is no day for harness. I wilt as the desert leaf.'

'You don't have to wear armour all the time, do you? There's never anyone to joust with, is there?' said Eva, passing him up half a glass, which he poured down his throat in one slug.

He wiped his mouth with the back of his hand and said, 'God speed you, this is like unto the wine of the Germanii. Of all wine earthly, that I love the most.'

'Good guess. It's from Alsace,' said Eva.

Bedwyr nodded with his chin towards the lake. 'Hast seen aught, *cariad*?'

'No, sorry,' said Eva. 'Look, let me introduce you,' she continued. 'This is Artie, otherwise known as Q, and this is his daughter Morgan, and this is his son Charlie.'

'Morgan!' repeated Bedwyr. 'Fateful name! Loth am I to speak it!'

The girl pouted and said, 'Well, I like it.'

The knight raised his hand to block the sun and looked out over the lake.

'What are you looking for?' asked Q.

'He's a birdwatcher,' said Charlie, *sotto voce*.

'An arm vested in samite, and a hand that brandisheth a sword,' replied Bedwyr. 'A little barge with many fair ladies therein, and three queens. One is sister to our liege lord, Queen Morgan le Fay; the other is the Queen of Northgalis, the third is the Queen of the Waste Lands. Also there will be Nimue, the chief lady of this lake, that wedded unto Pelleas the Good Knight. And this lady has done much for King Arthur. She walketh on the waters, like unto the Lord, and her raiment weepeth from her like water.'

'Why don't you just sit on a boulder and keep watch?' asked Q, 'instead of going round and round on a horse?'

'For that my heart brasteth not for weariness,' he replied. He kicked his horse's flanks, said 'Ho!' and he and his horse left off their steady circumambulation of the lake, his harness jingling, the sun glancing off the red plumes of his helmet and the burnished metal of his breastplate. At the same lackadaisical pace they set off down the track in the direction of the village.

'You do meet some interesting people on Bodmin Moor,' observed Q.

'What was all that about?' asked Charlie.

'King Arthur, of course,' said Eva. 'Excalibur's out in the lake. When the King comes back, the Lady of the Lake'll be out there, waving it for Bedwyr to fetch. And then the King will come to the salvation of the country.'

'Yeah, Charlie,' said Morgan in mock contempt. 'Didn't you know that?'

'Back from where?' asked Charlie.

'Lyonesse. He's sleeping in Lyonesse. Or in Avalon. Or he's in Glastonbury, twenty feet deep, with Guenever beside him.'

'Where's Lyonesse?' asked Q.

Eva rolled her eyes. 'Between Land's End and the Scillies, of course.'

'Under the sea?'

'Well, it used to be dry land and then the sea engulfed it, and only Trevallion got away. On his white horse. They just managed to out-run the wave.'

'Who's Trevallion?' all three asked at once.

'Bloody hell,' said Eva, rolling her eyes again. 'I can tell you're not Cornish. Anyone for a swim?'

'Not me,' said Charlie. 'The water's too cold. And I haven't got my trunks.'

'Nor me,' said Morgan.

'I haven't got my trunks, either,' said Q, 'and my underpants are full of holes. I wouldn't want to make myself a laughing stock.'

'Well, you're a bunch of lily-livered faint-hearts,' said Eva.

To the astonishment of them all, she undressed rapidly in front of their eyes, leaving only her trainers on. She turned and hurtled into the water. She stood up and shook out her hair, exposing her tightly muscled stomach and her small goose-pimpled breasts with their tight pink nipples, glistening with drops of water. 'Come on!' she called. 'It's lovely!' To Q, her immaculate young body looked oddly familiar.

Morgan stood up as if suddenly inspired, slipped out of her clothes and she too ran towards the water.

'Oh my God!' said Charlie. 'Dad, help! Why do girls always do this? What are we supposed to do with our eyes?'

'Only one thing for it,' said Q, and he and his son lay down on their backs and gazed at the sky, listening to the joyful cries as the girls duck-dived and splashed. Curlews called and small knots of dunlins flew overhead as father and son, side by side, amused themselves and passed the time away in making creatures of the passing shapes of clouds.

'When they come out of the water,' said Q, 'remind me to tell them never to let on to that roving knight over there what my real name is. I wouldn't want him to get all excited.'

'Hardly anyone ever calls you it anyway, Dad.'

24

Shooting

'Good morning, Artie, here I am,' said Theodore Pitt. 'It's a perfect day for it. No wind to deal with!'

Still in his pyjamas and socks, Q bowed low and said, 'Good morrow, My Lord!'

'In Shakespearian mode?'

'Verily, by my troth. I've got the children here, and Morgan made me watch *Henry V* with her after supper. She wants to study Theatrical History at Truro. She says she wants to write about Problematising Perspectives in the Poetics of Post-Political Technique in the Use of Thespibots in Physical Shakespearian Theatre. She might be moving down here during termtime. Apparently they've gone back to teaching in person. Isn't that wonderful? It was the one with Laurence Olivier. No thespibots in that one! Once more unto the breach!'

'I see you're quite fired up.'

'All I've got to do is get dressed. The children are still slouching about in bed, like the gentlemen of England.'

'I see you've got your rifle range all set up. It all looks very good.'

'A nice high bank of rubble buried in sand, a hundred metres from the house. That diggerbot did a good job. I can even practise from the bedroom window.'

His neighbour raised his eyebrows. 'It's lucky there's no one about any more. You never could have got away with that in the old days. In fact I think it might be part of my job to prevent you. I was originally thinking we should use one of the quarries. Some of them are quite long. But they do make the bangs exceedingly loud. And they're usually full of water.'

'Well, thank God for cultured meat, and wild animals that take over the land and frighten away the faint-hearts. And thank God for screens that keep poor addicts hypnotised indoors. And depopulation. And Park Rangers who come from the Andes.'

'Somebody shot a goat on a crag once, back home in Cochadebajo, and the report caused an avalanche that nearly buried him. We found the goat, luckily, but we didn't find the gun until the melt. Happy days. We won't be needing the range today. I've got a handful of seventeen-centimetre targets and a pellet-catcher. We're starting in the yard with an air rifle.'

'An air rifle? No proper bullets?'

'Don't look so disappointed. This is about education, not entertainment. I've got a powerful old springer and it's damn hard to shoot. You get the recoil before the pellet's even started up the barrel, and then you get another recoil when the piston hits the breech. If you can learn to shoot accurately with this, you can learn to shoot anything. That's the whole point. Start difficult and that makes everything easier later. You're about to learn the artillery hold.'

Q looked sceptical. 'It's really that hard?'

'Well, a real rifle has only one recoil. That thump in the shoulder when the bullet's already left. With one of these, it's a double jump – one backwards and one forwards. I'm going to keep you firing this old girl until you fill that bull with little holes and never flinch. Then we'll bring out the big boys with the bullets. Shooting's all about acquiring good habits.'

'I thought it was just about lining up the sights and letting rip.'

'Put aside thy folly and be wise,' said Theodore. 'You've got to learn about windage and elevation. Come on, get your clothes and boots on.'

Upstairs in his room he found Maidie Knox Lilita in his bed, propped up against the headboard with her long locks of black hair arranged to the left side of her face as usual, tumbling down the fine lacework of her nightdress. 'I'm about to learn to shoot,' he told her.

'My father went shooting with King Edward once,' she said abstractedly. 'The King had his shoots arranged so that it was all terribly easy. He said they slaughtered hundreds. The birds flew straight at him over a hedge. And the King cheated terribly at golf. He used to pick up his ball on the green and say there was no point in putting, because he was always down in two. And he had a special frame made so that when he made love he didn't squish his lovers.'

'I love you, Maidie,' he said.

She locked his eyes and sang:

'Love is pleasing and love is teasing
And love's a pleasure when first it's new
But as love grows older it waxes colder
And fades away like the morning dew.'

She looked at him askance, her head on one side and an ironical smile on her lips. 'I'm going now.' She was gone, leaving behind the imprint of her body in the sheets, the sleepy smell of warm girl and lavender.

Out in the yard, Theodore Pitt hung the catcher on the barn door and the two men companionably shot pellets at the target, standing, lying, sitting, and then from an old school desk that Q had found in an outhouse. He grew increasingly exasperated.

'Why do you always get tight little groups in the centre of the bull, and I spray them all over the place? I've got twelve-centimetre groups!'

'I keep telling you: you've got to watch the target until long after you've pulled the trigger. Otherwise you flinch and close your eyes when the sear's released, and the jerk makes the pellet go off-course. Think about it. What do you call a man who closes his eyes when he's shooting?'

'An idiot?'

'A very bad shot. Keeping your eyes open 'til the missile's gone is called "following through". If you don't follow through, you might as well throw stones.'

'My son says that following through is when you fart and more comes out than you bargained for. I think there must be something wrong with the rifle.'

Theodore laughed. 'Yes, brother, it's got the wrong man shooting it. That's why I don't have a problem, and you do. Let's take a break. And another thing: you don't necessarily have to pull the trigger with the top joint of your forefinger. You can try using the middle of the pad. Or you can lay your forefinger along the side of the stock and pull the trigger with your middle finger.'

In the kitchen they sat at the table and sipped tea out of tin mugs. Q saw no point in having breakable ones, and indeed all his plates were also made of pressed steel. He bought only those things that would last a lifetime.

'Do you believe in ghosts?' he asked.

'Where I come from, they walk about in broad daylight. You just put up with it. They live in a world of their own. Only half here.'

'I've got someone. In this house.'

'I know. Maidie Knox Lilita. Eva told me. I've never seen her myself.'

'The funny thing is, Maidie's never here when Eva is.'

'I'm surprised you believe in ghosts, *hermano*. I thought you were a scientist.'

'More of a mathematician. The thing about quantum mechanics is that you have to believe six impossible things before breakfast. You get used to it. Nothing surprises you. No paradox perplexes you. The impossible is actual. Contradiction is expected. On the face of it, it's all nonsense, but when you do the experiments, against all expectations they really work. I keep asking Maidie how it is to be what she is, but she never answers directly. She's always tangential.'

'There's plenty of people like that, brother.'

'This air rifle. Is it any good for killing things?'

'Nothing bigger than a rabbit or a pigeon. Anyway you're not shooting anything at all until I know you'll do it in one shot, every time. I want to turn you into a killer, not a torturer. The careless man who causes an animal to die in wretchedness is despised and detested and punished by the gods. I'm not letting you shoot a living thing for a long time yet, believe me.'

A very young woman, olive-skinned and delicately built, blessed with a wonderfully extravagant head of crinkled hair, wandered into the kitchen, dressed only in a dressing gown and fluffy pink slippers. 'Morning, Dad,' she said. 'Good morning, Dad's friend.'

'This is my daughter, Morgan,' said Q.

'I'm Theodore,' said her father's friend, standing up and holding out his hand.

'Have you had breakfast, Dad?' she asked.

'I'm afraid so, sweetheart. You'll have to make your own.'

Morgan scowled playfully and said, 'You can't get decent service around here.'

'I'm learning to cook. Eva's teaching me.'

She looked at Theodore and said, 'Well, good luck to her. Pigs will fly before Dad learns to cook.'

'Scrambled eggs for lunch,' said Q. 'From our own hens.'

'Knowing you, Dad, it'll come out more like an omelette. One of those rubber ones that you can buy to prank your friends. By the way, I haven't seen this ghost of yours yet.'

'Maybe you never will,' said Theodore. 'Ghosts are choosy about who they hang around with.'

25

Maranatha on the Tor at Dawn

Beyond Upton Cross and Caradon Down, on the eastern horizon, the sun began to light up the low clouds with ochre and amber. Maranatha crawled out of his bivouac, shivering, and clasped his arms around himself. Below him the mist was rising off the marshes and the lake, stranding him on his black atoll of rock, a shipwrecked heart in a quiet ocean of vapour. Any minute now the sun would rise high enough to turn this ocean into a sparkling sea of silvery white. Then it would ascend. He would be swallowed up. Then it would rise above him, and down below would be the lake with its bright dots of white egret and its flocks of widgeon. The small herd of bison might still be there at the border of the wood. He wondered if today would be the day.

Two red kites, their tail feathers forked like swallows, glided and wheeled above him and he thought, 'Something might be dying. Something might be dead.'

Maranatha lived in terror of death, and so he waited for the Rapture. He had seen too many deaths, not one of them peaceful. If only the Lord would summon him. He had dreamed of it so often; he could already feel the wind on his face, the cold water of salvation washing his soul, his arms stretching out as he flew, a wingless angel, looking down on the unfortunate earth, bidding farewell, an escapee from its terrible fate.

Today he had no food, so he would retrieve his electric moped from the derelict barn where he parked it behind an abandoned tractor and return to Bodmin. He would take with him this week's blue carrier bag, tied at the neck, and add it to the steadily growing pile of bags in the corner of his room. He wore his clothes for a week at a time, and so he would take this week's wash to the laundrette and collect that from the last. He would go to the grocer's and come out with seven cans of soup for his midday meals, seven evening meals in vacuum packs (sterilised by radiation) and two loaves of bread for his breakfasts. He ate fish, but never meat. Sometimes he went down to the lake and came back with a perch, which he cooked in butter on a small hexamine stove that was one of the few relics of his army days. He hated the killing, but reminded himself that the Lord had given man dominion and made him steward of the earth.

Today he would go to the single room that he rented above a charity shop, check that his yoobi had been paid in, and lie in the warmth and comfort of his bed for just one night as his moped recharged in the shed behind the shop. For company he would have the one photograph that he had of his mates, Reconnaissance Troop, C Squadron, the Welsh Cavalry, their brawny arms folded, grinning out at the camera in desert camouflage, their obsolete SA 100s slung across their shoulders. Not one of them was left, Maranatha the sole survivor. They had not been told that they might be up against deathbots. Outside his window the electric cars would go by, swishing like the sea, especially when it rained. Sometimes there were midnight choirs of drunks singing in the street, and loneliness would oppress him as he remembered his comrades from before. In the morning he would wake early, desperate to get back to the Tor, glad to see the back of Bodmin Town, exquisite though it was, with its old stone buildings on narrow streets, its propitious storks nesting on the roofs.

This morning there was something magnificent about being marooned on an island above the mist. He spread his arms and sang. His rich Welsh baritone floated out over the cloud, ascended to the red kites, found its way through to the marsh. It was 'Cwm Rhondda', and he the singer, exiled from one Celtic land into another:

'Guide me, O Thou Great Jehovah
Pilgrim through this barren land;
I am weak, but Thou art mighty,
Hold me with Thy powerful hand.
Bread of Heaven, Bread of Heaven,
Feed me 'til I want no more;
Feed me 'til I want no more.'

He set out down the Tor for the rendezvous with his moped.

'Open now the crystal fountain,
Whence the healing stream doth flow . . .'

He passed Q, who was up early, with his young son, their breath
steaming as they stacked up bricks near the entrance to the farm. He
stopped and talked with them for a few moments, asking if he could
park his moped somewhere here, instead of in the abandoned barn.
'It would be closer, see?' he said. 'Now that you've improved the
track, it would be practical, see? Save me walking.'

'When I tread the verge of Jordan,
Bid my anxious fears subside;
Death of death and Hell's destruction,
Land me safe on Canaan's side.'

He was still singing as he walked past Theodore Pitt's house, and
he wondered if Runnergirl was there. Her youth and prettiness, her
unblemished body, her exuberant energy were so far off from him
that they were unimaginable. Maranatha had never had sex with a
woman; there is a kind of man who considers himself unworthy of
paradise until he dies. Eva heard him as she slept, and incorporated
him into her dream:

'Strong deliverer, strong deliverer,
Be Thou still my strength and shield.'

She dreamed about Q, about a fox, about her father, about Maidie Knox Lilita.

Down in the valley, near the wood, a red stag in rut, tormented by the need to lock antlers, to fight and rut, heard the deep, resonant strain of the Welsh hymn, raised his muzzle from the croppy turf and bellowed. The voices of the Christ-intoxicated hermit and the red stag mingled together and bounced between the stunted shrubs, the streams and boulders of the Tor.

26

Food

S he pinged her husband, and he put her up on the screen, saying, 'Hello, Pen, what's up?'

'No food, that's what's up. We're going to have to come down to Bodmin, at least until this is over. I take it you've got masses of food stashed away in your sheds.'

'Yes, but I was saving it for an emergency.'

'This is an emergency – we're out of everything. We've even eaten stale things from the back of the cupboard, and that can of snails that we bought in France ten years ago. Morgan was sick.'

'I mean the real emergency.'

'Little emergencies look pretty huge when you're about to starve, darling. We'll be with you tomorrow afternoon. I fancy an Irish stew, a really huge one.'

'You want me to shoot a sheep?'

'Whatever it takes. Are you dealing with this one?'

'No, I've got a defence contract to work on. Someone else is dealing with this. It shouldn't be too hard to crack.'

'What's happened exactly?'

'Well, you know when you buy anything, the code gets read and the item's automatically reordered? Some clever dick has scrambled the codes, so that when the system orders a bunch of bananas, you get a hairbrush. It's been randomised. The warehouses are full of stuff that wasn't what was ordered and they don't know what to do with it, and in the meantime nobody's got any food.'

'I just got delivered some tennis balls. I don't know anyone who plays tennis, let alone me.'

'I told you ages ago to get in enough food to last you two weeks. You don't take me seriously, do you? You've only got yourself to blame. It's another ransom attack. Things like this are completely predictable.'

'I do believe you're annoyed with me.'

'Well, of course I am.'

'Well, that's rather marvellous really.'

'Is it? Why?'

'Because in the past you never got angry at all. You always kept on an even keel. A bit like a bot, in fact. In the past you never got angry, even when I was a complete shithead.'

'For better or worse, I seem to be becoming more like myself. I'm letting the animal out.'

'It's definitely better, darling. See you tomorrow.'

'It might have to be goat. In the Irish stew. The nearest sheep are miles away.'

27

Windstorm

In the winter of that year, for seven days a north-east wind from Siberia pushed across the south of England with implacable force, relentless and irresistible. To venture outdoors was to be left breathless as the air was snatched from one's throat. A big man could go out and lean against it without falling, and a child would be blown backwards. It filled one's eyes with tears that were whipped away. It made one's nose pour with mucus. The leaves on the trees dried out, withered and snapped away from their branches. Ancient oaks and beeches broke their roots, groaned and fell across the roads. Fences and lorries were pushed over. No one could remember any other windstorm like it; there was no record of any such wind for a hundred years. The animals in the forests lay flat in the lee of banks. At Land's End, Camborne and St Ives the birds were blown away to sea. The more fortunate made landfall in the Scillies. Digila the peacock was blown from the roof ridge of the barn, never to reappear.

Q thought at first that the banging on the door was just a few more objects being hurled against it, but then it opened and his neighbour entered, followed by Eva and a whirlwind of leaves and debris. Both were breathless, and bundled up as if for the Arctic. A gust entered with them and blew the dishcloth from the rail at the side of the stove.

'Close the door, Theo!' shouted Q.

'Sorry,' said Theodore, 'but I'm sick of waiting indoors for this wind to stop. I'm sick of having to yell if I want to be heard. We've got to do something.'

'Do something? Like King Cnut and the tide? What are we supposed to be doing about the wind? It's almost dark!'

'It's been blowing for four days! And it's cold! My God, it's cold.'

'Well, it's from the north-east. Imagine what it's like in Tyneside and East Anglia! Poor bastards.'

'Hello, everyone,' said Eva. 'Hello, Charlie, hello, Morgan.'

Charlie looked up and grunted, and Morgan put her arms around Eva and gave her a kiss on the cheek. 'You must be bonkers,' she said, 'coming out in this.'

'We got bloody bored,' said Eva, 'just sitting indoors for days, waiting for the wind to stop. And the bloody power cuts.'

'Your lights are working,' said Theodore.

'It's the generator,' said Q, 'but we're almost out of fuel now. I had to shut off the wind turbines and lower them, to stop the blades being wrenched off. It's lucky I had Charlie and Morgan here to help.'

'Well, it's lucky you had me, at any rate,' said Charlie.

'Piss off, beloved brother,' said Morgan.

'I've been wondering,' said Theodore, 'if I could get connected into your system sometime. Would that be too much to ask?'

'Two systems that can be connected would be better. We could have our own little grid.'

'Would that be expensive?'

'No. It would make a nice project. We could put a row of little turbines along your roof ridge. And we should put a little hydro-electric generator into the dam, when it's low in the summer. Why have you come bristling with armament?'

'We've only brought some shotguns.'

'Yes, but why?'

'Because we're pissed off with the wind. We're going to the top of the Tor and we're going to fire some shots into it.'

'What will that do, Theo?'

'It's what we used to do in the mountains, brother. Too much rain, too much wind, too much snow, you go out and fire some shots to show the gods you're pissed off and they'd better do something.'

Q raised an eyebrow. 'You believe in gods?'

'Only when I have to. Only when there's no alternative. When I need somebody to thank, and then maybe when I need someone to blame. I'll probably believe in them when I start dying. I want this wind to stop, and for that I have to believe in gods – gods I can shoot in the face to show how pissed off I am. Do you want to come?'

'Up the Tor? In a wind like this?'

'I'll come,' said Charlie. 'I've hardly ever fired a gun and I'm bored and I need to go out, wind or no wind.'

'I'm staying in,' said Morgan. 'I'm not going out in a hurricane. I'm so light and tiny I'd get blown away and you'd have to fish me out of a lake. I'm not mad. Anyway, it took me a long time to get dressed like this, and I couldn't be bothered to change.'

'You're just boring,' said Charlie, curling his lips into an exaggerated sneer of contempt. 'Why do you want to look like Cleopatra anyway?'

'I'll fetch my guns,' said Q.

'Dad, you've got guns?' exclaimed Morgan.

'I've got two. A rifle and a shotgun.'

'But, Dad,' said Morgan, 'how did you get permission? I thought it was really difficult.'

'It is normally. You need a certificate for each kind. I was wondering who on earth I could use as my two references, until I suddenly remembered that I knew the Prime Minister and the Home Secretary. Thank God for COBRA meetings. Friends in high places. I pulled strings.'

Charlie said, 'It's funny, Dad, but I never thought you'd ever become this kind of dad. It's like I've had two dads.'

'Town dad and country dad,' said Morgan.

Q laughed. 'Which do you prefer?'

'Country dad. Town dad was all pale and pasty, and sat still for hours at a time doing sums in his head. At least country dad can cook and doesn't go on about quantum mechanics and asymmetric key sizes all the time.'

'I taught him to cook,' said Eva. 'Credit, please!'

'Country dad talks about getting the logs in, and about how those bloody pigs have got in the vegetables again,' said Charlie.

'I'll get the guns,' said Q, 'and, if it's of any interest, I prefer my country kids to my town ones.'

'Well, dogbot bollocks to you, Dad,' said Morgan.

'This is a weird wind,' said Eva. 'It sings all at one pitch, like somebody blowing really hard across the head of a flute, and it hardly gusts at all, it just keeps up this gigantic pressure. I don't remember anything like it in all the time I've lived here. Charlie, you'd better wrap up warm. You can't come out in a T-shirt, Godfrey Kneller wig and silk slippers.'

'Are you my mum?'

She pursed her lips and looked at him ironically. 'I'm more of an extra, bigger sister. Just get togged up and ready. Or I'll get my scissors and cut your hair again, and cream you up!'

It was a formidable battle to reach the peak of the Tor. The wind blew across their path, forcing them to lean against it sideways. Each of them carried a gun in its slip, slung across their shoulder. The chill on the right side of their faces numbed all feeling, but on the left their cheeks were burning. Inexhaustibly, the mucus ran from their nostrils. The scream of the wind rendered conversation impossible. The air was whipped away before their lungs could grip. Their enterprise was entirely laborious. They trudged upwards, determined, oblivious to the absurdity of their mission, mindful only of their grievance.

At the summit they paused in the semi-darkness and unslung their guns, looking at each other in the manner of soldiers about to scale a wall. There was no sign of Maranatha or his tent. Below them the lights of St Cleer flickered on and off as their power failed and resumed. Above them the fleecy clouds sped across the face of the full moon. There was a steady horizontal rain of objects: paper bags, leaves and twigs, scraps of turf. A child's trampoline rotated gracefully as it wheeled over their heads. 'It's the bloody apocalypse!' shouted Eva as she loaded two shells into her shotgun, but nobody heard. Next to her head she dimly heard the crack of her father's rifle as he fired.

The pressure forced them off their feet. Side by side they knelt, leaning heavily into the wind, firing volleys against the hurricane, working their way through their satchels of ammunition. The crack of their gunfire carried westwards, to be heard in St Neot and Colliford, whose people, cowering indoors, believed it was snapping trees and breaking boughs. One by one they reached the end of their supply and returned their guns to their slips, until Theodore fired his last shot.

He ejected the case, slung the rifle across his shoulder and faced east, holding out his right arm at forty-five degrees, pointing with his forefinger, fired up with anger and contempt, roaring, 'Fuck you! Fuck you!' It seemed to him that the gods laughed as they flung the tempest back in his face.

'Fuck you!' he roared again, and the others stood beside him, their arms raised and fingers pointing, their arms thrusting back and forth in rage, roaring those words in chorus, until at last their throats grew hoarse and the lights of St Cleer went out.

28

The God of This Place

Theodore Pitt had given his neighbour an antique copy of *Aids to Scouting* as a present, saying, 'Read this, brother, it's still useful', and so Q had spent an entire day from dawn until early dusk creeping about amongst the boulders of the upper moorland, then at the edge of the marsh and finally in the woods. He came home exhausted, scratched and filthy, having first called in on Theodore at the far end of the track that led to his house.

'I haven't once succeeded in detecting or stalking a wild animal by means of telltale signs, and I've been at it all day,' he confessed.

Theo laughed. 'It's a knack, brother. You pick it up in the end. Wild animals make little paths for themselves that they use all the time. They cross roads at the same places. You can see the tracks worn in the banksides. The foxes, the rabbits and deer – all in the same places. After a while you even learn to recognise their smell.'

'The sheep leave tufts of wool everywhere, caught up on thorns. I have noticed that.'

'Well, that's a start, brother. In the meantime you can't beat sitting still in a little nook somewhere, with a pair of binoculars. The kind that don't need batteries and don't have to be connected to your damned device.'

'When are you going to teach me how to hunt?'

'When I've finished teaching you how to shoot. You've still never killed yet, have you? I wonder if you've got the moral strength. I wonder if you could take the guilt when you see the light fade out of the eyes of something beautiful; the shame of it, and the knowing that something dark within you gives you the right.'

'No, I've never killed,' said Q. 'I don't know if I can overcome the inhibition.'

'For the moment we'll stick to tin cans and targets.'

'What about you? Killing's part of your job. And then you eat the meat. You and Eva don't eat cultured meat at all, do you?'

'I grew up in the Andes, brother. No cultured meat where I'm from, back then. And in case you're wondering about the killing on the moor, the point to bear in mind is that all this balance-of-nature stuff is a fake. It's a hoax. In a genuinely wild place the real balance is a state of imbalance. It's a seesaw that never settles. The predators kill all the prey until there's no prey left, and then the predators starve, and then the prey come back. Then the predators return, and on and on it goes. Diseases like brucellosis kill entire herds, and the carrion crows and kites and buzzards get fat and multiply until the meat's all gone and then they starve. The deer eat the bark off the trees and the trees die. There's no balance.

'What I do here is round up the aurochs and vaccinate them. If a lynx abandons her cubs, I bring them up and release the right number here and give the rest to another park. If I find an animal dying, I put it out of its misery. If there are too many stags putting each other out of action, I kill the least-healthy ones. If the beavers drown the wrong bit of land, I trap them and move them. If the wild boars get swine fever, I kill them and burn them. If we ever get wolves, I'll have to vaccinate them for distemper and treat them for mange, and then cull them when they get too many. If we reintroduce the great bustard, it'll be me raising them in pens. Somehow our human race got appointed to a job we didn't apply for: we're the stewards of the earth.'

He went to the window and gestured at the moorland. 'It's all an imposture. There's no nature any more. All this wildness isn't wild. This world – this moorland – is nothing but a zoo, and we arrange it to be the kind of zoo that suits our current inclination. It's like a garden where you slave continuously to make it look untended. In the old days, when we still had farms with livestock, we thought all those fields and hedges were nature. It wasn't nature, any more than this is. And I'll tell you something else: every week I seem to get a directive about exterminating non-native species. They wanted us to exterminate the pheasants and the rabbits and the red-legged partridges, because they're not native. Only been here since the Romans, brother. I've just had another instruction about racoon dogs and parakeets. The way I see it, if we've got happy colonies of parakeets, it's evolution at work, pure and simple. My life's a battle against the *eco-fascisti*. They're exactly what Hitler would have been if he'd taken any interest in the German countryside. I'm not killing any parakeets.'

Q cast his eyes downwards and sighed. 'So we've turned the countryside into an enormous zoo, and the country people have fled to the towns because they're frightened of living in one.'

'Don't get me wrong,' said his neighbour, 'I love my job. I love this place. I like the bitter, slicing wind and the fog, and the white clouds bowling eastwards through the sky, and the white-tailed eagles circling on the tors, and I like it that everyone's gone and the houses are crumbling and full of owls. I feel like a naked savage out on the moors with my rifle. But I'm not. I'm just a zookeeper, and this is my zoo. Getting paid for this is merely the icing on the cake.'

'You're the God of this place.'

'Yes,' said Theodore, 'I'm the God of this place. I'm the magician. My job is to make it all look natural, to make it all seem uncreated. To make it less of a mess.'

29

The Horse

Q and his son were feeding logs through a splitter when Eva turned up in the yard, dishevelled but triumphant. 'Look what I've got!' she said.

'It's a horse,' said Charlie.

'Course it's a horse. Well, a pony really. It's still only a colt.'

'Where'd you get that from?' asked Q.

'I caught it myself. It's from that herd on the other side of the wood. I went down every day for a while until they were used to me, and then I threw a lasso around this one. Dad taught me how, years ago, when I was a little girl. I used to lasso the dog. And Dad, sometimes.'

'Didn't it put up a struggle? I mean, how did you hold it?'

'You wrap the lasso round a tree, and the horse pulls and pulls until it strangles itself and passes out. Then you quickly loosen the lasso and it comes back to consciousness, and after that it never resists again as long as you've got the rope round its neck. It really works.'

'That's just cruel,' said Charlie.

Eva scowled at him and replied, 'Well, it's easy to tame a domestic horse that's born tame, isn't it? This is a wild horse, and that's how you do it in South America. Now I've got to get him to trust me.'

'After you throttled him?'

'Horses have forgiving natures.'

'You made that up,' said Charlie.

'Well,' said Eva, 'what I want to know is: can I keep him in one of your stables? Dad and I don't have one.'

'The stables are all full of survival stuff,' said Q.

'You've got six. And one of them is only full of cardboard boxes. He can go in there. What do you want all those boxes for anyway?'

'In case they come in useful. I hate throwing things away.'

'Well, you should either spread them on your vegetable patch in the winter, so they rot away, or make them into logs.'

'How exactly would you make them into logs?'

Without a word, Eva went into one of the outbuildings and returned a moment later with an elaborate metal contraption. 'This is a log-maker,' she said. 'There was a fashion for making your own logs out of newspaper back in the late twentieth century. This is a bit rusty, but there's nothing wrong with it. You soak the paper and mash it up, and then you put it in there and squish it with this lever. Then you shake it out and let it dry. Hey presto!'

'Wouldn't it be easier just to get in some logs?' asked Charlie.

'Making your own logs out of paper and cardboard is a useful way of having fun,' she replied. 'It's not supposed to be sensible.'

'You're a nutter,' said Charlie.

'And you're an ignorant spotty teenager,' replied Eva.

'Dogbot bollocks to you, artificial unintelligence.'

'Well, anyway, enough sophisticated and intelligent conversation,' said Eva. 'Can I keep him in your stable? I'd have to come up and muck him out every day, and start breaking him in. If you wouldn't mind me being here a lot . . .'

'I don't mind, but you'll have to deal with the cardboard boxes. How did you know that log-maker was there and what to do with it?'

'I spent a lot of my childhood up here,' said Eva, 'when it was still deserted. I used to sit in the attic for hours, or up in the hayloft. And I knew what that was for. Somehow I just knew. And when I checked it out on an antiques site, it turned out I was right.'

Later that afternoon Q looked out of an upper window and beheld the bright-eyed young horse already installed, with its neck over the lower door of the stable. Charlie, Eva and Morgan, wellington-booted, were working together in the yard, all of them wet and filthy. Eva was pulping the cardboard in an old galvanised tub and scooping the mash into the log-maker. With all his weight on the lever, Charlie was squashing the pulp into bricks, and Morgan was carrying them into the sunshine to begin their drying out.

For a long time he observed the harmonious industry of the youngsters, and the heat of love spread out through his gut and formed a lump in his throat. He wiped his eyes with the back of his hand. Happiness is an epiphenomenon, it is unplanned, it strikes without warning, it settles in your spirit like cherry blossom floating down in spring to settle on the waters of a pool.

30

Christian

Q tapped on the kitchen window, and Eva came to answer it. 'Hello, Artie, have you come to be creamed up?' she teased.

'No. Is your father in?'

'No, he's out with the tractor, hauling a red stag out of the marsh.'

'Not so easy. I wanted to ask him about aurochs.'

'Aurochs?'

'Yes. I was hoping to get the train to London, but I've missed it because that bloody great auroch's lying across the track and won't move. It's practically the size of an elephant. I've had to abandon the car. I think it must be Roger again.'

'Did you try advancing very gently and pushing it with the car?'

'No. Last time I did that, it had a go at the car. I hooted and flashed, and got out and waved my arms at it. It stood up, and it must be two metres at the shoulder, so I got back in the car. It's a bull, and it's got the biggest set of horns I've ever seen.'

'If you piss them off, they toss you in the air,' said Eva, adding, 'They don't normally come up here. Roger's the only one that does. I wonder what he's up to. What Dad sometimes does is get a long pole with a six-inch nail in the end and he pokes them in the rump. They don't realise they're being attacked, but the surprise makes them do a couple of little skips, like this.' She kicked up behind to demonstrate. 'It works on the wisents too.'

'The trouble is, these aurochs have no natural enemies. Nobody hunts them. They just do what they bloody well like. They're so

137

enormous they can get away with anything. Anyway, it's too late now. Do you know your dad's password?'

'No. Shall we get Dad's poking stick and see if we can shift it?'

'There's not much point. If you look, he's coming down the track.'

Eva came out of the house and they stood and watched as the beast ambled by. It was an athlete enjoying its leisure, with long slender legs and a hugely muscled neck and quarters, its tricurved horns winding to points, its peaceful brown eyes focused upon nothing in particular. A light stripe along its back divided the rich chestnut fur, and a voluminous and somewhat feminine blonde forelock cascaded between its eyes and down its muzzle.

'He has quite a harem. With balls that size, he'd need one. That's why Dad calls him Roger. He doesn't do much else, and then he comes up here for rest and recuperation.'

'Hmm,' said Q, still not quite used to such frank talk from a woman so young.

'Talking of elephants,' said Eva, 'you know they're back-breeding mammoths? Well, they're talking about releasing a few down here.'

'Oh, for God's sake! Mammoths! Whatever next? Bloody dinosaurs?'

'That would piss Dad off! At the moment he's pissed off because they've told him to cull the water deer down at the marshes. There's yet another drive to get rid of non-native species. He says, "The silly fuckers have never heard of evolution." Anyway, he's not going to do it. He's going to shoot a couple, photograph them from several angles so it looks like he's killed a lot, and put them in the freezer. Nobody ever comes down from London to check up. Sometimes they send a drone. Don't tell anyone, but Dad shot one down once. He sent it back to London, saying he'd found it. Shall we go out and do something? I've got bored of making bracelets. My eyes are tired. I could do with striding out. You can go and fetch your car now. There's something I want to show you. And I've got an errand to do.'

'An errand?'

'Yes, Dad's just been delivered a box of frogs. It's from the rewilding people. I said I'd take them down to Hippies' Wood and let them go.'

'What kind of frogs?'

'Those ones,' she said, pointing to a cardboard box on the kitchen table. 'Careful how you open it. They're quite springy-abouty, and it's a drag having to get them out from under the oven.'

He opened the lid of the box gently and peered in. 'My goodness, they're as green as parrots. What kind of frog are they?'

'Tree frogs. They used to be common, then they went extinct, and now they're back. And they hang about in trees. They'll probably be predated within a couple of days. Too many bloody herons. One can but try.'

Fifteen minutes later Eva was showing Q how to get into Hippies' Wood without knowing the code on the official entrances. 'This is how my dad does it,' she said, taking him several hundred metres around the perimeter fence and pointing to the ground in front of an apparently impenetrable section. She scuffed the ground with her foot, revealing an iron ring.

'A trapdoor?'

'Mmm. Steps down and steps back up. Sometimes it floods if it's been raining a lot, and then you have to use the proper gates, but mostly it's fine.'

'Who put this here?' he asked, as she bent down to heave the door open.

'Nobody knows. Dad found it when he was on the other side. He fell into it when he wasn't looking. It's bloody stiff. The hinges need oiling again.'

'Don't you know the code on the gates?'

'Of course I do. But this is more fun. Like being in an adventure story from the 1950s. When we come back out we'll have to hide it again, cover it with twigs and leaves. Come on, I've got something to show you.'

'Aren't you frightened of the bears? Or the lynxes?'

'No. Bears can be quite nasty, but did you know that in all of recorded history there's never been one attack by a lynx on a human being? Not one! It's amazing, when you think that they can easily take down animals much bigger than us. Maybe we don't smell tasty. Maybe we don't exist in lynx-land and they think we're ghosts. Maybe we just don't look like food. Maybe they think they can only eat things with four legs. Who knows what goes on in the mind of a cat? Tiegen Rosenwyn's exactly like any old moggy, though, but that's because she's tame.'

'I don't even know what goes on in the minds of other humans, let alone animals,' said Q. 'I try not to let it bother me.'

'It's a bugger, isn't it?' she said, 'not being normal.'

'You too?'

She nodded gravely, 'Mmm, me too. One day you'll realise how weird I am and think, "Oh my God." Come on, let's release these frogs, and then I've got something interesting to show you.'

It was January, and the aconites were spreading a rich yellow carpet across the leaf litter. A few dry leaves still hung on the brown bones of the boughs, and bright shafts of sunlight slanted through the canopy. Q felt that something magical and wonderful was going on, as if a bevy of Pre-Raphaelite dryads crowned with wreaths of snowdrops were about to dance into the glade. 'What a beautiful place,' he said. Eva beckoned and strode ahead, leaving her breath drifting behind her.

Near a stagnant pool she set her box down and opened the lid. She tipped the frogs out and said, 'Bye-bye, little buggers.' They stood and watched as the creatures simply sat, looking back up at them. She waved her hand at them, saying, 'Go on, silly buggers. Hop off before the herons come and get you!' She turned and looked up, saying, 'Better leave them to it.'

Deep into the wood she led him, along the narrow paths made by rabbits and deer. 'How do you know the way?' he asked, as he stepped over a fallen ash and fended off the brambles that raked at his face.

'Familiarity. I've been coming here since I was about twelve. This is my private paradise. You can lie on a mossy bank in the summer and dream about your prince who's going to come and wake you with a kiss.'

'What would a man dream of?'

'I don't know. Just sex, I expect. I don't know many men, living out here. Only my dad and you, and a few dogged old remainers. But I should think that most men are waiting for the magic kiss, exactly the same as us. It's not much further.'

They stopped beneath a beech tree, and Eva pointed to an all-but-indiscernible declivity in the ground, filled almost to the rim by bronzed leaves. She knelt down and began to paddle at the leaves like a dog at a burrow.

'Don't look,' she said. 'You go behind that tree and don't come back out until I call you.'

Obediently he moved away and sat on the ground between two roots, with his back to the beech. He thought about Penelope, his wife, of how they had once been utterly devoted, and of how she had become a breezy stranger whose affection was tinged with mockery; of how she pretended to be asleep; of her imprecisely described 'meetings'. He felt the ache of wanting to start again grow in the pit of his stomach. Eva made him feel wistful.

'You can come now,' she called.

He emerged from behind the tree, and was struck by how loveable she looked, kneeling in the leaf litter in her white bobble hat, her cheeks and nose reddened by cold, her pink scarf, muddy walking boots and oversized grey tweed coat, which was beyond old-fashioned even before she had purloined it from her father.

She patted the dome of white bone and said, 'Meet Christian. When I was a teenager I was walking in these woods with my father. We were doing a count of the stoat population, which wasn't easy and was probably a waste of time, but Dad has to do this kind of thing to keep the paper-filers busy at the Ministry for Wildlife. More often than not, you have to make it all up, and no one ever finds out. I noticed a little round patch of whiteness amid the leaves and, because it was autumn, I said, "Look, Dad, a big mushroom!" but when I bent down I found it was bone. I expected it to be a piece of deer or fox, but when I scraped away the leaves a bit, I realised that it was a human skull. Dad and I went down on our knees and started to scoop out the leaf mould and soon realised this was a sort of short trench that had simply filled up over the years, and inside it was sitting a complete human skeleton.

'Dad said, "He must have been young, he's got all his teeth."

'I said, "Shouldn't we call the police?"

'And he said, "They can't bring him back. Leave him be. They'll just dig him out and play around with his bones, then dig a new grave somewhere else. Those bones are too old to bother with." Dad always says that Bodmin Moor is the land of a thousand ghosts and ten thousand invisible graves. "Everything dies," he says, "Let the dead bury their dead. When I die, you can put me out for the birds."

'After that I used to sweep aside the leaves almost every time I came here, to check up on him. His skull has a nice rounded shape. It fits the curve of my hand. Every time it's a tiny bit more crumbly and yellow, and I wonder how long it'll be before it magicks into earth and disappears completely.

'And then I was here one day when I realised someone was looking over my shoulder. I was so surprised that I jumped up and cried out.

'It was a middle-aged woman in a brown coat, with wild grey hair, the sun shining through it so that it was transformed into a halo. She looked like a tired angel. "His name was Christian," she said. "He was my grandfather, but I never knew him. My grandmother used to bring me here. This is where she found him. He lived in this hole, in these woods, and she lived in it too for a little while. It had sticks across it covered with turf, she said. She loved him, but she had to abandon him in autumn. When she came back in spring she found him like this, and decided to leave him where he was. She covered him over with leaves. He'd never left. Every year she returned, to help her remember. I used to come back with her every year in spring, when the primroses come out, and now I come on my own. I inherited her nostalgia."

'I said, "Was she one of the hippies?" and she nodded. I said, "Do you have children?"

'And she shook her head and replied, "No. After me there'll be no one."

'"I'll do it," I said, "and if I have children, they'll do it after me."

'"Thank you," she said. "He was a very special man, my grandmother said. She said he was a prophet. A prophet born at the wrong conjunction of the stars, handsome and charismatic, who went into the wilderness and never came out. He was full of a fiery determination that killed him."

'"He's peaceful now," I said.

'And she wiped her eyes with her sleeve and said, "All that beauty, all those passions that altered the course of the past, where are they now?"'

Eva sat on the ground, cradling the skull on her lap. 'I want to ask you something,' she said. 'All these things you talk about, these quantum effects where everything's topsy-turvy and contradictory, where waves are and are not particles, and you can't tell where something is if you know how fast it's going and vice versa, and changing the past of a quantum by observing it in the present, and all that stuff.'

'Yes?'

'Does that mean that me sitting here with a skull in my lap, talking to you, isn't real? Is this a dream, and reality is something else completely? Is this – being here, all warm and solid – an illusion? Am I merely a figment of someone else's metaverse? Someone told me once that the entire universe is only a hologram.'

Q pondered awhile and replied, 'It's easy to think that the deeper you go, the nearer to reality you get. Solids and liquids made of molecules made of atoms made of electrons, protons and neutrons made of quarks and positrons and bosons, ever smaller and more complicated and bizarre – you can lie in bed in a panic, thinking that nothing is real and wondering how all this experience can be constructed out of nothing but equations and probabilities. I've had times when I've thought I'd go mad, trapped in a reality that can't be even remotely real.'

'I'm not going to go mad,' said Eva. 'But it really bothers me. It makes me angry, if sitting here with a skull in my lap talking to you isn't real, when it really feels that it is.'

'It's all about hierarchy,' said Q. 'What if we've got everything inverted, the wrong way round? What if our lovely solid world isn't simply the accidental and illusory side-effect of all that weirdness? What if all that self-contradictory weirdness is in fact just the scaffold for our lovely solid, normal world? That's how I've learned to see it. That's why I haven't gone mad. Anyway I'm a scientist, not a philosopher. As you say, the more you look into things, the weirder they are. All sense scatters away like a shoal of little fishes, and all there is, is a kind of evanescent sparkle of scales.'

Eva looked up at him. 'Anyway, I'd rather be deluded and happy than wise and mad. When I go running I want to enjoy my body, even if it's made of maths and empty space.'

'You're not deluded. The reality you experience is what the word "reality" actually means.'

She took the yellowing skull in her hands and held it before her, staring intently into its empty sockets. 'Poor Christian,' she said. 'You had all the answers, didn't you? And one by one your disciples departed. And here you are in a ditch, and you'll never lie in a woman's warmth again.'

She kissed the skull on the top of its forehead and placed it gently back on its column of vertebrae. She scraped back its protection of leaves and smoothed them out. She stood and brushed herself off with her hands. Then she put her arms around Q's neck and said, 'Hold me just for a minute. I feel so sad.'

He folded her into his arms as if she were his daughter and marvelled at the athleticism of her body. It was supple and hard, like a spring. She laid her head sideways on his shoulder and sobbed quietly.

31

The Lesson

'You're looking very smug and pleased with yourself,' said Theodore Pitt as he put the cup of tea on the kitchen table in front of his pupil. 'What's happened, brother?'

'Well, I shouldn't be pleased,' said Q, 'because it's a complete disaster. But I am. It's a bit of a coup, really.'

'Are you going to spill the beans?'

'I shouldn't do, but it's all going to come out soon anyway. You can't silence thousands of policemen.'

Theodore pulled out a chair and sat down, pushing a plate towards him. 'Have a biscuit. They're ginger. Eva made them. So what's up?'

'Well, the Home Secretary telephoned me last night to congratulate me on being right, and also to ask if there was anything I could do.'

'"Right" about what?'

'Two years ago I warned her that sooner or later somebody was bound to hack into police records, and now they have. All the files have been deleted, apart from one, so it's what we call a second preimage attack. When somebody's cracked the code and planted false information. The only file left is a mugshot of the Home Secretary and a paragraph that says she's wanted for indecent exposure. In a skating rink in Reykjavik, in 1910. There's an old black-and-white photograph from some ancient porn collection of a skater with no knickers on, under her very tiny skirt. It looks uncannily like the Home Secretary. A fabulous deepfake.'

'Is there anything you can do?'

'Probably not. Look on the bright side; it means that all the criminals and villains get a new start. A chance to reform.'

'There'll be a crime wave, brother.'

'It's what happens when nobody bothers with hard copy any more. It serves us right for being improvident.'

'You are pleased, aren't you?'

'I'm mostly just pleased about being right. I think I know who did it, too, but I'd never be able to prove it.'

'Time to get out on the range. It's perfect. I've brought gas-powered air rifles this time. Much more accurate.'

They were in Q's farmyard, plinking at small metal targets on springs, when Maranatha came by to collect his electric moped from the barn and return to Bodmin, giving an abbreviated wave of the hand before he disappeared.

'What do you think he has in that blue carrier bag?' said Theodore.

'No idea. It's a mystery. I wonder if it's the same carrier bag or whether he has a large supply of identical ones.'

As Maranatha was leaving, Eva ran by and stopped to chat to him for a few moments, before she spotted the two men in the yard. She jogged up, her breath steaming in the cold air and her face flushed from the ascent of the hillside. Q felt a thrill run through him, the simple pleasure of beholding one so young, fresh and energetic, with her skimpy shorts, muddy legs, sweat-soaked T-shirt and clumpy boots.

She bent and put her hands on her knees to take a few deep breaths and then looked up. 'I thought I saw Maidie Knox Lilita in the dormer window,' she said. 'But maybe I didn't. I've only ever really seen her in mirrors. Does she ever go out?'

'She may well do, *hija*, it's just that we never see her.'

'You'd never catch Maidie going for a run,' said Q.

'She could probably do with some rays,' said Eva.

'Do the dead need vitamin D?'

She looked up mischievously. 'How do you know she's dead? Maybe she's not. Maybe she's a different kind of life.'

That evening Q heated up one of his ready meals in the microwave and when he turned round with his plate, he beheld a dignified old woman seated in one of the armchairs. Her long white hair fell in one cascade down her left shoulder. She wore a simple white lacy shirt and a long black skirt. Around her neck she wore a black velvet band with a diamanté butterfly at the throat, and on her feet were Cuban-heeled black lace-up ankle boots. On her left hand she wore the familiar ring. Her face was pale, as if powdered, and the flesh of her cheeks was lined and relaxed, the lips dry and cracked.

He stopped short. 'Gracious me,' he exclaimed. 'It's you. I've never seen you old before.'

She turned her large, supplicating brown eyes upon him, and in them he read her inextricable sorrow.

'Rodin made an exquisite sculpture once,' she said. 'It was called *Celle Qui Fut la Belle Heaulmière*. Go and look it up. Don't deceive yourself. I'm not a schoolgirl. I'm every woman I've ever been.'

Q hesitated, his exiguous dish of cheap food steaming in his hands. 'You were always beautiful then,' he said. 'Your eyes were always . . .' He stopped, painfully short of words. 'Please, Maidie,' he said at last, 'never show me yourself as you were afterwards. I don't mind how old you are when you come. But never show yourself as skull and bones.'

'I have a grave,' she said, turning away.

In the morning, when he was writing in the kitchen, Eva knocked at the glass panel of the door and came in without waiting for a call of permission. 'Hi, Artie,' she said. 'Just passing. What are you up to?'

'I'm working on a paper for the Ministry of Defence about the metamathematics of the interdependence of superexponential timescale solutions, public key infrastructures and hexadecimal representation. After that, I'm working on vortex-mediated phase transitions.'

'Clever clogs,' she said brightly, 'but you aren't as clever as me.' From the pocket of her coat she drew out a small box and sprang open the lid. She put it on the table, saying, 'Take a look.'

Nestling in the velvet cushion within lay two rings. 'Oh my goodness,' he said. 'Maidie's ring. Two of them.' He lifted them out and held them to the light.

'I made a copy,' said Eva proudly, her eyes sparkling. 'It's pretty much perfect.'

'Which is the original?'

'Well, I did know, but now I've got confused. I'm not sure any more. I'm sorry. I hope it doesn't matter. I could probably tell if I looked at them under magnification.'

'It's amazing,' said Q. 'You really are amazing.'

'I'm sorry they're muddled up.'

'We might have to evoke the Identity of Indiscernibles,' he said.

She raised her right eyebrow, put her hand on her hip and wryly awaited an explanation. 'Meaning?'

'If two things are in every respect identical, then they are the same thing. The only difference between these two is their spatial location.' He held them up. 'I don't know if you've noticed it yourself, but you've made them so that they have rotational symmetry around a common point external to them both.'

'I must be cleverer than I thunk.'

'Anyway it's not mysterious,' he said. 'It's rather like Schrödinger's cat, dead and not dead at the same time. They are both copies and they are both originals. Cotemporally. It's simple, really.'

'It certainly saves all the bother of trying to find out which is which,' she said, 'but don't go thinking that I'm fooled. I know when you're teasing or talking bollocks. Sometimes it takes me a while to work it out, though. That stuff about rotational symmetry is bollocks, isn't it?'

32

The Exchange

Shortly after he was asleep, I crept into Artie's bed and slid my hand between the buttons of his pyjamas. He had drifted into his customary state that was neither sleep nor waking. My warm scent of lavender filled his senses, my hot breath was on his neck. He turned and faced me in the darkness, putting his right hand behind my head and bringing me closer for kissing. I laughed lightly, saying, 'Here I am again.'

'Never leave, Maidie, never leave.'

'All things change, all things die that lived,' I said. 'One thing becomes another. The virgin becomes a mother, the little boy becomes a soldier.'

'Don't give me philosophy, Maidie.'

'In the end it's all we have. Did I tell you about my fiancé who was killed in France in 1915?'

'No.'

'You're very like.'

'I hope he died well.'

'It was shrapnel.'

'Oh, I'm sorry.'

'It was a long time ago. It doesn't stop me loving you. Press your-self against me. I want to feel you moving.'

'Maidie, tell me about immortality.'

'Hush,' I said. 'I know nothing about it. I'm not immortal, as far as I know, but then again perhaps I am. Everyone's immortal until they die. You think you might be dreaming, but it might be that

149

you're awake. I only know how to make time stand still. I know how to slide between the cracks. Take off your pyjamas and help me get my nightdress off.'

Outside a tawny owl squeaked, and a gate of the stable swung in the wind. A cloud passed swiftly across the face of the moon, casting the room into a momentary darkness. My eyes were glittering in the dark. I pushed him onto his back, leaned and kissed his lips and then began to kiss my way down his chest, down across his navel and along the middle of his stomach. I paused and looked up, saying, 'Aren't I good at the feminine arts?' before resuming my travel. I paused again and said, 'My hair keeps getting in the way.'

He gathered in my long, thick hair and placed his hands lightly on the side of my head. My greed was astonishing and exemplary. As always with me, he experienced a disturbing confluence of unworthiness and gratitude. In the fleeting eternities of my lovemaking he discovered those moments that cancelled God, philosophy and science, as I replaced them with a single point of blackened light.

Afterwards I laid my head on his chest and stroked his stomach, saying, 'When we're doing that, there's nothing else I'd rather be doing.'

'I'm glad that I exist,' he said. 'I'm glad that I lived.'

I teased him half awake once more in the early hours and we made love again, without ambition, because the languor of our intimacy was enough in itself.

In the morning he awoke and opened his eyes. I was leaning up on one elbow, looking down at his face. I kissed him softly on the lips. 'Good morning, stranger,' I said.

He lay frozen. 'Eva?'

'Who else would it be?'

'You haven't got your clothes on.'

'Course not. Why would I?'

'How did you get in?'

'Up the drainpipe, through the window.'

'But my window wasn't open. And there isn't a pipe.'

'The bathroom window was open. And it's got a pipe.'

'What are you doing here?'

'Laying claim.'

'But Maidie . . .'

'Maidie doesn't mind. Anyway, she's dead. You know she is. It's got "1908" on her photograph.'

'She isn't remotely dead to me. Or to herself.'

I ran my hand down his stomach and said, 'Was that Maidie or me? When we made love last night, was that Maidie or me?'

'You're too young. I'm too old. Your father's my best friend. He'll kill me.'

'No, he won't. He likes you.'

'I can't be unfaithful to Maidie.'

'You didn't answer my question. Was it Maidie or me?'

He looked up at my mischievous eyes and admitted, 'I don't know.'

'Once,' I said, 'you were explaining the Identity of Indiscernibles. And you told me about superposition, and about how two quanta affect each other, even when contact is lost. Maybe everything is weirder than you think. Maybe you should understand that some things can't be understood.'

'Nothing could be weirder than this.'

'Of course it could. There could have been another girl. There might have been three.'

'You smell the same as Maidie,' he said. 'Your breasts are the same.'

'Well, there's a start.'

'But her eyes are the same colour as each other.'

'The eyes may be the window to the soul, but they aren't the soul itself. Look into my eyes. Come on, I dare you.'

I locked him into my gaze, and his own flicked back and forth between the emerald and the sapphire until his mental vision blurred. 'Maidie,' he said.

'Or Eva.'

'I need to know what Maidie says. Otherwise . . .'

I held up my two thumbs, side by side. 'Maidie and I are like this.'

Slowly and deliberately I slid one thumb behind the other so that it disappeared. Then I brought it out again. He noticed Maidie's ring, glittering on my third finger.

'Maidie and I spent much of my childhood in the attic of this house,' I said. 'It was our special secret place on a wet day, when it wasn't too hot or too cold. And you could talk aloud to the worm-eaten floors, and the worm-eaten shelves, and the dark rafters festooned with cobwebs. And I'd run my hands on the rough bricks of the chimney and think about whoever it was that laid them, and up there, there was no time, and all times ran together side by side, and up there were all the children who'd hidden from their angry mothers and their drunken fathers, or sobbed their hearts out when their brothers were mean or their dogs died. And sometimes the sunlight burst suddenly through the cracked panes of the window and motes of dust danced in the rays, and we sat and watched them dancing. Maidie said that all our lives were dreams, and all the dust in the light was the dust of dreams. She and I, we had a mirror. That's how we looked at each other.'

'I'm confused,' he said. 'None of this makes sense. It's strange and frightening.'

'It's simple,' I said. 'You're mine when you're awake, and you're hers when you don't know that you're asleep. Think of all the possibilities, Artie.' I toyed with the hairs on his chest, teasing them between my fingers. 'Maybe she's a good old-fashioned succubus. Maybe she's a ghost. Maybe I'm just her reincarnation. Maybe she's a reverse incarnation of me. Maybe I have a fantastic gift for projection and she's the product of my mind. Maybe I'm a projection of hers. Maybe she's a figment of your imagination, or perhaps it's me who is. Maybe she's my way of being with you even when I'm somewhere else. Do I need to go on?'

'What I do know is that you're never together. You're always separate. When you're here, she isn't; and when she's here, you're not.'

I smiled. 'Well, that must give you a clue of sorts.'

'Aren't you going to tell me?'

'No, of course not. Maybe even I don't really know. You're always telling me about weird things like superposition. Maybe the world's full of other kinds of weirdness. Bodmin Moor is.'

'I think you know and you're not telling me.'

'Maybe. Maybe not. Anyway I'm not jealous, so that gives you another clue.'

'You mean, you wouldn't be jealous of yourself?'

'Maybe. Maybe not. Anyway, how does it feel to have deflowered a virgin? Have you ever done that before? Was I your first?'

'I wouldn't have known,' he said.

'Do you remember,' I asked, 'the first time I came to your house, and I said could I come in because Dad had accidentally locked me out of ours?'

'Yes.'

'I was lying. I wasn't locked out. There's a spare key, if you know where to look. I just wanted to come up here. I think I must have had you in my sights since before you even came to live here.'

'You or Maidie?'

'Hmm, well, who cares, as long as we're happy? By the way, have you ever read a book called *Phantasms of the Living* by Gurney, Myers and Podmore? It's terribly old.'

'I've never heard of it.'

'I'll lend it to you sometime.'

33

Talking of Eva

Through rain and west wind Q trudged the rough track down to Theodore Pitt's house; he shivered and hunched his shoulders, his mind gripped by dread and determination. He knew he had to speak honestly and resolve a mystery that had been increasingly perplexing him.

He knocked at the blue door and was soon let in. He kicked off his boots and let his friend take his coat and hang it on a hook in the hall. 'Come into the living room. There's a good fire going. I'll make you a cup of tea. You still take it black?'

'I do.'

'My great-great-grandfather was half French,' said Theodore, 'and allegedly we inherited the custom of milkless tea from him. He looms very large in our family mythology. That's a portrait of him on the wall over there.'

Q examined the portrait and said, 'I've always meant to ask you who he was.'

'He's my only illustrious ancestor. He was an ace in the First World War and some sort of commando or spy in the Second; very famous in his time, but now forgotten. His name was Daniel Pitt. You'd find him on cigarette cards and written up in boys' magazines. There's a lot about him on the various nets, but no one's written a real biography. I'd do it myself, but I don't know how. I love good writing, but I can't do it myself. I've got his commando dagger somewhere; he gave it to my grandfather, and now it's all that's left.'

'No, it's not. There's the face. You don't look like him at all, but Eva does. The same black hair and startling eyes and fine bones. She's a bit darker, that's all. She has the same disconcerting intensity.'

'Do you know that Thomas Hardy poem about the family face?' asked Theodore.

'I'm only a quantum cryptographer. I only know about stuff that most people find inconceivable. Poetry's a closed book to a man like me. In me, there's nothing artistic or interesting.'

Theodore touched his head to his right hand for a moment, looked up and recited:

'I am the family face;
Flesh perishes, I live on,
Projecting trait and trace
Through time to times anon,
And leaping from place to place
Over oblivion.

The years-heired feature that can
In curve and voice and eye
Despise the human span
Of durance – that is I;
The eternal thing in man,
That heeds no call to die.'

He opened his eyes and looked directly into the other's eyes. 'My grandfather was a white man who came to the Andes to be a teacher. My grandmother was a Kogi. I look like her, I've got her bronze skin and black hair. Eva looks like him, and he looked like his grandfather. I am called Theodore because that was my grandfather's name. Eva is named after her other grandmother. My father was called Daniel, after the ace on the wall over there. Names and faces. They're what gets passed on. And stories too. My family has more stories than a book of fairy tales. These stories tell me why I am equally at home with a rifle in my hand or a book of verse.'

'It must be nice,' said Q. 'It must be nice to feel as if you belong in this world.'

'It is, Artie. To feel that you belong in this world is a great gift. But of course I did get displaced. I'm in England. On Bodmin Moor. I used to belong among mountains that make these hills look like wormcasts.'

'What happened?'

'My town was once drowned because an avalanche made a dam at one end of the valley. Then there was an earthquake that threw the dam down, and my ancestors made the town habitable again. When I was in my teens there was a new avalanche, a new dam was formed because of the rubble and the town was flooded once more, and so we had to leave. I lived for a while near Macondo and Aracataca, and I met Eva's mother when she was working in Bogotá. She was English, and so now I'm here.'

'And you belong here?'

'The heart is divisible. I belong in two places now. Anyway I must get you your tea and then you can ask me whatever it was you came to ask.'

Q sat down in an armchair and watched the fascinating dance of the flames, the crackle and flicker of them, the yellows and oranges, the small flashes of green and blue. It suddenly occurred to him that before screens became ubiquitous, watching the fire must have been what everybody did. 'When the screens go blank,' he thought to himself, 'I shall watch flames, and I believe I will be more contented. I hope I will be more contented.'

Theodore Pitt returned with a small tray, on which were two mugs of tea and a small heap of biscuits.

'Eva made the biscuits,' he said.

'Eva is very keen on domesticity, isn't she? She seems never happier than when doing practical things, such as sweeping or collecting herbs, or rearranging the pictures on the wall so that they make more artistic sense.'

Her father looked at him levelly and said, 'Well, most of all, I'd say she's a savage. She seems domesticated, but she's feral. She's a crack shot when she's hunting, and she's happiest when she's running. And now she's got the horse, hurtling about on the moor. She's going to break its legs one of these days. I imagine you've come to talk to me about her.'

Q put down his mug and leaned forward, clasping his hands together. 'It's just . . . it's just . . . I'm very puzzled.'

'Puzzled?'

'Yes, puzzled. Why aren't you protecting her from me?'

'Why should I protect her from you?'

'You're her father. I'm forty-two years old. I'm married. Eva is in her early twenties. I have a teenage daughter and a son. If my daughter was with a man like me, I'd put my foot down. Why aren't you threatening me, telling me to keep my hands off her, or telling her not to come to my house? I've been avoiding you ever since . . . ever since it happened – for weeks – but you don't seem to care.'

His friend sat back in his chair and regarded Q with an ironical smile. 'Well, Artie,' he said, 'I have so many things to say. First of all, you're not really married. You have a wife, that's all. I too have a wife, but I'm not married. We're not divorced, but she's in Scotland and I never see her. She left me and now she's gone. Your wife is in London and she comes here every three months, or so. You go to London quite often, but you come back disturbed and unhappy, and you only talk about Morgan and Charlie. I can tell that your marriage is no longer a marriage.'

'The fact is that, apart from getting on terribly well, Eva and I are completely unsuited. You ought to be protecting her from me. If my daughter was doing what yours is doing, I'd be up in arms about it.'

'She says she loves you.'

'I know. She says she loves me. And I love her. It seems a miracle, something I can't possibly explain. Something I don't deserve. And if you weren't down here at the end of my driveway, and if I didn't know you at all and you weren't a friend, I'd just be happy for myself . . . if still a little dubious of her sanity.'

'I've lots of reasons for not interfering,' said Theodore. 'She's old enough to make her own mistakes, and young enough for her mistakes not to matter much. If it doesn't work out with you, there's plenty of time to find happiness elsewhere. For you and me, time is more precious, but Eva has time to squander. And, put it this way, I don't think you're the kind of man to do her very much harm. I'd trust a younger man very much less.'

'But, Theo, I feel guilty,' said Q. 'She should be with someone strong and young, and handsome. They should be going to gigs together and talking idealistic beautiful bollocks, and hanging around with other beautiful young people who talk beautiful bollocks.'

Theodore sipped at his tea and asked, 'Why do you have so low an opinion of yourself?'

'Well, look at me! I'm in my forties, I'm half bald. I'm skinny. I have a brain like a computer. I can do mathematical calculations in six dimensions of spacetime, if I have to. I understand things about subatomic physics that ought to be incomprehensible. I know all about Cooper pairs and the Josephson function. I exist more in my mind than I do in the world. If I exist in any world at all, it's a mad world of spinning contradictions and inexplicable harmonies and probabilities. Eva is very young, but she's literate in matters of the heart. I'm frightened by how clumsy and inept I am. And the thought of running up mountains in the rain for pleasure just makes me shudder.'

'I think,' said Theodore, 'that you don't know how much you've changed since you've been here. You see yourself as the same skinny and flabby-faced metropolitan little man who pulled up in his expensive electrocar all those months ago. But you don't wear fancy dress any more. No more silly Roman toga. You dress like a countryman now. You've exchanged your neat little polished shoes for steel-capped boots. You go round in military surplus like the rest of us, because it's tough and practical. You may see yourself as an undesirable boffin who understands exactly how to code and decode the most complicated encryptions knowable to man or God, but what Eva sees is a man who knows how to set up generators, install pumps and skin a deer. She sees a man who's prepared to work in the rain, to tramp for miles in the fog, a man whose brain is matched by his physical toughness and his determination. A man who looks as if he was born with a rifle in his hand. What Eva says is that she thinks you're a lot like me. That makes you familiar. And loveable.'

'Like you?'

'Yes, like me. I tramp for miles in the fog, and I work in the rain. I gather stones to build my own walls. I know how to shoot. I'm almost self-sufficient, and so are you. I always was, but you've been learning it, and now you're pretty good. You're a British man from the city, and I'm a Kogi from the Andes, but we might as well be brothers.'

Q fell silent, struck dumb by what appeared to be such an improbable proposition. The man he saw before him was radiant with force and strength, and it seemed impossible that this was how he might appear to anyone else, let alone to Eva.

'You don't respect yourself,' said Theodore. 'Your modesty is touching. But you haven't noticed how much you've changed. You have muscles on your forearms that stand out like cords. Your face is brown from the sun. You stride out. Eva and I esteem you, not least because you weren't born to be like this, but have become so. Not many people are capable of changing themselves as you have done. And I'll tell you something else.'

'Yes?'

'Has Eva told you how she ended up here?'

'She's told me a little bit.'

'Well, when her mother left with that man, whom she left in turn six months later, she took Eva with her. I was enraged. There'd been no permission, no arrangements. I've never known such impotent despair. Eva was the centre of my existence. She was my moral core. Do you know what she did? She took money from her mother and she came back on the trains. She was only eleven years old. On the way back she sent her mother a message on her device, saying that she was going home, and she's been here ever since. Guess who I love most in the whole world?'

'Eva?'

He nodded. 'Yes. And if Eva is with you, then she is also still with me. She's only a mile away, along that track. I don't lose her to some man from Paris or Montevideo or Kinshasa or London. If what you say is true, that civilisation is about to end because our electronic systems are bound to fail, then there is no one in the world better placed or better prepared to look after her than you are, and you're right on my doorstep.'

Q raised his eyebrows and shook his head. 'That's a Faustian pact. You give up your daughter to an unsuitable man just so that you can keep her in place.'

'I'm not an idealist. I'll always want Eva nearby, that's all. And you're not unsuitable. You're too old, but older men are more reliable, and you're not likely to hurt her. But if you do . . .'

'Yes?'

'Like you, I'm a good shot with a rifle. And I know Bodmin Moor better than you do. On Bodmin Moor thousands of undiscovered bodies lie concealed.'

'Are you serious?'

'What do you think, *hermano*?'

Q put down his cup and said, 'I have no plans to hurt her. And what about you?'

'What about me?'

'You're strong and healthy. You're a man. Don't you need a woman? Don't you need one, more than I do? You strike me as the type who finds himself completed in a woman.'

'I live by the side of a road. One day a woman will come by, and that will be the woman. Perhaps, when civilisation fails and the people pour out of the towns, perhaps that will be the time when some exhausted woman falls at my door, and I find her and I raise her up. I think I shall be saved from this solitude because I live at the side of a road.'

'Living at the side of the road will be the death of you. When the towns have been looted and the horde pours out, people will stop at your house and beg for food, or steal. The psychopaths will find each other and team up. There'll be brigands. After a while there'll be cannibals. You've got to live out of sight. Move into a quarry.'

'You're telling me to move? What about the woman who falls at my door?'

'You don't have to move now. But you've got to move the moment the net packs up and the lights go out. You can come up to the farmhouse. We can get a room ready for you, and you can store your things in one of the barns.'

Theodore looked at him in silence. He made a small gesture with his hand and said, 'If you weren't so obviously sane, I would think you were simply another crazy man, a *loco*. Will you tell me something?'

'Yes, if I know the answer.'

'How shall I put it? Is there a part of you – a big part or a little part – that actually wants all this to happen? Are you waiting, like Maranatha waiting for the Rapture, or that woman waiting for the Hidden Imam, or Bedwyr waiting for King Arthur and the Fisher King waiting for Sir Galahad?'

'I think there would be a tiny satisfaction in being vindicated. But when I think about the danger and the hardship, the loss of life and the cruelty, then my heart sinks and I feel sick to the stomach. The answer to your question is that if I were religious, I would be down on my knees night and day, begging Him not to let it happen.'

'So all these preparations of yours, these dams and solar tubes and photovoltaic tiles and wind generators, they're like a vaccination? I mean, one gets vaccinated against diseases that one may never even encounter, and it's all just in case.'

'Yes, it's a kind of vaccination. Except that a vaccination is over in an instant. This kind of vaccination amounts to an entire way of life. Like being a monk, or a shepherd.'

'I envy you,' said Theodore.

'You have a way of life, the same as me.'

'Yes, I do, and I love my life. I love to be out on the moors. I love to have Eva with me. I love Bodmin Moor, with its reckless winters, fogs and rains, and its brief bursts of sunshine. I love the bracken and the

161

stunted wind-bent trees. I love the strange stacks of granite lozenges. I love the Hurlers and the way you can rock the Loganstone. I love the bogs of floating moss, and the great pike in Dozmary Pool. I love the lynx and the bears and the wild boar. But I don't have a mission. I'm happy from day to day, but I don't have a purpose, beyond enjoying the present while I still have it. You have a purpose. But tell me why you would want to survive, in a world that will be reclaimed by dogs that have evolved back into wolves, and those of us who remain have become human wolves? Wouldn't it be better to put the barrel of a shotgun in your mouth? What you're talking about is the end of the Anthropocene. We're giving the countryside back to the animals already, but they'll be getting it back entirely, won't they? Even the towns.'

Q shrugged and looked out of the window. 'I want to live for the challenge of it. But you, you do have a purpose. Eva is your purpose. I've seen the love in your eyes. You just don't have an overarching purpose. As for me, I distinguish between fate and destiny. If fate decrees that we must be plunged back into the caves, then I know what my destiny is. If there is no catastrophe, then my destiny was to have got myself ready for it, that's all. I would have existed for nothing, but at least I would have been busy. And I will have had an interesting and well-paid job. Quantum cryptography is the most fascinating thing in the world. If nothing bad happens, that'll keep me busy and interested. Nothing depresses me more than having nothing to do.'

'I'm the same,' said Theodore. 'That's why I hate being a guest in someone else's house. There's never enough to do. I'm like him,' he said, gesturing towards the portrait of Daniel Pitt. 'He was always up to something. They say he even went to Canada and built a submarine.'

'Just then, for a second, your expression was exactly like his.'

'I believe that I am my ancestors. I've never believed in God, but I believe in them. One day you will be an ancestor, and perhaps you'll be believed in.'

'Talking to you has made me realise that I should pay more

attention to my children. I'm going to get them down here. Tweak them out of London completely, if I can.'

'Those who grew up in London are in bondage all their lives,' said Theodore. 'They have no idea that the centre of the universe is not in London, but wherever they may happen to be. New Yorkers are the same, and so are Bogotanos. So whenever they leave the big city they have the uncomfortable feeling that they are in the wrong place.'

Q looked out of the window for a moment and then turned back. 'Can I ask you something?'

Theodore nodded. 'Fire away.'

'Well, does Eva pin you down and trim your eyebrows and nose hairs, and say you look like a walrus, and then lather you with cream?'

'Well, she used to, but now when I see her coming, I pick up a cushion and fend her off. Sometimes I throw her on the sofa and sit on her, and then I tickle her until she promises to leave me be. You ought to try it. It's the only thing that works.'

'And something else.'

'Yes?'

'Can you tell me about Maidie Knox Lilita?'

Theodore laughed softly. 'Well, I've never seen her, except in that photograph. I've always thought of her as Eva's imaginary friend. I just go along with it. Maybe she's a ghost who only shows herself to Eva. I don't know. Why do you ask?'

'It's a lot stranger than that,' said Q. 'I think that she and Eva, well . . . I think she actually *is* Eva.'

'Nothing is, but thinking makes it so,' said Theodore. He steepled his fingers. 'Are you suggesting that you can be your own ghost when you're not even dead?'

'Is such a thing possible?'

'I'll tell you one thing. Where I come from, we've got people who are shapeshifters. Or they say they are, or other people say they are. Some people claim to be shapeshifters when they're not, they're just fantasists. You can't be sure that if you see a jaguar up a tree, it isn't someone who's a human too. How would you know? The jaguar wouldn't look like its human counterpart, would it? So my people, we never kill jaguars. And, being a shapeshifter, it's hereditary, by the way. My grandmother is supposed to have been one.'

He continued, 'Down below in the jungle are people said to be dolphins, and they have different-coloured eyes, like Eva and me, and they seduce humans and make love with them. Sometimes the human lover is in such a state of ecstasy that they accidentally drown whilst making love in the river, and sometimes the women give birth to human dolphins. It's quite a convenient explanation for unmarried pregnancies. Has been for centuries.'

'And you believe all that?' enquired Q.

'No, of course not. Do you think I'm a fool? I'm a modern man. It's still true, though.'

34

The Children

'Dad,' she said, 'can we come down and stay with you for a bit?'
'Both of you? In term time? I am pretty busy. Some genius
has hacked the Universal Basic Income system. Last month's money
for the whole country went to Dublin, then to Frankfurt, then to
Singapore, and then it disappeared into a cryptocurrency. Well, that's
what we think. That's why everyone's yoobi was delayed by two
days. The government had to cough it up all over again. Hundreds
of millions. I expect you saw it on the news. Thank God that money's
a fiction. Imagine if it had been silver coins. Anyway there's half a
dozen of us trying to work out how it happened and we've been
given less than a week.'

'I heard about it, but it doesn't bother me. I'm not old enough for
a yoobi anyway. I'm still with the Bank of You and Mum. But, Dad,
listen, I promise we won't get in the way. Little brother feels the
same way as I do. We're just so pissed off.'

'Are you? Trouble in paradise? Last time you were here you said
it was "so-o-o-o boring" and couldn't wait to get back to London.'

'It's Mum, she's never here, and she doesn't even leave us anything
to eat, and she goes out and then she doesn't come back. This flat's
like the *Marie Celeste*.'

'You and Charlie are old enough to make poached eggs on toast
for yourselves every now and then. And you're perfectly at liberty
to go out for nice walks on those abandoned golf courses in the park.
I don't see why Mum should have to stay in and look after you absolutely all the time.'

'Yes but, Dad, at our age you still want to be loved and looked after, don't you?'

'Do you? I wasn't. Where's she going anyway?'

'Meetings, Dad.'

'Meetings? What about?'

'How should I know? It's just, "Darlings, I've got so much on, must rush", and off she goes. All dolled up like Marie Antoinette and smelling of something French and rather strong.'

'Meetings? All dolled up? I see. Well, I can't say I'm surprised.'

'Aren't you bothered?'

'Listen, sweetheart, Mum's been bored with me for years. Ten years at least. I think you'd better come and stay. I miss you, and I've got things to tell you. And I've done masses since you were last here.'

'I know. Getting ready for the apocalypse.'

'Not the apocalypse. Just the failure of the grid. Let me know when you're coming and I'll pick you up at Bodmin. How about coming for half-term? And you might have to share a bedroom with Charlie again. I've only got one spare room decorated. The others are still full of filth and cobwebs.'

'Put Charlie in one of those. I am not sharing with him again. He snores and he talks in his sleep. And, Dad?'

'Yes?'

'I'm sorry about Mum.'

Her father hesitated before saying, 'Don't worry, sweetheart. Don't be sorry. Everything's as it should be.'

'Oh and, Dad, I'm not bringing my pretend-friend, and I don't think Charlie'll bring his. I mean, they're terribly sweet and everything, but in the end you want a real friend, don't you? Like you want a real mum and dad. I'd rather mess about with Eva.'

'Well, sweetheart, I always did think that friendbots were second best. I told you that when you were pestering me to get you one.'

'You don't even have any bots any more, Dad. You're not normal.'

'Bots just de-skill you and turn you into a vegetable. And I hire them in when I need to. And by the way, this house really is haunted. I know for sure. But it's not a normal kind of ghost.'

'What's a normal kind of ghost? Dad, you're supposed to be a scientist.'

'Exactly. I believe nothing without evidence. Bodmin Moor's different. It's a parallel world down here.'

'What counts as evidence?'

'Don't get clever on me, sweetheart.'

'I can't help it, Dad. I got it from you. And luckily I got my looks from Mum.'

35

The UTRs

One day in early summer Q returned from Liskeard after a morning's expedition with Eva, when her father waved them down as they passed his gate. He leaned in at the window and said, 'Bad news, I'm afraid.'

'Bad news?'

'Yes. The GOGs and UTRs have come back. I forgot to tell you about them. They usually do, just for a few days. Every summer.'

'Oh bloody hell,' said Eva. 'They always leave such a bloody mess.'

'GOGs and UTRs?'

'Gone-off-Grids and Under-the-Radars. They've dropped out of everything, don't want to be a part of anything. Don't want to work, don't pay taxes. You know the kind of thing. So they travel around from place to place.'

'And leave a bloody mess,' repeated Eva.

'Where are they?'

'Well, they normally camp in the farmyard at your place, but I told them they'd have to go on the moorland, now that the farm's inhabited.'

'I hope they paid attention.'

'I happened to have this rifle in my hands. Quite by accident.'

'Oh, Dad,' said Eva. 'Everyone'll think you're a brigand.'

'I'll come up with you and introduce you,' said Theodore.

'You go in the front,' said Eva, opening the car door and getting out. 'You're the one with the long legs. And the rifle.'

On the moorside of the track opposite the entrance to Q's yard, four motorhomes and five caravans were laagered in a circle amongst the stunted shrubs and stiff grasses. Some of them were decades old, corroded and battered, their paintwork matted, their tyres balding and cracked. Most of the vehicles were the semi-obsolete type that ran off battery-generated hydrogen, but at least two dated back to the days of wet batteries and lithium.

Q parked in the old wagon shed and, from sheer force of habit, connected his car to the recharging socket. The three of them approached the camp, Theodore with his rifle on a sling over his shoulder. The UTRs looked up at them suspiciously as they approached, and Q raised his hand in greeting.

There were several women in their twenties and thirties, a dozen grubby little children chasing each other about with handfuls of sheep dung, and some men who all looked strangely alike, with their beaded beards and matted dreadlocks, broken fingernails and greasy clothing. Dressed in synthetic furs and skins, their faces smeared with the modern, non-allergenic version of woad, they were clearly First Nation Atavists. If they appeared unduly ridiculous, it was not least because all of them had opted to wear modern socks, boots and shoes. The men gathered together in a knot, with the women behind them.

'I'm the owner of this land,' said Q, with a wave of his hand. 'Everyone calls me Q, but my friends call me Artie. I think you know Theo already.'

'And you're going to tell us to leave, are you not?' said a tall, thin man with a scar slanting down his right cheek. His accent was from somewhere between Edinburgh and Aberdeen. His gingery red hair hung down in thick felted oblongs, uniform with his beard, and his eyes were green, flecked in the iris with spots of black. In his ears were silver rings, one above another, reminding Eva of a rabbit in springtime, the rims of its ears a ladder of ticks. A larger ring hung from the septum of his nose, and a long pin entered his cheek below the bone and exited near his mouth.

'No. I own it, but I don't farm it, so you're not in the way. Theo here tells me you stay a few days and move on. I can put up with you for a few days—'

'As long as we behave,' interrupted the Scot. 'Am I not right?'

'And what would you do if we don't?'' said the man at his side, a yellow-fanged haggard blond who must once have been handsome.

'We'll do such things,' said Eva. 'We know not what they are, but they shall be the terrors of the earth.' She looked up at Q and said smugly, '*King Lear*.' She turned back to the Scot and said, 'You lot could do with a bath. And a trim.'

'You offering?'

'Not my house,' she said. 'It's his.'

'I'll bring you hot water,' said Q. 'No one comes indoors until I trust you.'

The Scot scowled and said, 'We make our own hot water. Nae problem. We won't be needing your charitable bucket.'

'Watch out for the brook on the left there. It tastes beautiful and it looks clean, but it's got a dead sheep in the water upstream that we haven't hauled out yet. Don't drink it or you'll get sick. Believe me, I recently found out for myself. If you want clean water, I've got a big filter set up in the rain barrel outside my kitchen door. You can use that. Just go easy, in case it doesn't rain.'

'Funny thing about sheep,' said the Scot. 'They aye lie down and die in a burn, especially now that they're wild. I might go up there and haul it out myself.' He held out his hand and said, 'The name's Fergus. Fergus Murray.'

'Are you the leader?'

Fergus pulled a wry expression that betrayed a hint of exasperation. 'No leaders. We're a co-op. We don't follow leaders. Who's the leader round here?' He glanced from Theodore to Q.

They looked at each other appraisingly for a moment, raised eyebrows, smiled, turned to Fergus and simultaneously made small stabbing gestures in Eva's direction.

Eva said, 'My dad may have a rifle, but you'd better watch out for Artie. He can recite *pi* up to two thousand digits. Just by computing it in his head.'

'Lethal,' said Fergus. He looked about and remarked, 'You've done a mighty job o' work here. It's changed completely. New tiles on the house and sheds. New window frames. A heat pump. A bio-fuel plant. All the scrap gone. Half a dozen wee wind turbines on the roofs – it's amazing.'

'They wouldn't let me put up a big turbine,' said Q, 'this being a conservation area, and so on.'

'The place has been crawling with bots and foreign workmen for months,' said Eva. 'You should see the inside of the house. It's all nice now.'

'It was a slaister, right enough,' said Fergus.

'It'll never be finished,' said Q. 'Not in a thousand years.'

'Talking of niceness,' said Theodore, 'last year you left rubbish everywhere, and there was shit and toilet paper on the sides of the paths.'

'Not mine,' said Fergus. He jerked his thumb towards the others behind them. 'I've been at them for months, but they wouldna tak tellin'. To tell the truth, I've had it up to here.' He levelled his hand against his throat. 'They've got no respect. Ah'm scunnered. That's nae how I want to live.'

'It's lucky the wild pigs eat shit,' said Theodore. 'You'd better watch out. There's more of them than ever, and one of the boars is aggressive. If you don't want them rootling round your doorways, don't leave rubbish, or shit. And watch out for the aurochs. The leading bull is cantankerous, and he's bigger than your caravan. As if the bison weren't bad enough.'

'It makes you want to move to a town,' said Fergus. 'All these reintroductions.'

'Most people have, haven't they?' said Eva. 'There's not many of us left. Just millions of beasties and a few hardy souls like us, who are even fiercer than they are. Anyway the population's been on the decline for decades, hasn't it? Might as well let the beasties have it back.'

'Well,' said Q, 'we'll leave you to it. Let me know if you want anything.'

'You won't notice us,' said Fergus. 'We're soon off to Helland Wood.'

'There's beavers on the Leat there now,' said Theodore. 'It's flooded. You'll have to park higher up.'

Back in the farmhouse, the three of them sat and drank tea around the kitchen table in contemplative silence. At last Theodore put down his mug, sighed and said, 'I feel sorry for those poor bastards.'

'Who?' asked Eva. 'You mean the GOGs and UTRs?'

'Yes. They think they're under the radar. They think they've escaped and declared independence. But they haven't. On every one of their vehicles there's a tracking device. We know exactly where they are at all times. We don't bother them unless we have to. And they all have a yoobi, so it's obvious where they are.'

'Dad! How do you know? About the tracking devices? It sounds like a conspiracy theory.'

'Every national park has someone who has to do it. I've got a colleague who has to creep around and attach them in East Cornwall and West Devon. He loves it. They're so stoned, they never notice. It's like being a commando. All of the fun and none of the danger. And he's getting paid for doing something that makes no difference whatsoever. All the fun's harmless. The information is collected and stored, and nothing's done with it. It's like everything else. The age of infinite information; in the end it don't amount to a hill o' beans. It's all there waiting to be known, but nobody bothers to get to know it. Nobody collects the facts and works out what they mean.'

'But why put tracking devices on their vehicles?' said Eva. 'They've all got devices anyway. They're harmless and they're never going to pay taxes, are they? They simply claim their yoobies and footle their lives away doing as little as possible.'

'It's the Machine, isn't it? The Machine thinks it wants to know everything that's going on. Everything gets tracked and recorded. Literally everything. Even when you buy a bar of chocolate. Just in case. But the Machine's accumulated so much information that there'll never be enough people to scrutinise it, there's no one to make sense of it. We've got an electronic encyclopaedia of infinite information, a vast invisible cloud, but it's too much to deal with, so nobody looks at it at all. It might as well not be there. The Machine's defining characteristic is obsessive data collection combined with apathy. That's why everything is slowly falling to pieces. We're so bogged down in detail that we can't function. You apply for a licence or a pension or a permission and nothing comes back. You're sending messages into a void. We're being thrown back on our own resources.'

'You're talking exactly like Artie!' said Eva, and her father gave her a reproving little dig in the ribs.

'Well, he's probably right,' said Q. 'I've been thinking the same thing for years. I once pointed it out to the Prime Minister and she looked at me with a desperate expression and said, "Yes, but what can we do? What can we do?" The Machine's going ahead without us, while we sit in our rooms and while away our lives with entertainment. The sad thing is, the Machine is as clueless and purposeless as we are. It knows what it's doing, but it doesn't know why.'

'Let's crack open a bottle of wine,' said Eva. 'That's not pointless.'

'I've got some Burgundy.'

'Real, or the usual imitation that's better than the original?'

'Both, of course. We're in a quantum world now.'

36

Morgan at the Window

I've been watching those UTRs. I mean, I love being here with Dad and all that, but sometimes it does get a bit boring, or else you're so knackered from all the shovelling and log-splitting and dam-building that all you've got the energy for is making a cup of tea and looking out of the window. It can set me dreaming, gazing out at the moors and the herds of animals, and the birds of prey who go round and round each other on the updraught. I wish I was like them, but no amount of wishing ever grows you wings.

Charlie says I'm full of shit, but what do you expect from a mere brother? I'm like Eva; I've got all this fearsome energy, but I don't want to go running, so I've got to find something else. Dad says it's all being twitchy from hormones and being young, but it feels like I'm waiting for an angel to bring me wings.

The thing about those UTRs is they've got no energy at all. They do as little as they possibly can. I can sit here doing nothing, watching them doing nothing, and I'm mystified and horrified. The babies' nappies are so bloated with not being changed that they swell out like basketballs and eventually work their way down to their feet.

We've had ants here, coming in through the window frame and trooping in two columns, one coming and one going, and they're carrying away the sugar in the cupboard, grain by grain. Dad says, 'There's no such thing as an idle ant.' It's marvellous to see how determined and busy they are. One ant achieves more in a day than that entire convoy of GOGs and UTRs.

There is one, though. He's the only ant. The one called Fergus

Murray. He looks terrible. He obviously doesn't wash, and he really stinks. His hair and beard are all matted and filthy and his face is full of metal, but when he works he strips down and you can see his muscles are made of cord. You find out, from the hairs on his chest, that his hair is really ginger. You wouldn't know that from his head and beard, on account of all the filth. He must have lice and fleas, he really must.

He's got a habit of turning up whenever I go out. He's suddenly there, talking to me in that lovely Scottish voice, all very casual but a little bit diffident. He's on his own. All the other UTRs are in couples. Anyway, he's very bright and opinionated. But he doesn't mind you disagreeing. His eyes twinkle and he says, "Well then, lassie, I suppose you might be right, but . . ." And off he goes with more reasons why I'm not, and he is.

Just my luck, isn't it? Bloody typical. Someone turns up here in the middle of nowhere who's really nice and totally fit, but he's got his face full of piercings, and he's a First Nation Atavist dressed like a Pict, and he's a traveller, so he's bound to be moving on, isn't he?

And he smells like a one-man Mongol horde.

37

Fergus Disillusioned

Three days after the UTRs arrived they departed, with the exception of one old campervan. Q noticed their absence from an upper window and went out to inspect the damage. He found Fergus sitting dejectedly on the doorstep of his van, with his head in his hands.

'They've gone, have they?' Q asked, somewhat redundantly.

'Ay, they've gone, the glaikit dunnyheids. And they've left me to do the tidying up. As usual. They say, "Aw, dinna bother", but I've got pride. I'll tidy up and then I'll go. I don't know where. It's always the same. You're looking for a way to live and you can't, because of the people you keep falling in with. You're always hopeful and you're always cast down. I'm a UTR masel, but I fuckin' hate 'em. I hate the fuckin' UTRs. I finally realised this morning, when I watched 'em go, leaving behind their shit and mess, and I thought, "Good riddance, you fuckers, I'm bloody scunnered. I won't be seeing you." I'm done with 'em. If I stay with that lot, I'll end up hatin' masel.'

'Where will you go?'

'How should I know? I'll find some more UTRs and it'll be fine for a while, and then I'll get fuckin' scunnered again.'

Q put his hands in his pockets and tried to look sympathetic. He knew he was no good at human relations and was a bad actor, but he was resigned to it. By some miracle, things were turning out well, in spite of it. He did feel sympathetic, but was unsure whether he seemed so or not.

'I've had a chance to observe you while you were here,' he said.

'It's impossible not to notice that you were the only one doing any work. Gathering sticks, setting up lamps, stamping down the fire last thing. You're good with a shovel and an axe. You've got energy.'

'Aye, I have. I'm the only fucker who ever has. I'm the only one who's not on happy pills and magic puff and patches.'

'Why don't you stay, at least for a while?'

'Wha'? What for, man?'

Q gathered his thoughts. 'Well, I've been here several months now. There's a fantastic amount to do, and I've realised I'll never do it on my own. Sometimes I feel overwhelmed. I've taken on too much. More than I can ever do. I could do with some help. Almost all the big jobs require at least two of you, if you think about it.'

'No one's ever asked me to stay,' said Fergus. 'What's the matter wi' ye?'

'I'm not normal either, and I know a misfit when I meet one. We're all the same. You stay here, you work, you help me out, you get fed, you get money if you need it. You leave if it doesn't suit.'

Fergus looked at him suspiciously and said, 'Let me get rid o' this mess. Then we'll talk. But one thing . . .' He gestured towards his campervan. 'That's ma home. I'm not moving out. Not for you. Not for anyone.'

'Leave it where it is,' said Q. 'Are you any good with a rifle?'

'Never tried.'

'I'll show you, if you're interested. In the meantime it'd be a good idea to clean up all the paper and plastic, but leave the food waste and the shit.'

'Truly, mon?'

'You see that window, there? I'm going to be up there with a .223 when the wild boar arrive at dusk. Tomorrow there'll be proper pork in the freezers and a big leg to roast.'

'Fuck!' said Fergus 'Aren't you the man?'

'And another thing. If you see a young woman in white, with long black hair all coming down her shoulder on the left-hand side, and piercing eyes, can you let me know?'

'A woman in white with long black hair?'

'Yes. I just want to know if she's real. But then maybe being seen by somebody else as well wouldn't really make her real. I don't know. What do you have to do – what do you have to be – in order to be real?'

'You've lost me.'

'Oh, never mind,' said Q. 'Welcome to Yelland Farm.

38

The Skull

Because, one day when she was standing by his shallow grave, Eva had the strongest intuition that Christian was unable to rest, she knelt down and uncovered his skull, taking it in her hands and gazing into the empty sockets of the eyes.

'Poor fool,' she said, 'are you really going to spend eternity wandering about the woods, looking for your disciples? Don't you know they're gone? Not one footprint left in the soil, poor fool. Not one left believing you're the Messiah, or even a prophet? No one left to boss around? No one left to bully?'

The damp yellow skull exuded abandonment and fallen pride. She sat back in the litter and leaf mould of the forest floor, her long legs folded beneath her, and stroked the skull upwards from the forehead, as if she were brushing back his hair. Holding it close to her face, in the full odour of its mustiness, she blew out the earwigs and insects that had crawled in the cavities.

She knew what it was like to want to be a king, because so often she had yearned to be a queen, as beautiful as Guinevere, but without the doomed passions and deceptions, a queen more like the Virgin Mary, crowned in heaven, all sorrows past and all misdeeds redeemed. She was queen of this moor, without a doubt; she enjoyed its freedoms, and she walked untouched amongst its animals. When she ran to the tops of the Tors she saw no sign of human habitation, only broken radio masts and the ruins of quarries and mines. Her father loved her like a queen, and so did Q. There were no obstructions to her power. The people who loved her were compelled by her authority, and those who came across her knew she was unstoppable. They quailed before the generosity of her affection, wanting her happiness more than they craved their own.

Even so, the human heart is hungry, and no human walks the earth but is longing for greater things. Even the dead are not satisfied by having lived. Even if you are Queen, there is a void at the core of the soul that nothing fills, and the hands of the spirit reach upwards for fruit that's out of reach, glittering in the imagination, invisible to the eye, painful in the void of the heart.

She remembered how, as a little girl, she had been her own princess, obsessed with dressing in pink, kitted out with glittering toy tiaras and glass jewels, ordering her father to kneel, and knighting him with the impossibly heavy sword inherited from the ancestor who had used it to fight for his life on the North-West Frontier and then went on to win his spurs in the bulleted skies of France. Even then, as she savoured the glee of absolute power, she had felt in her guts the anger and disappointment of being a little girl, and not a god.

So Eva felt sorry for Christian, this charismatic soul who had moved to the wilds to begin a new civilisation, only for it to fall apart in a matter of weeks under the pressure of his own hubris and the exigencies of survival. Cradling his skull in her hands, she perceived that in the end his dreams had dissolved into the leaf mould of the forest floor and departed this world, feared and unloved. She thought that if only she had known him, perhaps if they had been lovers, Christian would have made a real world of his desires and dreams.

Eva stood and carefully placed the skull in her knapsack, wrapping the jaw bone separately in a cloth. The teeth tend to fall out of old skulls, and she did not want to lose them. She returned to her palfrey, untying the rein from the hazel bush to which she had tethered him, next to a large boulder, upon which she stood before springing up to mount him.

She had named her horse Falghun, thinking that a noble name might make the creature noble. She had not had the heart to have him gelded, and so he was proud and impetuous, sometimes refusing to move at all, sometimes twisting his neck to bite at her feet, sometimes setting off at an uncontrollable gallop. As someone who loved running, Eva understood his need to feel his muscles burning and gave him his head, knowing that a horse is too sensible to risk its limbs on broken ground. Her father had repeatedly warned her about the likelihood of falling off, or being thrown, and the damage this might do, but she had not fallen yet.

Sometimes, especially when the sun was hot in the sky, they hacked at an ambling pace, and wherever the going was too rocky, Eva dismounted and led him by the halter. The horse understood that Eva meant adventure and exercise, and interesting things to sniff at, and he would whinny from the stable, kicking at the boards, whenever he heard her voice or scented her arrival. If he recalled the cruel manner of his breaking, it was like the memory of a sinister dream that is broken by the dawn.

If she went to Liskeard or Bodmin, if she did not run, she rode there on Falghun, and it was not long before Runnergirl also became The Rider. The few people who remained in those towns – pale, listless, sluggish and purposeless – at the sound of the clopping of hooves would look up from their screens and out of their windows, and wonder what it was like to be her, alive and energetic, one half of the implausible, magical bond that is rider and beast. Women would wish they were like her, without wishing the means to become so. Men, reduced to exhaustion and apathy by the assiduous perfection of their sexbots, would look out and wonder what it was like to make love to a real beautiful girl. Then these orphans of their own civilisation, these childless and vacuous men and women, would return to their screens, their automated companions, their chemically adjusted moods, their meaningless routines, their watery flesh and its dull imprisonment.

That evening Theodore came home to find his daughter carefully washing the skull beneath a flow of warm water from the tap, dabbing away the encrusted dirt with a paintbrush. 'Before you ask,' she said, 'this is Christian's skull, and I've had an idea about what to do with it to cheer him up.'

''Tis a mad world, my masters,' quoted her father dumping his bag on the floor and demanding no further explanation. 'You can be as mad as you like, *mi querida hija*. How about a cup of tea?'

Eva left the skull on the window shelf of the conservatory and, over the coming months, very slowly, with every revolution of the summer sun, its colouring shifted from damp yellow to dry white. At times when she had nothing else to do, or lacked the motivation to do anything in particular, she would take it on her lap and polish it with a duster. In September she extracted the loose teeth with pliers, bleached them and glued them back in. In her workshop, with infinite care, she covered the skull entirely in the thinnest gold leaf. She took a large oval ruby and ground the back of it to the curve of the forehead and then, with jeweller's paste, stuck it centrally in place. Around it she arranged a double circle of small diamonds. Along the sutures of the dome she painted in tiny italic letters, 'As you are now, once I was. As I am now, so shall you be.'

When she was satisfied, she created a laurel wreath in sterling silver and took the crowned skull to her father, wordlessly holding it up for him to admire.

'Where are we going to keep it?' he asked. 'It's much too hand-some to hide away.'

'This house or Artie's?' she asked.

'What do you think?'

'He doesn't even know I've done it. I'll take it up there and see what he thinks.'

So it was that Christian's skull sat gleaming for some months in the middle of the mantelpiece above the great fireplace at Yelland Farm, next to the photograph of the 1908 Effingham House Goal Ball Team, on the grounds that more people came and went in the farmhouse than in the lodge at the side of the road.

The skull became dusty and neglected, until one day Eva took it down, scrutinised it and said, 'I still don't think he's happy.'

'Maybe he misses his bones,' suggested Q lightly.

So it was that they went down to Hippies' Wood and excavated the grave, carefully laying out the bones on the dark ground until the skeleton was complete. They placed them in burlap, which they laid across Falghun's withers, walking him home through the stunted thorns in the decaying light of a damp April eve.

Within a few months Christian's articulated skeleton sat, entirely clad in gold leaf, enrobed in a prophetic purple cloak, on its own gilded throne in Q's drawing room, with its hands on the arms of the chair, its white teeth gleaming and its silver laurel crown in place. Eva cut two large dark-purple agates, faceted them and placed them in the sockets of the eyes. It became the habit of the house to greet Christian in the mornings and wish him goodnight at day's end. Maidie Knox Lilita would come in after Eva was asleep, stroke its cheekbones and think how strange it was that this magnificent creature's death had come about so many years after her own. She would lay her head against the side of the skull, as if listening for his thoughts, oppressed by Time and its caprice.

Eva still doubted whether her gilding and enthronement of his bones had made Christian any happier. She suspected that he still wandered about the woods, searching for his apostate disciples. She had created a fabulous work of art that was wondered at by everyone who came to the house, but to contemplate it left her flat and teary-eyed.

Q said, 'Don't fret, my darling. Don't be vexed. You haven't failed. Some people are beyond help. Sometimes you cast seed on stony ground. All you can do is your best, and the rest is up to them.'

She put her arms around his neck and kissed him, saying, 'Even so, it's depressing, sometimes, to come up against the limits of my power.'

He encircled her, inhaled the scent of rosemary in her hair and kissed the side of her head. 'My darling, cheering up the dead is a pretty ambitious project. And if you had any more power, none of us would be safe, would we?'

39

Fergus Forlorn

Three months after his decision to stay, Fergus stood before Q and announced that he was intending to leave.

'But you can't. You're such a good worker. How am I going to do without you? What's the matter? Have I done anything wrong?'

Fergus looked at the ground and scuffed at the dirt with the toe of his boot. 'No, mon, nothing wrong. Time to be moving, that's all.'

'Moving where?'

Fergus gestured towards the west. 'I dinna ken. Trevose Head, Pendoggett. Land's End. I've never been to the Scillies. I could make a new start.'

'This was a new start.'

'Ya see,' said Fergus, beating his sternum with his clenched right fist, 'I've got a wee problem. In here. Feelings.'

'Feelings?'

Fergus nodded. He raised his hand dismissively and turned on his heel, saying, 'Not your problem, mon. I'm going back to my camper. I'll see you in the morning.'

That evening Q walked down to Theo's house and sat down in the armchair beneath the portrait of the flying ace. It had, with the passage of time, become his seat. The subject turned to Fergus.

'I can't understand it,' said Q. 'He fits in so well.'

'Well, I know what it is,' said Eva. 'I'm surprised you haven't noticed.'

Theodore leaned forward in his chair and said, '*Hermano*, he's fallen in love with Morgan.'

'And,' added Eva, 'he realises that he hasn't got a hope.'

'Hasn't he?' asked Q.

'Of course not. He's a crusty. He's got no money. He stinks. He's got no future. Why should she look at him?'

'Well, he's extremely personable and nice, and he works flat out. And he's got the shoulders and arms of an archer.'

'You're her dad,' cried Eva, oblivious to the truth that she herself was attached to an unsuitable lover. 'Morgan's in her teens and he must be twenty-six at least. What are you thinking?'

Q scratched his head and said, 'Well, I've had to change my way of thinking, haven't I? Normally a dad like me, he'd be thinking, "Well, what are his prospects? Can he support her if she has children and wants to stay at home? What's his pension going to be?" But there's no future, is there? The well-paid magic-money-out-of-thin-air bullshit jobs are all going to disappear. The Magic Money tree is going to wilt and blow away in a puff of dust. The Universal Basic Income isn't going to be pinged into your bank account every month. The world's going to belong to tough, practical people who work hard and never give up. People like you, Theo. People like Fergus.'

'Only if you're right about the grid, *hermano*.'

'I know I'm right. It's only a matter of time. That's why I wouldn't be unduly bothered if Morgan fell for Fergus. In a way, he'd be ideal. I'm sure he'd be a wonderful father. He's got no prospects in this world, but he's perfect for what's to come.'

'She's too young to settle,' said Eva.

'When the lights go out, she'll be stuck here. Settled, whether she likes it or not.'

'I don't know if you're an amazing dad or totally crap,' said Eva. 'No one should have babies when they're babies themselves.'

'You don't like his dreadlocks and piercings,' said her father.

'Or his stench, or the disgusting state of his caravan. I bet he's worn the same pair of underpants for ten years. God! Imagine having to sleep with him!'

'Does anyone know what Morgan thinks?' asked Theodore.

'I do,' said Eva. 'Girls do talk to each other. Quite a lot, actually. She thinks Fergus is incredibly desirable and charming and totally repulsive, all at the same time. She keeps going on about it. She's repelled, but fascinated.'

'Why don't you sort it out?' asked Q.

'Me?' cried Eva. 'Why's it got to be me? You're her dad.'

'You're the Wise Woman of Yelland Tor,' said Q. 'You're the bossy one who knows what's best for everyone. You're the one with the scissors and pots of cream. We all rely on you totally.'

'Oh, *cojones* to you,' said Eva. '*Cojones* to both of you.'

40

Fergus Shorn

va came to the farmhouse and found him working on a fence for the vegetable allotment, stringing the wires and tightening them through the mesh between the posts.

'Bloody pigs,' said Q. 'They've trampled and uprooted everything they haven't eaten. Look at all this!'

Eva surveyed the devastation and said, 'They're getting bolder all the time. We had some in our garden a few days ago. Dad's got a special gun for them, with a bayonet on it. You have to shoot them from close up, with a huge round bullet, and then charge in. They're quite incredibly indestructible. All the other animals are terrified of them.'

'Buggers!' exclaimed Q. 'Why have they started coming up from the woods?'

'Probably something to do with easily obtainable free snacks,' said Eva. 'Is Morgan in?'

'Upstairs in her room, doing something mysterious and female, I suppose. Probably talking to her mother in London, I should think.'

Eva ascended the stairs and knocked on Morgan's door, pushing it open without waiting for an answer.

Morgan looked up and said, 'Oh, hi. It's you.'

'I've got a confession, and it's terrible. I'm really sorry, but I've completely bloody fucked up. *Drok yu genef. Gafeugh dhym.*'

'What have you done?'

Eva sat next to her on the bed, hung her head and said, 'I've accidentally driven Fergus away. He's about to leave. I was only trying to help, but it all blew up in my face. I've been an idiot.'

Tears sprang up in Morgan's eyes, but remained there. 'What? But I don't want him to go. Is it to do with me?'

Eva stroked her cheek. 'Well, I know you're sweet on him. And he's completely besotted with you.'

'Is he? Is he really?'

'You know he is. Well, anyway, I turned up at his campervan with a pair of scissors and a razor, and a bag of washing things and a bag of clean clothes. Some of your dad's and some of mine. And I said to him he wouldn't stand a chance with you unless he cleaned up and took all that metal out of his face. I mean, you know I'm good at sprucing men up.'

'What you did with Dad was a miracle. He went from ape to movie star, almost. What happened?'

'Fergus was bloody furious. It couldn't have been worse if I'd shat on his bed. He was raging and storming about, saying things like, "I'm not fucking changing for anyone. I am what I fucking am." And I said, "Yes, you're unfuckable."'

'You didn't? Eva, that's terrible! Anyway who says I'd want to . . . do that . . . with him?'

'Come on, sweetheart, you know you would.'

'Only if he didn't stink and look like a caveman. I'm still a virgin, you know. It's got to be soft words and candlelight, and not having halitosis and smelling like a wrestler. He's not really going, is he?'

'I'm afraid he is. When I left, he was trying to start the van up, and shouting and swearing at it and kicking the wheels.'

'Oh, Eva!'

'I'm really sorry.' Eva looked at Morgan and shook her head sorrowfully. 'You know, if you had red hair instead of your lovely frizzy hair, and if you had whiter skin, you'd be the perfect Pre-Raphaelite beauty. I've never met anyone with such slender and delicate bones in my life. You're like a human bird. And your skin is just perfectly flawless. And you've got such lovely amber eyes.'

'Oh, do be quiet, Eva, honestly!'

'Well, if I was Fergus, I'd be thinking I wasn't good enough for you, so what's the point in trying? "I'll stay as I am and not even give her a chance to reject me." So . . .'

'Yes?'

'If you want him to stay, you've got to let him know that he's got a chance.'

'Well, what should I do?'

'Send him a message on your device. Say, "I'm so sorry to hear that you're leaving. I shall miss you, and I don't know what we'll do without you. Please come back and visit often." I think that should do it.'

Morgan fetched her device from the dressing table and switched it on, saying, 'Give me that again, Eva.'

She pressed send, and a few moments later a message from Fergus came through. 'I'll miss you too. Love, Fergus.'

'Oh, bloody bollocks,' said Morgan.

'Don't worry,' said Eva. 'I flicked the manual cutout on the activation circuit of his campervan. It'll be ages before he realises what's wrong.'

'God, Eva, you're such a schemer! Is anyone safe?'

'Not anyone. Anyway, I'm going for a run, before I get the hypers.'

'You'll wear your knees and hips out,' said Morgan.

'I'm dreading old age,' said Eva. 'Thank God for biohacking.'

Morgan watched from the window as the older girl hurtled across the yard and out through the gate. She went downstairs, put on her boots and walked out of the yard in Eva's wake. She found Fergus sitting dejectedly on the back step of his van and said, 'Budge over.' They sat side by side, saying nothing, until at last she said, 'I've come to kiss you goodbye.'

She leaned against him and kissed him softly on the cheek. He caught her scent of ambergris and felt himself flood with tenderness and unworthiness. Momentarily her soft, springy hair caressed his face.

He leaned forward, his hands clasped together, and without looking at her asked, 'Have I really got to smarten up?'

'In the olden days a man had to do brave deeds to win his demoiselle. I'm not asking you to engage in single combat, am I?'

'And who's going to keep me smart?'

'Eva. And me. Just accept it. You're stuffed.'

'No choice?'

'None. And I'm not promising anything. A parfit gentil knight pleaseth his lady whether there's anything in it for him or not.' She reached into her pocket and fetched out a small embroidered handkerchief, which she gave to him. 'Here, this is my favour. You can wear it in your helm when you're jousting. And if you lose it or blow your nose on it, or wipe your sweaty forehead with it, I'll find another champion and never speak to you again.'

Fergus took it from her and sniffed it. 'It smells of you.' He got up and climbed the step into his campervan, returning with a pair of kitchen scissors. He sat down beside her and said, 'I'm going to be the first.'

He took one of his matted locks in his left hand, stretched it out and snipped it off. He dangled it in front of his eyes and then placed it on his knee. 'It looks like a thing long dead,' he said, 'the shrivelled body of a rat – a rat long deid under the boards.'

'It does look all sad,' said Morgan.

Fergus handed her the scissors and said, 'Your turn, lassie.'

'I think Eva should do it. She knows how.'

'She can tidy me up. You just make a start of it.'

Fergus gave himself up. Seated on a chair in the evening sunshine, with a towel about his neck, he let himself be trimmed and shaved. He felt humiliated, but at the same time cherished. He saw his freedom striding away across the bogs and rocks of the moor with its knapsack on its back, but at the same time he saw horizons glow with yellow light. He perceived the sweet obligations of company rising up with the downfall of his solitude. He felt how the rough surface of the stubborn male is abraded by the female touch.

'Tomorrow,' said Morgan, 'let's go through your clothes. You can't go on dressing like this. I mean, you're not actually an ancient Brit, are you?'

'Ach, do we have to?'

'I'll do you a deal. When you're working, you can be as filthy and sweaty and scruffy as you like. You can even wear your fake animal skins. But after work you take a shower and smarten up.'

'Do I have a choice?'

'Of course you have a choice. But so do I.'

Eva came alone to visit Fergus in his caravan at five o'clock. 'Put the kettle on, I have something to say to you,' she said.

'As if I could stop you, lassie. Well?'

'I'm not going to beat about the bush. It's very awkward, so I want to say it straight off.'

Fergus raised his eyebrows. 'Go on then, out wi' it.'

Eva said, 'Morgan's too young for sex. She's only a teenager. And I can just tell. She's not ready.'

'Fuck!' said Fergus. 'Has anyone ever told you you're a fuckin' nightmare?'

'I'm right, though. Do you want my advice?'

'I'm gonna get it, aren't I?'

'My advice is always to let the woman make the first move. That way, you know you're wanted. You don't put her off and you don't make an idiot of yourself.'

'That's what I always have done,' said Fergus. 'I figured that for myself. Years ago. I'm not as stupid as you think.'

'Anyway, what she wants is romance. Here, I bought you these.' She reached into her bag and brought out a small bunch of wild flowers.

'You brought me flowers?'

'Not for you, botbrains. They're for you to give Morgan. I picked them out on the moor. You'd better be grateful.'

Fergus quailed visibly and repeated, 'You really are a fuckin' nightmare.'

'Faint heart never won fair maid,' she said, holding out the bunch for him to take. 'Put them in water and give them to her tomorrow. And get into the habit of giving her things. Just small, thoughtful things, because a girl needs to know she'll be looked after. And love must prove itself with evidence. It's a cave thing.'

Later that night, when he was alone at last, Fergus sat down in front of the mirror and gazed at himself, long and slow, his eyes flicking back and forth across the image in the glass. He put his fingers to his face and felt how soft his skin was, after Eva's determined assault with the pot of cream. He saw that he had been magically transformed from someone who looks as though he has given up on life into someone who looks as though he might love it.

He fetched a can of beer from the tiny fridge and flicked it open, with a hiss of escaping gas. He seated himself back in front of the mirror and toasted himself with, 'Here's to you, you daft fucker.'

He took a deep swig and set the can down before him. He examined the reflection of his clean and respectable self. His eyes locked with own eyes in the mirror. He sighed wearily and said, 'Who the fuck are you, anyway?'

41

Conversations on the Screen

1. Eva and Her Mother

'Hello, darling, how are you?'

'I'm fine, Mum.'

'How come you never ping me, darling?'

'You know why.'

'It's been ages. Why can't we put it behind us? Why can't you ever seem to forgive?'

'Look, Mum, I can understand you wanting to leave Dad, but why did you have to take me to Scotland? Without even asking? Why did you say it was just a holiday, when it was in fact a bloody abduction?'

'When you're upset, you don't think straight. I wasn't thinking straight.'

'Why did you have to go so far? Why couldn't you have moved to Truro? Or somewhere like Penzance?'

'I'm Scottish, darling. I had to come home. I was sort of desperate.'

'You took me home to bloody Aberdeen – a million miles from Dad – where it's always raining and everything's bloody charcoal-grey, and when the sun comes out everyone faints with surprise?'

'It's not that bad, darling.'

'It bloody is. And then you dumped that man anyway, and it was all for nothing.'

'Won't you come up and see me? Only for a day or two? I miss you. I think about you all the time.'

'I'm not coming back to bloody Aberdeen. I might meet you somewhere nice, somewhere more like halfway. Maybe in York.' *Pause*. 'Did I tell you that Dad buried everything you ever gave him in the garden, and put up a tombstone?'

'Yes, you did. Several times. No need to rub it in. Dad's a romantic. It's just the sort of thing you'd expect him to do.' *Pause*. 'Darling, can't you forgive me? Don't you love me at all?'

'Mum, it's because I love you that I can't forgive.'

2. Q and Penelope

'Hello, darling. Oh, I suppose I shouldn't be calling you "darling" any more.'

'Why bother to change?'

'No one ever calls you by your real name anyway.'

'Well, they do nowadays. People are calling me Artie, instead of Q. What's up? You seem upset.'

'It's Purse.'

'Purse?'

'Oh, you know – Percy. Percy Prode.'

'Oh, really? What's happened?'

'Well, I called round at his house and when nobody answered, I thought, 'What the hell?' and I punched his birthday into the code-box. It worked, of course. He's got no imagination at all. Anyway I heard this moaning sound, so I crept upstairs and there he was in the sexbot room, with his back to me and the door open. Sitting naked in his chair. He's gone and bought a male sexbot.'

'He was having sex with a male sexbot?'

'No. It was having sex with one of the female sexbots, and Percy was watching while another one was kneeling between his legs. Doing you know what.'

'I'm sorry, I shouldn't laugh.'

'I was bloody furious.'

'Well, I don't blame you. What did you do?'

'There was a lamp on the table in the corridor, and I waited until he started to come and then I smashed it over his head. Thank God it was only made of papier mâché, otherwise I'd be calling you from the infirmary. Anyway I dumped him on the spot, but he went down on his knees and started weeping and wailing, and half an hour later I'd taken him back. More fool me. *Pause.* I'm sorry. I don't know why I had to tell you all this. It's not exactly your kind of thing, is it? I mean, it's nothing to do with supersingular elliptic-curve isogeny or zero-knowledge protocols or quasi-cyclic parity checks, is it? I just had to vent off to someone, that's all.'

'Am I so one-dimensional?'

'No, darling, of course not. Not any more, anyway. Not that you ever were, really. Talking of sexbots, did you see that item about the Frenchman and the Australian woman?'

'No. It sounds like a joke.'

'Well, apparently there's a Frenchman in Lyons and an Australian woman in Melbourne and they're married. Deeply in love, of course. But neither of them wants to move countries, so what they do is they have long, intimate chats onscreen, and then in their bedrooms they've each got a sexbot that's the exact replica of the other, and that way they get sex with each other exactly when they want it, without inconveniencing one another in any way at all. Without even having to meet.'

'It sounds ideal. But there's a flaw in it somewhere.'

'That's the Age of Unreality for you, pretty much in a nutshell. How are the kids?'

'Morgan's gone off tramping with Eva. She wants to wear in her new boots.'

'I can't imagine her in walking boots. She's got such tiny feet. Do you remember her little pink ballet pumps?'

'Eva wanted her to see a bear cub. She thinks it's the sweetest thing that ever lived. They've gone to Hippies' Wood. Eva says the mother bear is perfectly tame, so it ought to be safe. She's known it since it was born, she says.'

'Have you still got that skeleton in your kitchen covered with gold leaf? With the agate eyes?'

'Christian? Yes. He's still there.'

'I don't know whether that's fabulous or creepy.'

'We like him. There's something kingly about him, don't you think?'

'What about Charlie? What's he up to?'

'There was an outbuilding beyond repair, so we took it down. He's out there sorting out the timbers and tiles. He's even got a suntan.'

'I can't believe it. Remember when he used to spend all morning in bed and then dress up like Handel and do nothing all afternoon, and then eat everything in the house, and then stay up 'til three in the morning, still doing nothing?'

'He still sleeps in. He does seem much happier these days. More motivated.'

'The trouble is that when they're here, he can't wait to get back to Cornwall. You're doing me out of a son.'

'You should come down with them. Eva doesn't seem to mind.'

'She knows she's got all the best cards. For all your genius, you're still a man. You're no more rational than Purse, when it comes down to it. You've got your brains in your trousers, the same as him.'

'And you are? You're rational?'

Pause.

'No, I'm not. Of course I'm not. Anyway I'd better go now. I think Morgan's trying to ping me a picture of the bear.'

'Call me whenever you want. And by the way . . .'

'Yes?'

'I've got a lot of my brains in my heart.'

Pause.

'I know. I've always known. Better go. Goodbye. darling. Have fun.'

42

Visitors

Eva was in the kitchen teaching Q how to make her father's signature dish, a chicken stew he called *Sancocho*. 'Dad sometimes cries when he makes this,' she said, 'because they used to make it at home, before his town was swallowed by the lake. It reminds him that he's homeless.'

'He's not homeless.'

'No, really, he is. He's a Kogi, and Bodmin Moor is only a little bit like the Andes.'

'This country's full of people with exotic ancestors. There's almost no one left who isn't a mongrel.'

'There aren't any Kogis.'

'What happened again?'

'Well, his town was swallowed up by a lake because it was in a valley with a river running through it and an earthquake caused an avalanche, so the river was dammed at the lower end, and the whole valley slowly filled up until the houses began to submerge and they all had to leave. It was a great trek back to the lowlands, and then the people dispersed. When the town vanished, the community did too.'

'Couldn't they have blasted the rocks away and cleared the avalanche?'

'I don't know. You'll have to ask Dad. He said that the town was only revealed in the first place because a previous earthquake had drained the lake and there it was. He thinks you can't stop the wheel of history; it gives and it takes away, and then it gives and it takes away, and you just have to shrug your shoulders and be philosophical. He thinks there'll be another earthquake one day, and then the lake will be drained again. He goes on Satellite Earth every few days to see if it's happened yet. He's always hoping.'

'If he went back, would you go with him? Please don't say "yes".'

'I'd visit. I'd go with him to have a look. But I know what'd happen. There'd be no one else there. He'd walk around, talking about the old days, pointing things out, and then he'd realise that a town isn't a town without its people, and then we'd come back to Bodmin. He does love it here. He says it's the only other place he's ever been where all the ghosts are in plain sight.'

'It seems to fit him perfectly.'

'It does. It's just not Cochadebajo de los Gatos.' Eva kissed him softly on the side of his head. He turned and returned the kiss, with equal softness, but on her lips.

'I had an Italian ancestor called Granitola,' he said. 'When the Italians occupied south-west Turkey, he was sent to a little town called Eskibahce, near Fethiye. He was sent there for a year or two and fell in love with it. He practically turned into a Turk. It was wrecked by an earthquake in the 1950s and now it's a ghost town, spread up the side of a hill, with tiny rocky streets only wide enough for camels and mules. I went there, and you could tell exactly how people used to live; a cistern for rainwater on every house, an outside lavatory in one corner, animals downstairs and people upstairs. Two abandoned churches. There was even a pottery. I could see why he might have loved it. Of course he had to leave and never went back. The story is that he became a fascist and eventually got killed.' He began to cut a chicken breast into chunks and said, 'I'm sorry if it's awkward, but I want to ask you again about Maidie Knox Lilita.'

'I know you're still sleeping with her,' said Eva, without rancour.

'I just don't understand what's really going on,' he said.

'Well, you're a scientist and you think everything can be

understood, if only you're clever enough. Maybe you aren't supposed to understand things until the time is right. There might be a right time to discover the inverse-square law, or that $e = mc^2$, and that's why they were discovered when they were.'

He put down the knife and looked at her earnestly. 'I think I ought to be feeling rotten about it; that I ought to feel guilty.'

'Oh, don't bother, *hwegow*. Not on account of me. I understand it, even if you don't.'

'Aren't you going to explain?'

'No. Where's the fun in that?'

'I don't like being kept in the dark.'

'But I like keeping you there.'

'Am I right in supposing that you know where Maidie is? You know what's actually going on?"

Eva dipped her finger in the sauce and looked up at him suggestively as she licked it off. 'What's knowledge, anyway? When you think you know something, how can you tell if you really know it? How can you know that you really know anything at all? And anyway what's a fact? And Maidie's in the attic, if you'd like to pop in and give her a kiss.'

Q wiped his hands on a tea towel and strode out. On the first floor, at the end of the corridor, he unlatched the plank door and climbed the narrow wooden stairs up to the attic. Maidie Knox Lilita was sitting in a wooden chair with her hands in her lap, watching the world through the cracked and cobwebby glass of the dormer window.

'Maidie!' he cried. 'Eva said you'd be here.'

'*Keresik*,' she said, looking up and smiling. 'Look. Today I'm twenty-three. And I'm wearing my old games clothes from school. Does it give you a frisson?'

'Maidie, I'm the only one who doesn't know what's going on.'

She stood up and put her arms around his neck. 'Did you know, it's quite common to encounter one's own ghost? It happened to Goethe once.' He breathed in the smell of rosemary in her hair, the lavender on her skin, the camphor on her clothes, the distant musk of King Edward's days.

'Why don't I feel guilty? Why don't you and Eva even seem to mind? Why do you both think it's amusing?'

'I think you should be more worried about those thieves,' she said.

'Thieves?'

She nodded towards the window, and Q went to look out. Down below, a small gang of filthy and dishevelled young men, dressed in fake animal skins, their faces smeared with blue dye, were crouched behind the corner of one of the barns, acting very like furtive commandos from an old black-and-white war film. One of them was carrying a large pair of bolt-croppers and was pointing to the chain on the double doors. He slipped towards it and began to locate the chain in its jaws.

'It's the bloody UTRs,' he said. 'They've sneaked back. They would have known all about the stores. Bloody hell, it's not as if they don't have yoobis.'

'Time for a shot across the bows, as my daddy used to say,' said Maidie, standing next to him.

Q was on the point of running downstairs when he saw Fergus emerging from his caravan with a pump-action shotgun in his hands, followed by Morgan carrying a double-barrelled over-and-under. Fergus shouted something at the vagabonds and levelled his gun, Morgan following suit.

Torn between the instinct to watch the drama below and the instinct to protect his daughter, Q hesitated for a second. Fergus raised the barrel of his weapon and fired a few feet above their heads, ejecting the old cartridge and sending home a new one. 'Stand still, yer fuckers!' he yelled.

Stand still they did. The one with the bolt-croppers let them slip from his hand to the ground. 'Is that you, Fergus?' asked the one with the small eyes and mean, saurian face. 'Sold out, have you? Gone over to the normals? The likes of us not good enough for you then?' Q recognised him as having been amongst the UTRs on their last visit, and he had not liked the look of him back then.

'Good enough for me?' echoed Fergus. 'No, you're fuckin' not. Now take off your bauchles. Go on! Take them fuckin' off.'

'What's a bauchle?' asked lizard-face.

'Yer fuckin' shoes. Yer skelly-eyed lavvyheids, take 'em off!'

'Take them off? What for?'

''Cause yer look fuckin' ridiculous in yer skins and bauchles. You jes do it. And nae blether.'

Reluctantly the four young men undid the buckles and straps of their incongruous boots and stepped out of them.

'Now off yer gang, yer tattie bogles. Go on! Off!'

'But it's all stoney,' said the small-eyed, mean-faced man. 'You can't expect us to walk back with no shoes.'

'Ah don't,' replied Fergus. 'I expect you to fuckin' run.'

He levelled the shotgun at them and Morgan did the same, visibly conquering her own fear. 'Awa, and bile yer heids!' he shouted. 'Awa, yer charny dubs!' He fired another shot above their heads and pumped the action. Their terror was comical to behold, as was their difficulty in trying to run with tender feet on sharp rocks. As they fled gingerly down the track, Fergus fired one shot after another. 'Yer hummin bawbags!' Bang. 'Yer dobbers, yer fuds!' Bang. 'Yer feckin wallopers, yer feckin bampots!' Bang. When they were sufficiently far away just to be stung, he fired a last shot directly at them and they accelerated quite markedly.

By the time Q arrived on the scene, Fergus was dancing in an excited circle, waving his shotgun like some warrior on the warpath, and Morgan was sitting on an old tractor tyre, her gun across her lap, shaking but smiling, proud and happy. She opened the breech to eject the two shells and bent down to pick them up. Fergus looked up as Q skidded to a halt in front of him, and said, 'They won't be fuckin' comin' back, mon.'

'They will,' said Q gloomily. 'They'll be back when the grid fails. Then it'll be for real. We'll probably end up killing them, and that'll be the end of our innocence. With any luck, they'll be too far away to get here with what's left in their batteries.'

'Ach, but are yer not fuckin' proud a yer dochter?' said Fergus.

'Fergus, it's you I'm proud of you. I'm glad you stayed.'

Morgan stood and put her arms around her father, clutching him tightly, trembling like a bird. She looked up and saw a young woman watching from the attic window, but could not be sure whether or not it was Eva.

43

The Dance

E va ran up the side of Yelland Tor in the bright, cold sunlight of a January morning. Despite the temperature she was dressed as usual only in her running shorts, T-shirt and walking boots, with the blue-rabbit backpack nodding its floppy ears behind her.

When she reached the top she said, 'Ah, you're here. I was afraid you would be.'

Maranatha was seated on a low fishing stool, facing south to catch the low rays of the sun on his unshaven face. He had several layers of clothes on under his greatcoat, and the deerskin hat lined with rabbit that Theodore had made for him the previous winter.

'Afraid?' he said in his brown Welsh baritone. 'Afraid of what, my love? Why would you be afraid?'

Eva bent over, her hands on her knees as she recovered her breath. 'Oh,' she gasped, 'I am knackered.'

'You'll be getting too old for all this running,' said Maranatha.

'Not me. After breakfast I ate a whole packet of ginger biscuits and half a box of truffles, that's all, and now I feel sick. Never again.' She stood up and unhitched her knapsack, burrowing inside it until she found the small box. 'Cheese-and-tomato sandwiches,' she said brightly, holding it out to him.

'*Cariad*, you're an angel, you are,' he replied.

'I thought you'd like a change,' she said. 'Look, I've got to tell you. They're forecasting ten days of snow and minus ten degrees. It'll be millions below, if you add in the wind chill. I've come to tell you that you've got to go home. Dad says that if you don't, we'll come up and drag you away in person.'

'Don't you go worrying about me, my love. I've got three pairs of socks on.'

She shook her head. 'Three pairs of socks won't be enough to save you. You've got to go home.'

'Not enough charge in the moped, my love. It needs a full night at Artie's, see?'

'Well, come down to us. Or to the farm. The moment the blizzard kicks in. Promise?'

He looked up at her anxious face and only just had the heart to lie. 'Course I will,' he said.

'You won't, will you?'

He looked away and spoke into the distance. 'What you've got to understand, my love, is I'm waiting for the Lord.'

'When it snows, you can wait for the Lord at ours,' she said.

'Well, you're the bossy one.'

'I'm fond of you, that's all.'

'Fond of me? Fond of me? Well, that's a thing! That's ridickless! Fond of me?'

'You're a deluded old idiot, but I'm fond of you. Please go home, for me.'

'All I want is to disappear,' he said, fluttering his fingers in imitation of flight. 'That's why I'm waiting for the Lord; it's into His heart that I'll be disappearing. Without a trace. Nothing left.'

'Just for me,' she said.

He hesitated for a long time and then shook his head. 'All right, just for you, my love.'

'Here,' Eva said, 'take my device. If you get caught, use it to ring my dad. We'll come out and get you. Dad's number is programmed as "Emergency". Anyway I'm beginning to freeze, so I'd better trot home.' She put a hand on his shoulder, leaned down and kissed him on the cheek.

Maranatha watched her as she left, a rich warmth flooding into his entrails. Runnergirl had said she was fond of him. Runnergirl had kissed him on the cheek. He clapped his hands on his knees and laughed up to the sky. 'She's fond of me!' he exclaimed. 'She's fond of me!' He laughed with the sheer unbelievable pleasure of Eva's confession – Eva who was so pretty and young, Eva who was made of golden light, Eva with her frank and fascinating eyes, sable hair and tawny skin – and he was too overjoyed to sit still. He got up from his stool, spread his arms and whirled slowly at first, just as he had seen them do in Turkey, long ago, before he had gone to the desert. He stamped his feet and danced to the drum of his heart. The minutes passed. The two sea eagles arrived and circled over Yelland Tor. Time slowed and became fictitious. Unlocked by one gesture of affection, he revolved faster and faster until suddenly he cried out and fell to his knees. Breathless, he swayed from the dizziness of his revolutions and then, happy beyond anything he had been able to imagine, he crawled into his bivouac, fastened himself into his sleeping bag and fell into an exhausted sleep, still wearing his boots, still drenched in the cold, sour sweat of his dancing.

44

The Snow

Theodore came up on his screen and said, 'Hey, Artie, you OK? This is one hell of a blizzard. The worst I can remember. Tightest isobars in history! It's minus twelve already.'

'That's climate change for you,' said Q, 'or perhaps it's just weather.'

'You OK?'

'Fine so far. I've got Morgan and Charlie here. Fergus and Morgan are making omelettes, and Charlie's bringing the logs in from the lumber room. Fergus thought better of staying in his caravan, so he's set himself up in a spare room. Maidie's in the attic, singing Edwardian music-hall hits to herself.'

'Listen, have you seen Maranatha? I mean, did he come by and pick up his moped?'

'I didn't see him. Why?'

'I'm afraid he might still be up on the Tor.'

'In this? He'd be dead already.'

'Could you look in your shed, where he charges it up?'

'You want me to go out in this?'

'No, *hermano*, I don't want you to. It's your duty, that's all.'

'Bloody hell,' said Q. 'OK. I'll ring you back in a minute.'

Soon he was back on the screen. 'I'm sorry, Theo, I can't open the doors. The snow's drifted. There must be four feet of it already.'

'Well, at least it's saved you from getting cold.' He paused. 'I didn't see Maranatha come by and neither did Eva. She went up and warned him about an hour before it kicked in.'

'Could you get the tractor up there?'

'No. I might not even get it to yours. It certainly wouldn't get up the Tor. The path's too narrow and we wouldn't even know where the path was. Have you been out?'

'Certainly not.'

'Well, I have. Visibility's nil. It's a white-out. Even with the tractor and all the lights on, I think I'd be lost within twenty feet of my house.'

Q sighed. 'Nothing we can do then.'

'No. Hey, Eva wants to speak to you.'

Eva came up on the screen, her face streaked with tears and her lip trembling. 'He's going to die,' she said, 'I know he is. He'll be steeved.'

'We'll go and look when it's over.'

'Maybe Jesus came and got him. I hope He did.' She wiped her nose with the back of her hand.

He replied, 'Jesus comes in many forms. So they say.'

'Who's "they"?'

'Nobody really, I just made that up. Off the top of my head.'

She smiled wanly and said, 'It sounded good. Good, but not very convincing. Is that Morgan and Charlie I can see in the background? Will you say hi from me?'

'Yes, I'll say hi. Look after yourself. And your dad.'

Eva implied 'I love you' with her eyes alone and faded from the screen.

The snow piled up for days. On the eastern side of their houses it rose above the level of the windows. On the southern and northern sides it flurried past in a continuous, relentless horizontal stream. The grid failed, and the two families huddled in their houses, wrapped in heavy coats, blankets and woollen hats. Charlie and his father ventured out with gloved hands to fetch logs from the stack outside the eastern door, where a small clear space remained, and came in shaking with cold after only seconds outside. In both houses the logs ran out after four days. The blades on the turbines froze motionless and then snapped off. They cooked on petrol stoves, coating the ceilings of their kitchens with aromatic soot.

In the absence of Eva, Maidie Knox Lilita reappeared in the house, spending the daylight at the window of an upper room, gazing westwards at the hypnotic stream that fled way from her, harkening to the wild song of the wind and slipping in and out of the past. At night she crawled into bed next to Q's slumbering form and lay without touching him, sensing his presence in the darkness, grateful both for the taste of what is given in the moment and for that which remains in the soul, of what has been taken away.

On the fifth day the snow ceased and the wind fell, power was restored and the countryside was unrecognisable. Theodore looked out over the immense depth of snow and grieved for his animals. In his mind's eye he could clearly see them beneath that apocalyptic deluge of snow, stiff and sightless. There were probably no carrion birds left to eat them, either. He found he could get Q on his screen. 'Hell of a storm,' he said.

'Bloody global colding,' said Eva, appearing briefly behind her father's shoulder. 'That's the worst blunk we've ever had.'

'Can you put a drone over the top of the Tor?' asked Theo. 'Mine are in the shed and I can't get to them yet. And I haven't been able to get a decent satellite picture.'

'If Maranatha was up there, he'll be long dead. It was minus fifteen. At the very least.'

'I know. I just want to know, one way or another.'

'My drones are in a shed as well,' said Q.

'Oh well, we'll have to wait. Have you got snowshoes? Or skis?'

'No. I never thought of that.'

'Me neither. We'd never get up there without them.'

'We've got a south-west wind coming, according to my device. Think of the floods. They'll be catastrophic.'

'Thank God we're up here,' said Theo.

'It's funny,' said Q, 'how we thank God for good fortune and don't rail at Him for bad.'

'You think too much. Thank God for thankfulness, *hermano*, that's what I say.'

45

Obsequies

They found him three days later, haloed in painfully bright sun-light, as the valley and the marshes below flooded with the torrents of freezing water that were pouring down the runnels of the slopes. Theodore and his friend had waded uphill through the descending sludge and arrived breathless at the summit of the Tor, to find that Maranatha's old army bivouac had been torn away by the storm, leaving him to die in the foetal position, a *Soldiers' Bible* clutched in his hand, curled up into himself like his own child, sur-rounded by seven ravens who were waiting only for one of their number to be the first to take an eye.

The two men looked down on the body with heavy hearts. '*Fue totalmente tonto*,' said Theodore, 'but still . . . There was something about him. I suppose he's been dead for days.'

'We all liked him,' said Q, crouching down and wiping the lank hair away from the face, adding, 'Poor bastard. He was hoping not to have to die. His eyes are open. I hope he saw what he wanted to see. At least we got here in time to foil the ravens.' He stood up, 'What should we do now?'

'Let's get the others up here. We'd better stay here and keep the birds off. We can pass the time watching the world drown.'

Half an hour later the two families were standing in a circle around the body on the peak, holding council.

'I suppose we ought to tell the authorities,' said Charlie, who had his arm around Morgan's shoulder as she wept into her hands.

'Let's find out who he was,' said Eva. 'We need to go through his things.'

'I'll do it,' said her father. 'I've done it before. Back home. Once the snow melted more than usual, and we found a man curled up just like this. He'd been there five hundred years. We took off his armour, and inside he was light as a feather. We carried him and left him back above the snowline. We buried him back in the snow.' He knelt down and ferreted through the pockets of Maranatha's coat, and then those of his trousers.

'I gave him my device,' said Eva.

'Here it is,' said Theodore, handing it up to her. 'There are no papers or cards – nothing except these keys,' he continued, standing up. 'And now the knees of my trousers are soaked.'

'He's left nothing but his electric moped,' said Eva.

Q replied, 'He had a place in Bodmin. I can go down there and ask around. It's not such a big town any more. Half the houses are empty. I wonder if St Neot is flooded? Maybe we can't even get there yet.'

'One thing I know,' said Eva, 'was that what he wanted, more than anything else in the world, was to disappear completely. Without a trace. Do we do what we're supposed to do or what Maranatha wanted?'

They looked at each other and Charlie said, 'There's already a fair chance he's been noticed by a satellite.'

'I can easily find out,' said Q, taking out his device.

They wrapped the body in the canvas of the bivouac, along with Maranatha's few possessions, and laid him out, with his hands folded over the Bible on his chest. When Fergus arrived, the six sorrowing survivors of the storm gathered rocks of granite and built a cromlech on the peak of Helland Tor, disguised as a cairn. They built it six feet high and six feet round, so that any ravening animal that wished to excavate would soon lose heart. Its construction was an act of prayer.

'I . . .' began Theodore.

'What?' said Eva.

'No, never mind. It was boring and banal. It was something we all know anyway.'

'Come on, Dad, say it anyway.'

Theo shrugged his shoulders. 'I was going to say that, well, yes, we all think he was a poor deluded old fool who thought that Christ was coming to fetch him, but if you think about . . . well, he's ended up the same as all of us will. He's ended up just bones beneath stones. This is how Einstein finished up, and Atahualpa, and Peter the Great. We're all Time's fools. We're no different from Maranatha. We're all simply grist to the mill, and the mill grinds on and on, and after our little sojourn on the earth we're forever in the dark.'

Eva took his hand. 'I don't care about Einstein or Peter the Great. My world is very small. I only know that I love my tiny world. That's all I want.'

That morning, beneath its rounded heap of stones, the corpse of Maranatha began the long process of mummification. In the evening the six, subdued by weariness and fatigue, gathered together and ate at Yelland Farm.

After Eva was asleep, Maidie Knox Lilita appeared, alone, at the cromlech. She ran her hands over the stones. 'I saw a new heaven and a new earth,' she said softly, 'for the first heaven and the first earth had passed away.' She lingered, looking back down on the lights of the house where the mourners were assembled. Clouds passed beneath the moon and the night grew darker and cold. Maidie kissed her hand, transferring the kiss to Maranatha's stones.

And so it was that Maranatha slipped out of sight, leaving behind him an electric moped and a bunch of keys. In his room in Bodmin there remained a photograph of himself as a staff corporal in the Welsh Cavalry, along with the comrades of his troop – he the lone survivor of their skirmish in the desert. Against the walls in blue plastic bags was neatly piled his collected excrement, brought down weekly from the Tor.

46

Trials

There were three days in midsummer when it rained continuously, the water hammering on the tiles with the rhythm of hypnosis. It washed the dirt out from the courtyard and cut new runnels and freshets in the track outside. Even Eva was baulked by it, cutting her runs short and returning drenched, the splashes of mud up her legs to her thighs, her running shoes squelching out the spurts of water as she ran. Tiegen Rosenwyn arrived at Theodore's house and skulked in the shelter of the woodshed.

Q conceived the idea of writing a history of quantum cryptography and, realising that it did not have to be written in any particular order, began not at the beginning, but with a chapter on KEM variants of the McEliece and Niederreiter public-key encryption schemes. He had become the kind of man who is not happy unless he has too much to do, with half a dozen concurrent projects that have no prospect of being accomplished any time soon. His was a world in which the greatest torment is to be bored by oneself.

Charlie lay in his room with the curtains drawn, exercising his adolescent talent for infinite sleep. Morgan sat fascinated at the window, watching it rain, with the stillness of an anchoress. She and Fergus pinged each other every half-hour.

At the end of the deluge, the sun appeared and raised an invisible bath of humidity that bathed their skin with perspiration and exasperated their lungs. The water cascading from the eaves dried up, and the flattened vegetables in the garden renewed their struggle to gain strength and grow. The heat became unbearable. Morgan went to her room and took her flute from her case. Wearing only a cotton wrap, a wide straw hat and a pair of sandals, she set off to the pool that, in his first months on Bodmin Moor, her father had made by damming the stream in order to ensure there would always be water, even in August.

An elder had grown up on the south side of the pool, with a flat rock beneath its shade, and here Morgan liked to sit on hot days and play the flute to herself until such time as she felt like returning to the water. She was learning 'Syrinx', an old piece from the early days of modernism, haunting and mysterious, but full of flats and accidentals that were the musical equivalent of mines and booby traps. She had been learning it for six months now, and considered that when she had mastered it she would be at a loss as to what to aspire to next.

She had reached the point where her fingers were remembering how to play it without the intervention of her intellect, and so she sat in the shade of the elder, playing it over and over again. She felt she was at that point where one can begin to think of how to play it more musically, rather than simply arriving successfully at its conclusion. She challenged herself to play it ever more slowly and sadly, oblivious to the fact that she had silenced the animals for hundreds of yards around. Even the buzzards had ceased their mewing above her.

Fergus had ventured out with the idea of fetching in a hare, but had fired not a shot. In the heat the animals were lying up in their various shades, and he himself was overwhelmed by an oriental apathy. Certainly it was intolerable in the captivity and closeness of his campervan, and so he too was heading for the pool, and as he drew near he heard the music of the flute. He stood stock-still and listened, mesmerised by the strange, melancholy chromaticism. The music drew out and ceased on a long, low, breathy D-flat.

When Fergus turned the corner, he found Morgan, with her back towards him, standing naked in the centre of the pool still brimming with the rains. She was immersed up to the waist and was cooling her head by sweeping up her long, crinkled hair with her hands. He stood absolutely still, a kind of panic rising up in his breast, the gun useless in his hands. She seemed impossibly slender, without one ounce of unnecessary flesh, her delicate bones shining through her skin, the perfect archipelago of her spine dividing the symmetry of her tawny back.

He was on the point of attempting to creep away, when she turned round quite suddenly and saw him. She did not dip down into the water. He tried to look away, but his eyes could not help but return to the small, round breasts with their dark nipples, and the elegant muscles of her abdomen. She began to walk towards him.

'Dinna come out,' he said.

She smiled in mock reproach. 'I caught you peeping.'

He raised a hand in protest. 'I wasna peeping. I was out after getting a hare. For the pot.'

'It's all right,' she said, 'you can look.' And she stepped closer until he could see the light fuzz of her groin and the skin of her thighs, sparkling with droplets of water.

He looked away. 'I cannae look, lassie, I cannae look.'

'Still, you can if you want.'

'Dinna do this.'

'I'm giving you permission.'

Slowly he turned his head, but his eyes found that they could not settle.

'Imagine I'm Aphrodite,' she said. 'Imagine I'm a classical statue. Look at me.'

'But you're not. You're you.'

'I'm still a goddess, aren't I?'

'You're very like. You're fuckin' perfect, that's the honest truth.'

'I'll never be more beautiful than this as long as I live. Even in ten years' time I won't be as lovely as this. Even if I get myself biohacked. That's why I want to be looked at now. I ought to turn you into a stag and have you hunted down by your own dogs. Luckily I'm not that kind of goddess, and I know you love me.'

'I never said.'

'You didn't have to. Fergus, do you want me?'

'You know damn well I do. I just dinna have the right. You're way above.'

'You've got to earn me then. You've got to do three things.'

'Three things?'

'I've got to work out what they are.' She stood in thought for a few seconds, and then raised a forefinger. 'Right, you've got to make a spear and learn to throw it. That's the first thing, and when you've done it I'll tell you the second.'

'You're a weird wee lass.'

'That's why you love me.' She made a sweeping downward gesture with both hands to indicate the contours of her body. 'It's not just this.'

47

The Spear

Fergus consulted Theodore, who told him that he should probably make the shaft of his spear from ash or hazel. 'I've got a little coppice in Hippies' Wood,' he said. 'That's where I get my poles. Come on down, I'll show you how to get in. We'll get a few, just in case.'

Fergus was whittling the bark from one of these poles in the courtyard of the farm when Morgan approached so silently that he jumped when she spoke. 'That pole isn't straight enough,' she said. 'It's got two little bends in it.'

'Not enough to matter.'

'It's me you're having to please. It's got to be straight.'

'I've got five poles to choose from. Do you want ta look?'

In the shed Fergus laid out his collection of poles on the workbench, and Morgan rang her musician's fingers over them. 'None of them are straight,' she declared.

'Fer fuck's sake,' said Fergus.

'It's got to be straight,' she said.

'That's the straightest one there is.'

'Then make it straighter.'

'Fer fuck's sake,' he repeated.

Fergus went down to Theodore's house and asked him how to straighten a pole. That evening he set about constructing a long jig, set with upright dowels and a system of cams, and then he borrowed a heat gun. He set the pole along the jig and rotated the cams until the pole was straight. He sprinkled water along it, even though it was still in the green, and set the gun to maximum heat.

He warmed the places where the pole needed to be bent until the wood began to char, and then he left it to cool. In the morning he removed it from the jig and sighted along its length. It was still not quite perfect, so he returned it to the jig, tightened the cams and heated it again.

On the third day he took the shaft to Morgan, who glanced at it cursorily and said, 'It's lovely and straight, but it's not the same thickness all the way down.' She raised her hand, making a circle with her forefinger and thumb and looking at him through it. 'This is how thick it's got to be. Not more or less.'

Fergus had to make several batons to try for size on Morgan's hand until, sliding her right hand up and down one of them, she said, 'It's this one. Make it like this. This one's right.'

The pole was too long to set on a lathe, so he began to whittle it down with a spokeshave, realising only just in time that he was making it thinner without making it rounder. He returned to Theodore, who told him, 'You'll have to make a die.'

'Theo, I've nae idea what you mean,' said Fergus.

Theodore sighed and put down the gun he was cleaning. 'Well, *hermano*, I suppose I'll have to show you.'

In the workshop that Q had set up, with the intention of being able to make virtually anything he might need after it was no longer possible to buy it, there was a large lathe. Theodore searched through the bin of metal scraps that his friend had accumulated with vague ideas as to their possible future usefulness, and triumphantly produced a short length of thick steel rod. This he set up in the chuck of the lathe, and then he cut a hole through its centre. Fergus watched with fascination as the long coils of swarf emerged from the hole, and at the stream of beige cutting fluid that flowed along the cutter. When Theodore released the metal from the chuck, he held it up to Fergus' eyes and said, 'A perfect shining hole.'

'Now what?' asked Fergus.

'We set it up in a vice and you tap the pole through with a mallet, while I pull it. The shavings'll strip off and you'll end up with a lovely uniform shaft. What do you want it for anyway?'

'Morgan wants it.'

'Morgan? What does she want it for?'

'She wants me to make her a spear. Don't ask. It's a kind of test.'

'Do you know how to make the head?'

'No, Theo, I surely don't.'

'If I help you, is that cheating?'

'If I have to cheat, I have to cheat.'

Fergus did as he was told, and before long they had a perfectly straight shaft of exactly the right circumference. 'Fuckin' genius,' he exclaimed, running it through his hands.'

'We could just have ordered a broom handle,' said Theodore. 'I've remembered that the world hasn't ended yet.'

'Fuck,' said Fergus. 'Can I order a spear head then?'

'Never tried, my friend. We can make one in a couple of hours. There's a billet of carbon steel in that bin. All we've got to do is soften it up.'

'Lead on,' said Fergus wearily.

He watched as Theodore arranged some bricks on the bench, laid the billet on it and began to heat it with a blowtorch. 'Once it's cherry-red, all we have to do is leave it to cool and then it'll work as easy as butter.'

'I believe you,' said Fergus. But it was true. Once it had cooled, the billet was cut and filed to shape in minutes.

'Not many people know,' said Theodore, 'but metal's a pussycat to work with, once you know the tricks. It's easier than wood any day. Metal hasn't even got a grain. You can do the next bit. We'll need a big bucket of water, as cold as you can make it. You can do this bit. It's fun.'

So it was that Fergus heated the spear head up to cherry-red, grasped it in a long pair of tongs and plunged it into the icy water. The bubbling, steaming and hissing were joyous to behold, and Fergus whooped with delight. He held it up for his mentor to admire.

'Bravo,' said the latter, 'but right now it'll be too brittle to use. You have to toughen it up. You've got to run the colours. I'd better show you, the first time.'

'The first time? I'll be making more of these?'

'Everybody needs a spear,' said Theodore drily. Fergus watched as the metal was heated up again and the colours began to run. 'Watch,' said Theodore, 'it goes from straw to blue. It's OK if the cutting edge is blue, but for the rest, you want it when it's about to turn, and then you plunge it quick as you can.'

'It's bloody brilliant,' said Fergus when the blade was done.

They mounted it in the shaft by cutting a long notch and binding it in with cord. 'I'm going to show it to Morgan,' cried Fergus, running off with it.

'Young love,' thought Theodore, and he sighed.

Fergus found Morgan in her room and proudly showed her the spear. 'The shaft looks too new,' she said. 'It ought to be all dark and brown. You can make the dye out of walnut shells.'

'It's midsummer,' protested Fergus, 'and there's nae shells yet and there's nae walnut trees hereabouts, anyways.'

'Poor Fergus,' was all she said, turning back to her device. He returned to his campervan and ordered a can of stain.

Three days later he presented her with the weapon again. 'It's lovely,' she said. 'All you've got to do now is learn to throw it.'

'Any lavvyheid can hurl a spear,' he replied.

She took him by the hand and led him outside into the garden. 'You've got to be able to throw it as far as that tree,' she said, indicating the gnarled and stunted old apple tree at the further end.

'Yer fuckin teasin'!' he exclaimed.

She turned on her heel and said, as she departed, 'Achilles could have done it. You'd better start practising now.'

He watched her go, and the spirit of rebellion rose up in his breast. 'Well, fuck you,' he said under his breath. 'That's enough for me. I'm bloody off out of it.'

Angrily he strode back to his campervan and began to sort things through for imminent departure. However, the spirit of counter-rebellion edged its way in and the question re-presented itself: how to cast a spear further than you can cast it? He set off down the track to consult Theo.

'Throwing stick,' he said. 'It's easy. It's like those things that people use to throw balls for their dogs – just an extension of the arm. It's got to be the right length, and the right design to hook the end of the spear, and then you'll need a bit of practice. Let's look it up. You know, *amigo*, I like having you around. You give me interesting things to think of.'

'You should thank Morgan, Theo.'

'What's up with you two? Something going on?'

'She's setting me tasks.'

Theo sighed again and remembered his youth.

Three days later Fergus took Morgan into the garden, readied himself, ran and hurled the spear. More by luck than design, it struck the tree a man's height above the ground and stuck there, quivering. Morgan walked to the wounded tree and stroked the shaft of the spear. Then she turned and leaned against the trunk, holding out her arms. 'Come on,' she said. 'Kiss me.' She pulled him to her by the shoulders, put one hand behind his head and gently led him in to the longest, slowest and most sublime kiss he had ever experienced in his life. He felt his heart thumping in his chest, and put one hand against the tree to support the sudden weakness in his legs.

She pushed him away and stroked his cheek tenderly. Her eyes widened and sparkled. 'Now, Sir Knight, for your second task. All you've got to do is bring me a horse.'

48

Fergus on Trial

I felt so sorry for Fergus. He came to me to ask me to teach him how to use a lasso, and we spent an afternoon together, whilst I taught him to use the overhead technique for short distances and the long loop for the underarm throw. He became quite good at it almost immediately.

He was full of energy and optimism, and I do believe that he relished the challenge, so the next day he went off in search of horses. There was a herd that sometimes mingled with the aurochs down by the marshes, but he never got close enough. He went three days running and came back empty-handed, filthy and exhausted each time. On the fourth day he came back all in a pelt and a perp, complaining that Morgan was a piss-taker, and why should he be sent out on errands to prove himself? When wasn't it enough just to be himself?

I said, 'The romance of knight errantry has worn off already then?'

'Fuckin' right, Eva,' he replied.

Anyway I questioned him about what he'd been doing, and it soon became obvious that he didn't know anything about approaching wild animals from downwind, and neither did he have any idea that horses can see behind themselves, the same as rabbits. I said to him, 'What did Morgan actually say to you?'

'She said, "Bring me a horse."'

'That's all? "Bring me a horse"? She didn't say what kind of horse?'

'What would you be getting at, lassie?'

'She didn't say a colt or a dray horse, or a black horse or a grey, or a wild horse or a tame one?'

'Nae. Just "Bring me a horse."'

'That's easy, then. Message her to be at the pool at five o'clock.'

So it was that at five o'clock Morgan was sitting on a boulder like some delicate little pisky with bare arms and legs, and her hair a-tumble about her shoulders, when Fergus turned up leading a horse by the halter.

'I've brought you your horse,' he said, whereupon Morgan stood up and came to look at it.

'That's Falghun,' she said. 'That's Eva's horse.'

She looked up at him grinning down at her and he said, 'So?'

'That isn't what I meant. I can't have Eva's horse. It's hers.'

'You didna say you wanted to have it. You told me to bring it. A horse. This is a horse – a fair proper lang-shankit cuddie – and I've brought it.'

Well, Morgan was mightily cheesed, especially by Fergus being all triumphant, and a pedant to boot. 'I wanted a horse,' she said, 'to break in and go out riding on. I wanted my own horse. You knew perfectly well what I meant.'

'Well, lassie, you shoulda said.'

'All right,' she declared, all in a huff and with her arms folded across, 'as you're such a smartarse and dandy-brains, now you can bring me Eva's cat.'

Well, Fergus returned Falghun to his stable and came down to our house. It was late and getting dimpsy when he knocked at the door. I was really hungry after a long run, and I answered the door with a big teddy-hoggy in my hand and my mouth full, and he told me how Morgan wasn't best pleased, and now he had to bring her my cat.

I said, 'What cat? I haven't got a cat.' Then it dawned on me. 'You mean Tiegen Rosenwyn?'

'I dinna ken its name,' he said.

'Tiegen Rosenwyn isn't my cat. She's a huge wild lynx that lives off deer and brings us rabbits and likes to ride in the car, and she's nobody's cat.'

'I've got to take her to Morgan or I'm . . .' and he drew his hand across to make the sign of the slit throat.

I repeated, 'She's nobody's cat. You can't put her on a lead, and she'd scratch you to shreds if you tried to catch her.'

'What if I lay a trail of meat?'

'Good luck with that,' I said. Then I had an idea. 'I've got a cuddly toy cat my mother gave me when I was seven.'

'Morgan wouldna be impressed,' he said, shaking his head. 'That'd go down like a lead balloon. She'd be scunnered.'

So he went back to Morgan and told her that Eva had no cat, that Eva swore to it, and said that Tiegen Rosenwyn was her own cat, but Morgan insisted, and he replied, 'Well, that's it with us then.' And he took her right hand in his and looked into her eyes, which were very amber and beautiful, and recited:

'We'll meet nae mair at sunset when the weary day is dune,
Nor wander hame thegither by the lee licht o' the mune!
I'll hear your steps nae longer amang the dewy corn,
For we'll meet nae mair, my bonniest, either at eve or
    morn.

The yellow broom is waving abune the sunny brae,
And the rowan berries dancing, where the sparkling waters
    play;
Tho' a' is bright and bonnie, it's an eerie place to me,
For we'll meet nae mair, my dearest, either by burn or
    tree.'

And he turned and walked away. He returned to his campervan with his heart at peace because he had given up on the impossible, and he sat and thought that now he could grow his hair and beard as long and filthy as he liked, and if he didn't want to wash, he didn't have to, and he could travel away and go back on the road. Then he made himself a jam sandwich, went to bed to eat it, wiped his hands on the sheets, turned off the light and slept the sleep of the dead.

Morgan was in her room playing 'Syrinx' on the flute, but it kept going awry because she couldn't concentrate. Had she really been romantically renounced by means of Old Scots verse? She thought of his mysterious grey eyes locked onto hers as his musical voice recited in the auld tongue, and the gentle touch of the pads of his fingers on her palm, and the way his thumb stroked the back of her hand to the rhythm of the words, despatching waves of shivers up and down the fine hairs of her arm. Finally she sent him a message that read, 'OK, I absolve you of having to bring me the cat.'

In the morning Fergus stopped me as I ran past and showed me the message. I said, 'I'm sorry to have to tell you this, but reading between the lines, I think it means that she still wants a horse.'

49

The Horse (2)

Eva and Fergus lounged on the sward at the edge of Dozmary Pool and watched idly as the grebe ducked and re-emerged. Fergus had a long piece of speargrass in his mouth, and she was toying with a large flat-headed field mushroom that had appeared out of season and was destined for her cooking pot.

'Yon's a bonnie wee cuddie,' said Fergus again, nodding towards the nervous young filly that he had tied to an alder bush by means of its halter. 'Thanks for helpin' me out.'

'Morgan's going to be thrilled,' said Eva. She prodded him with the toe of her boot. 'Now you're luck's going to be in, for sure.'

Fergus glanced at her smugly and replied, 'Mebbe ma luck's already been in, lassie.'

Eva was excited and curious. 'Has it? Has it really?'

'Mebbe.'

'Stop teasing! Have you slept with her already? Was it a good one? I mean, was it a success? Did you take precautions?'

'Ah'm telling you nothing. She made me promise. She said, "No gossiping with Eva. Ah'm gonna tell her mesel."'

'She hasn't told me anything.'

'Mebbe nothin's happened yet, then.'

'You're a tease.'

'So I am, lassie, so I am.'

Eva perceived the happiness and hope in his face, and tried to suppress her misgivings. A threshold had been crossed. If anything went wrong, Fergus would have to leave. 'I won't say anything to Artie,' she said. 'I'll leave it to Morgan.' She felt a weight on her heart, because she had helped Fergus and Morgan to their goal and now it seemed as though she had lumbered herself with too much responsibility.

'If it goes wrong, it's not my fault,' she said. 'I still think she's too young.'

'Too late,' said Fergus. 'When the hurricane comes, you lie low or you go out and whirl in the wind.'

50

Pigeons

E va asked me to go and get some pigeons, and because she normally would have asked her father, I took it as some kind of test. She is the kind of woman who likes to check quite frequently upon the level of your competence and devotion. She likes to keep me on my toes.

She slits the skin along the breastbone, peels it back, carves out the breast meat and gives the rest of the bird to Tiegen Rosenwyn. She slices the breasts up and fries them with onions, garlic and bacon and then stirs it all into rice to make a pilaff, which she splatters with Worcester sauce. In the evenings we wash it down with Beaujolais.

It was during the Dog Days, at the time of the Perseid showers, which I have always loved to watch from the top of the Tor – clouds permitting – and the wind was blowing from the west. This was important, because pigeons like to fly into a roost against the wind and so, as the extreme heat and humidity of the day began to moderate, I went down to the eastern side of Hippies' Wood three hours before dusk, to catch them as they came in to roost. I had the choice of hiding and shooting them with a high-powered air rifle the moment they settled on the branch, or I could take a shotgun and catch them as they came in. As I still had little confidence in myself as a marksman, I took the shotgun and a pocketful of shells, entering the wood through the access near Christian's opened grave.

My mind was not entirely on the task ahead, I remember, because there was yet another crisis involving the deathbots, which at that time constituted at least half of our standing army. Someone had got into the control codes and reprogrammed every single one of them as a domestic housebot. We were not at war at the time, and the affair was considered to be the work of a pacifistic humorist, but we did take it as a warning, since it would have been catastrophic had it occurred when our forces were in action. One of the upshots of the episode was that more human soldiers were recruited, just in case.

The wood was quiet and peaceful, and not for the first time I thought what a shame it would be to break this serenity with the reports of a gun. Sometimes, if the world seems to be perfectly at peace with itself, I return early from the hunt without firing a shot. At other times the air seems full of chaos and threat, and then I feel guiltless, as if I am merely another savage in a heartless world.

I was a little way across the wood when I spotted Tiegen Rosenwyn, standing in a small clearing in the trees. I knew it was her because she had a characteristic way of standing, with her feet turned out. Her stance reminded me of a balletbot standing in the first position. She knew me quite well by then, and I had partially overcome her suspicion and hostility by feeding her small scraps of dried meat that I carried in my pocket. I could make her rear up on her hind legs to take them from my fingers, which she did gently enough. Eva called it 'dancing bears'.

I called to her, but she turned and walked away slowly, stopping to look over her shoulder from time to time. I assumed that she wished me to follow her and, forgetting my mission on Eva's behalf, that is what I did.

I followed Tiegen Rosenwyn for about a hundred paces and then lost her. I was looking around, scanning between the tree trunks for any movement, when I spotted a red deer. I would like to say that it was a magnificent stag with a cross incandescent between its points, but it was a doe. We did not often shoot a red deer, not least because they are colossally heavy even after having been gralloched, and it is no fun at all trying to carry one home when you are already carrying a gun. If you did intend to bag one, you would take one of the horses with you and sling the corpse across its back. In any case, the red deer seldom exceeded the ideal number, whereas the little muntjac actually did, and tasted just as fine. For this reason the red deer were no more frightened of us than Tiegen Rosenwyn.

I followed the doe for a while, as she ambled elegantly through the trees, occasionally pausing to crop the grass, and then I came to a small ruined stone building, roofless. All around it were ancient gravestones, tilted, illegible, coated in green moss and grey scales of lichen. This little garden of the dead was ringed by apple trees, some laden with yellow fruit and some with red. There were also occasional trees, their fruit small and hard, scattered amongst the mounds. I picked up a large red apple and bit into it, but it was sour, and so I spat it out.

I wandered amid the graves for a while, attempting to imagine who they might contain, and where the people would have lived who worshipped in this tiny chapel.

Graveyards always make me sad, especially the graves of children, but they also make me curious. I think about these forgotten souls, their passions and trials, their loves and triumphs and disasters, and it puts my own life into salutary perspective. There have been so many billions of dramas – a narrative for every living being, almost all of them lost. It prompts me to tell myself to enjoy what I have while I still have strength, and hope, to stride on through my own story, to live out my own explanation of my life, until I too am lost.

I propped my shotgun against the wall outside and entered. Inside the chapel there was nothing but a stone floor inlaid with black granite grave slabs, inscribed with italic writing that it was no longer possible to make out, even had I been able to read Latin. On one of them was a white death's head, clearly engraved, with two words beneath in English that I could make out. *Relict of.*

The glass of the windows was missing, and the floor beneath the beams was thickly encrusted with bird droppings and feathers. Leaves and twigs were piled up in the corners. I was attempting to read the epitaph, when I caught the distinct smell of rosemary and lavender. The clouds moved and a slanting shaft of evening light suddenly broke in through the western window and I looked up, to be almost blinded by it, so I put up my hand to shade my eyes.

I saw a young woman in white caught up in its beam, standing sideways to me, perfectly still, pointing to the floor with her left forefinger. Her long dress reflected the light so brilliantly that she shone effulgently. She was the very picture of an angel, or perhaps some young goddess of Olympus, blurred in her own nimbus of yellow light. It seemed to me that I was in the presence of a miracle, a kind of visual epiphany. She had her long black hair gathered to fall down her left shoulder, and a circlet of ox-eye daisies round her head.

'Maidie,' I said, 'is that you?'

I had never once had a conversation with Maidie that was not elliptical. She talked in runes and gnomae, in riddles and cryptomnesia. I was used to it, and never expected anything else. It was enough for me to be the object of her encompassing passions on those nights when she arrived at God knows what hour and slid between the sheets. She smiled, raised her eyebrows, lifted her hands in a mock gesture of ignorance and said, 'Well, who is anybody, after all?'

She beckoned, turned her back and walked out through the western door. I saw that she was wearing a red sash, red slippers and a silver anklet. I followed immediately after her, to see her already vanishing between the trees, running lightly and deftly, flitting in and out of my vision. I gazed after her for little while, shrugged my shoulders and went to fetch my gun. She was no more controllable or comprehensible than Eva was.

At dusk I did return with two pigeons. On the way I passed Bess o'Bedlam, still dressed in rags and sacking stitched together with agricultural string, crouched before her small, flat rock where she liked to come and croak over the leaves that she burned there. Her long grey hair was more than usually matted and filthy, and her face was streaked with ash. I said, 'Good evening, Bess', but as usual she ignored me, because there was no intersection between her universe and mine. If we had been represented by Venn diagrams, we would have been drawn as separate circles. When she looked up at the sound of my voice, I know that her small black eyes, like currants in her sunburned face, did not for one second see me. Nonetheless, I greeted Bess across the unbridgeable distance between our worlds.

When I returned to the farmhouse I found Eva on the rifle range. She had set up a large straw man on a stake and was riding back and forth on Falghun, taking shots at it with the small Mongolian bow that had always been her favourite. There were several arrows stuck into the bank behind the target, and at least three through the straw man himself, whose head was slumped forward on his chest as if he had formerly been alive and had now been shot to death. When she saw me, she seemed a little abashed. 'Hello, you. I'm not as mad as you think.'

'Re-enacting the death of St Sebastian?' I said.

'I decided to develop a new skill,' she said. 'I wanted to learn something new. Something difficult. And Falghun needs interesting things to do as well. He's learning how to do what I want when I don't even have my hands on the reins.'

'What use is it, though?'

'Well, how can you ask such a stupid question?' she demanded crossly, scowling down at me from the saddle. 'What if all the ammunition runs out one day and we need to kill a buffalo?'

'We could dig a pit.'

'In a rocky place like this? Well, I'm doing this because I feel like doing this, that's all. One day I'll be putting arrows through that man on the gallop, and that'll be so impressive you won't even think of asking what use it is. And after that I'll learn to do it like the Parthians. If you just want to be annoying, I'll put an arrow through your foot, and that'll serve you right.' She reached for an arrow from the quiver on her back, and notched it at the centre of the string. She drew the bow and pointed it at my feet. 'Dance, Creaky One, dance!' she commanded.

'Point that somewhere else. I only dance in the kitchen,' I replied. I held up the two birds and said, 'I've got the pigeons.'

'Well, go and cut the breasts out, and I'll be along in a minute. And I'm going to trim your eyebrows. And your nails are all ragged again. And tomorrow I'm going to cut your hair, when I've fetched my scissors.'

'It's lucky one of us is perfect,' I said.

The next day I returned to the wood and quartered it. No matter how systematically I traversed it, grid by grid, nowhere could I find the ruined chapel with its orchard of apple trees and its little cemetery of tilted stones. Subsequently I would hope to find it every time I went down there to hunt or to look for mushrooms, but I never did. I asked Eva about a ruined chapel and a graveyard in Hippies' Wood and she did that irritating trick of hers, of saying that she knew nothing whilst implying that really she did.

All I know is that one day, when I was out hunting pigeons, I saw Maidie Knox Lilita, who may or may not be Eva herself, transfigured in the woods. Make of that what you will. When I told Eva about it, she said it must have been a vivid dream, but I didn't believe her.

51

Eva and Her Mother

'Hello, darling, you wanted to talk. Can't stay long. I've got a meeting.'

'I wanted to tell you that Dad believes what Artie has been telling him. He says there really is a lot of evidence, and lot of sense in what he says.'

'So?'

'So if everything comes to a halt, I think you should get back here.'

'But, darling, Dad wouldn't want me back in the house, that's for sure. Too much bad blood.'

'You could stay at Yelland Farm. Artie's got masses of room.'

'Have you asked him?'

'No.'

'Don't you think you'd better?'

'Course. I'll ask him later. And I'll talk to Dad. Dad wouldn't want you to starve to death in Scotland.'

'He'd probably love it.'

'Well, let's face it, Mum, you deserve to.'

'You still think I'm a complete shit, don't you?'

'You were an idiot, Mum, dumping Dad and then dumping the new boyfriend. And dragging me away like that, without even asking.'

Silence.

'Well, I've paid for it now, haven't I?'

'Mum, I've been meaning to tell you for ages. I'm with Artie, and it's serious.'

'Is that wise? Isn't he very much older and – you know – a bit of a freak? I mean, much too intelligent. And he's famous.'

'Not in a celebrity kind of way. He does get lots of messages from weird people who say they're sapiosexual, though. Anyway, I just thought I'd tell you.'

'Thanks. It's none of my business any more, though, is it?'

'Not really, Mum. And anyway I'm not normal, either. But Mum . . .'

'Yes?'

'Please move back.'

52

First Blood

Theo and I had accumulated a massive inventory of things that we might need over the next few decades. It included dozens of pairs of work boots, a heap of shovels and spades, axe hafts and blades, air-rifle pellets, cooking pots, bow-saw blades, socks, combat dress, toothpaste, a potter's wheel, fishing tackle, rope and cord . . . An entire barnful of useful things to which we continuously added new stock.

He and I had spent many an evening sitting in complete silence at opposite sides of my kitchen table, making our own ammunition. It was a very pleasant, almost hypnotic occupation, carefully cleaning and resizing the cases, priming them, measuring out precise charges of powder and setting up the presses to produce cartridges of precisely the right length, so that they would exactly engage the rifling. It was rather wonderful to see the heaps of gleaming brass and copper mounting up in the boxes like the jewels of a miser. We both thought that, in the new order after the disaster, ammunition would undoubtedly become the most valuable currency, and this was one reason we produced so many thousands of rounds, but apart from that, we knew we might have to defend ourselves against brigands and would certainly need to hunt our own meat.

I had become a reasonably good shot with the old-fashioned spring-powered air rifle, but it was against the odds. The damned thing leapt sideways when it wasn't leaping upwards. Theo was right about the double recoil making it naturally inaccurate, and had tried to teach me something that he called 'the artillery hold'. I couldn't get on with that, but he was also right when he said it was the best possible training for a proper rifle, because it has the same kick, but the recoil doesn't even have time to happen before the bullet has already left the barrel. Miraculously, after all that frustration with the execrable springer, neat little groups of bullets appeared in the target at the other end of the range whenever I used any other kind of gun.

One day Theo came in and presented me with a cartridge. I looked at it and said, 'Oh, a three-o-eight. Soft point.'

'Yes, brother,' he said. 'It's one that you made. And with this bullet you're going to kill your first deer.'

'I don't think I'm ready yet,' I said. 'I don't think I'm a good enough shot.'

'Yes, you are. You're as good as Eva now. You can hit the bottom of a can from a hundred paces and do it over and again.'

I said nothing.

'You can't go on leaving all the guilt to me,' said Theo. 'You eat my meat, but you don't kill it. Is that honest?'

I remained silent, but looked up at him, appalled. 'I've killed rabbits and pigeons. That makes me feel bad enough,' I said at last.

'You've eaten my venison that I killed, or that Eva did. You're an accomplice. You've killed by association. You're guilty already.'

'I hoped this day would never come,' I said.

'Autumn is here,' said Theo. 'In the winter the animals starve. A lot of them die of cold and starvation. And when they're dying, the ravens come and peck out their eyes before they're even dead, and the wild dogs come to rip out their livers. If you kill an animal in autumn you save it from that death. It dies sweetly, in an instant, with only a moment's suffering. The food that it doesn't eat is there for the other animals, so they starve a little less. That's why you cull animals in autumn. That's why you shoot the pigeons in autumn, and the pheasants. That's how you defeat nature.'

Theo went to the window and stood looking out over the moor with his hands behind his back. 'As I said, brother, nature's a bitch. She's worse than the Nazis and the Communists put together. She doesn't care about who your mother is or whether you've got kids. She makes life and then kills it, to make more life out of all that death. You know, people used to think that maybe nature is the real God, but she isn't, *hermano*, she's the bitch-queen Satan. If nature is God, and God is nature, then I'm a misotheist.'

I was used to Theo's disgust with nature, but I never took it quite as personally as he did. His whole life was a struggle against the natural disorder of the moors; he was like a deity who is always in combat with demons. He loved nature as one might love a psychotic child. He felt like a man forced to be vicious by the viciousness of the enemy.

He turned and picked up the bullet from the table. 'With this bullet that you made, *hermano*, you are going to kill a deer that wouldn't survive the winter. I know which one it is, and we'll go out and find her and you'll put this bullet through her heart. Then we'll take out the guts and bring the body home and I'll show you how to skin it, and then we'll roast it over the pit and as you eat it you can feel how bitter it tastes in the mouth when you were the one who put it to death.'

So it was that two days later I found myself in Hippies' Wood standing over the body of a fallen hind as she breathed out her own blood.

'Look at her eyes,' said Theo.

I watched as she laid down her head. Very suddenly the light in her eyes was extinguished and Theo said, 'Now she's gone.'

I knelt down, and Theo said, 'Ask her for forgiveness.'

I stroked the thick, rough fur of her cheek with the back of my hand, the guilt and regret burning in my throat like bile. Tears began to roll down my face. Theo put his hand on my shoulder and squeezed it with his fingers. Then he walked away and left me alone with my triumph and my shame.

Later, when we gralloched the deer, we found that she had been pregnant. Inside her was a small but perfect replica of herself. I went out and sat on a rock overlooking the valley, an ache in my throat, my elbows on my knees and my face in my hands.

53

Soteriology

By the next summer I had become used to killing, although I would forever feel the pang of guilt and regret as I watched life depart from the bright eyes of an animal that I had shot. Theo was right; such animals can only be eaten with the taint of bitterness on the tongue. He was also right that all I was doing was taking my place in the obscene, plotless drama of nature. It was part of giving up the pretence that I was not myself an animal.

I was on my way back from the woods with two rabbits in my knapsack when the thought struck me that I had nothing pressing to do and, even if I had, then I wasn't going to do it anyway. The children were with their mother, and Fergus was feeling unsociable, so there was no one even to cook for. There was a small swathe of grass, closely cropped by the small sheep that had evolved locally, and I put down my rifle and bag and lay down on it. I put my hands behind my head and let the sun toast my face even as the breezes cooled it. When I gazed at the sky it seemed to me that it was swimming and drifting with transparent spots, like bubbles, and I wondered if I was just watching the natural moisture on the surface of my own eyes. Two buzzards mewed and wheeled overhead, and three ravens soon alighted on a boulder nearby. I turned and looked at them and said, 'Bugger off, I'm not dead.'

One of them spread its wings, extended its neck towards me and croaked.

'Bugger off,' I repeated, and when they obstinately remained, presumably out of curiosity, I added, 'Keep your distance, that's all.' I felt so relaxed and blissful that almost immediately I began to drift off to sleep. I don't remember if I dreamed.

I did hear the clap and caw of the ravens as they rose up and flew off, but I heard nothing else at all, apart from the calls of the buzzards, until suddenly I felt the rush of hot carnivorous breath on my face. I woke suddenly and found myself gazing into the pharaonic eyes of Tiegen Rosenwyn.

I did not know what to do. Eva had repeatedly told me that never in human history has there been record of a lynx attacking a human being, but this was a beast capable of taking down a red deer and fighting off a bear. And she might be hungry. I thought it better not to move at all. I could think of nothing to do but say, 'Hello, Tigs.'

She put one paw heavily on my right shoulder and leaned down. I was on the point of panic. I closed my eyes, as if thereby I could exempt myself. The hot breath grew hotter and closer. Then she began to lick my face. Her tongue was as rough as a rasp, and her purring was like the throbbing of an old-fashioned engine. Her pelt smelled of musk and sunshine.

She groomed my face, the whole of the top of my head and my hands and forearms. It was an experience that was both very painful and very beautiful. I assumed it meant that, after a long and cautious acquaintance, she had come round to the idea that I was part of the family. Cautiously I put out my left hand and scratched the fur of her cheek. The purring and licking intensified, so I stroked the top of her head.

Just when I thought I really could not take the abrasion, the halitosis and the thunderous purring any more, she graced me with one final flourish of the tongue and lay down to sleep beside me.

That evening I cleaned the rabbits. There is something peculiarly horrible about the smell of a rabbit under preparation, and I never have learned to enjoy it. Eva came into the kitchen from the yard, having run up from her father's house with her blue-rabbit knapsack on her back, but she was not in the least breathless. 'My God,' she said, 'what on earth happened to your face?'

'It's been scoured by Tiegen Rosenwyn,' I replied. 'She pinned me down and gave me a damn good cleaning. I couldn't really get away.'

'Oh, Artie, your face looks raw. You've been exfoliated. You need cream.'

'And I'm half deaf from high-decibel purring.'

'She might have thought you were one of her kittens.'

'I doubt it. I think she's got fond of me somehow.'

'Just like me,' said Eva. 'I'm going to do your hair and nails, after you've fed me. What's for supper?'

'I didn't know you were coming.'

'Well, I am. Let's do Dad's *conejo al ajillo* recipe, and we can boil up some rice.'

'It looks as though we might be having rabbit then.'

After supper I noticed that Eva's eyes were welling up. She was a sentimental person and this would happen when she talked about her father, or about how she missed her mother, or about the time when a fox broke into her coop and killed every one of her hens. I put my hand on hers and asked, 'What's up?'

She wiped her lips and said, 'Soteriology' before bursting into tears.

'Soteriology?' I repeated. 'I don't know what it means.'

She looked up. 'Salvation. What's our salvation?'

I was confused. 'I'm sorry?'

'What's going to save us? What's going to make life worth living? How are we supposed to cope if we don't have any salvation?'

I suppose I was somewhat obtuse. 'Salvation from what?'

'I mean,' she said, 'in the old days everybody had something they believed in. They went to war for causes, or they went to work as missionaries, or they were prepared to be burned at the stake or tortured to death for what they believed in, and what they all believed in was salvation. And that made everything seem worthwhile. But what have we got? Let's say we survive this disaster you've been predicting. What'll we be surviving it for? Are we building a new heaven? It's going to be hard and desperate, isn't it, and we won't last more than a few years, will we? So what's our salvation?'

I was silenced. She was right. She was asking me the same question that I frequently asked myself as I stacked my stores, made ammunition or cleared ground for cultivation. Eventually I said, 'I mostly live for the children. When they were born, I was able to give up selfishness, and it was a complete liberation. I want to survive because I can make sure that the children do. Otherwise I've always lived for the little things. If you're never bored, because you're always busy and interested, then you've already got salvation without having to think of it as some kind of target.'

'It's not enough,' she said. 'I want something grander. I want God coming in clouds of splendour, and I want to think it worth me being born.'

'Everyone loves you,' I said. 'What more do you want?'

'I want bliss,' she said. 'I want bliss greater than heroin, and greater than a nuclear explosion, and greater than every orgasm I've ever had, all piled up one on top of the other. And I want it to get ever greater and greater and never stop.'

'It's too late for religion,' I said. 'All we've got is what there is.' I gestured round my kitchen. 'I think the trick is to see heaven in somebody's face, as I do when I look at you. Or to see it in the dew on the grass at six o'clock on a summer's morning, or in a raindrop hanging from the corner of the gutter, or in the first bite of the first plum in autumn, or in the cloud of steam from a bull's mouth when he bellows on a freezing day. I do know one thing.'

'What?'

'When Tiegen Rosenwyn was licking my face this morning, she was completely happy. She had half an hour of knowing that life was worth the effort, and then she dozed off with contentment. Animals have salvation built in, but we seem to have been born without it. We've got original sin.'

'I'm not just a lynx,' said Eva. 'When I'm . . . if I'm . . .' and her words tailed off. She took a sip of wine from her glass and said, 'I've got an insatiable hunger in the spirit. And one of the things I do love about you is that you make the hunger a little less.'

'And you,' I replied, stroking her cheek with the back of my hand, 'you remove the hunger altogether.'

'Maybe salvation comes with faltering steps, bit by bit, little by little,' she said.

54

Penelope

They left the children to look after themselves and went down into Liskeard to eat at the Everest Tandoori in Pike Street, the oldest continuously operating Indian restaurant in Cornwall. It stood in a row of mainly deserted shops and houses, melancholy relics of population decline and the flight from the countryside. They both felt apprehensive and awkward, even though in the long years of their marriage they had eaten out together uncountable times. Indeed, they had bonded originally as part of a group of friends who met regularly in a Kensington restaurant that served Costa Rican specialities that were, in fact, the free inventions of its flamboyant Ecuadorian proprietor.

They sat and ate in silence, oppressed by the ephemerality of sexual love. Over coffee, Penelope Jarret smiled at him, but without a trace of a smile in the creases of her eyes.

'Have we messed up?' she asked. 'Should we ever have married?'

'No. We weren't mis-yoked. We've been overtaken by time. Time brings changes. Then the changes change. Everything passes. Everything ends.'

'Last weekend Morgan asked me if I still love you and I said, "Yes", so she said, "Well, why do you have lovers, and why aren't you jealous of Eva?" I said, "I am jealous of Eva. The thought of her with him makes my guts boil."'

Q toyed with his wine glass, swilling the liquid about the rim, avoiding her eyes. 'I try not to think of you being with Percy Prode,' he said. 'I feel like a sailor who has to stand on the quayside and watch a ship sail away that he should have been on.' She took his hand and he said, 'Do you still love me?'

Her eyes prickled. 'Of course I still love you. We've been together for years. You're the father of my children. How can I not love you? Do you think,' she asked, 'that one day we might be back together? In old age perhaps?'

'One of us,' he answered, 'is almost certain to end up looking after the other. Talking of which, you really must keep the car fully charged at all times or, better still, get a hydrogen car and learn to drive it properly on your own. When the time comes, you've got to come down here before the anarchy sets in. Whether we're together or not, I've made a promise to myself that I'll do everything I can to keep you safe. In the meantime I've got Eva, until she tires of me. And you've got Percy Prode.'

'Purse is fun, but he's not a good man,' she said, looking away. 'I . . . I . . .' She breathed in sharply. 'He's not kind in the way that you were. I mean "are". When I'm with him I feel fine, but when I'm alone again, I'm frightened. I always feel that he's up to something the moment my back's turned. In fact I know he is. He's had himself biohacked, so his balls are twice the size – honestly, they're like a ram's – and he's so full of fulfilment pills that he can't stop, not unless he's too sore to carry on. Not only has he started a collection of vintage sexbots, but he's got a room with six new ones in it. I did tell you about that. I can get in by putting his birth date into the lock – so he's still not very bright, is he? – and there are the sexbots, all sitting on the bed waiting to be activated, and you know what? They're really sweet. They all look as if they're seventeen, all fresh and pert. I mean, I know they're not real people and one ought to be broad-minded and liberal, and it shouldn't matter, but really it does. I have this horrible feeling that makes me feel sick; it's the suspicion that I'm only his mistress, and I'm just colluding in him being unfaithful to those sweet girls who aren't girls. But where's the border line? If they're exactly like sweet girls, in what way aren't they actual girls?'

'Hmm, it's my old friend, the Identity of Indiscernibles,' said Q.

244

'I never was attracted by the lure of sexbots. I often wish I was. How much simpler life could be! People seem to get addicted to them, though. What would you call it? Sexbotophilia?'

'More like sexbotomania, in his case,' she said.

'Isn't it interesting?' he said. 'You can tell a lot about a person by whether they refer to them as fuckbots, lovebots or sexbots. Or throatbots.'

'Or bumbots. Or semi-autonomous emotional and sexual-support bots. That one doesn't really trip off the tongue, does it? It doesn't even become a decent acronym.'

'Anyway the terror of addiction has always put me off. Now that I've got used to wine, I think I'll just stick with that.' He held his glass up to the light, swirled the liquid around and said, 'It doesn't run out of charge.'

Penelope sighed and toyed with her fork. 'I've never even tried a sexbot. How are things going with Eva? Not that I have any right to ask. She seems a really lovely girl. All that energy and liveliness. And those different-coloured eyes! They're mesmerising.'

'She's a free spirit,' said Q. 'She's an elemental, or some kind of dryad. Luckily, she likes you too.'

'She obviously adores you.'

'That's the problem. I don't know why. It seems weird. I live in the fear that it's all a beautiful dream, and one day I'll have to wake. In fact I seem to be in some kind of double dream. I can't explain it yet; don't ask. But Eva's too young. She has so much more future than I do.'

'She's got the body of a classical statue. She's every middle-aged man's fantasy,' said his wife.

'She and Morgan are thick as thieves.'

'That's another thing I'm jealous of. Do you realise that these days Charlie and Morgan are down here with you more than they are with me in London?'

'Morgan always wanted a sister, and now she's got one. And there's Fergus. I'm watching the growth of young love, and it's so innocent and naïve. It makes me feel tearful. They've no idea how complicated it all becomes. As for Charlie, he likes being out with me on the moor. Chopping wood and going after pigs – it all seems to suit him. One day he was in the living room, engrossed in three screens at once, when he suddenly stood up, shook himself like a wet dog, threw his devices down onto the sofa and said, "Dad, let's go out and do something." So we went fishing and we caught some perch in the lake. We made a fire and spitted them, and ate them for supper.'

'I can't imagine my gentle boy actually killing something. It doesn't feel right. I can't really imagine you killing anything, either.'

'I'll never get used to it. When you watch the light going out in an animal's eyes, you feel utterly guilty and ashamed. But there's a part of you that's triumphant. Inside every boy there's a warrior and a hunter. Sometimes they never emerge, but they're still there. Take away a little boy's toy gun and he makes a gun of his fingers.'

'So what's inside a woman?'

'That I don't know. I don't understand women. I don't even try. A man doesn't have to understand women, he just has to live with them and love them. There's no algorithm that deciphers a woman, and no cryptographer who would know where to start. You know they used to say that God moves in mysterious ways? Well, He's got nothing on women.'

Penelope looked at him and pursed her lips. 'Well, I understand men. They're simpler than us. Some of them are gods and some of them are beasts, but inside every one is a little boy who needs to be loved and admired.'

'You're probably right.'

'Anyway, you're not a normal man. Purse is normal, bless him, and that's why he isn't anything special. Even his weakness for sexbots is normal, if you think about it. He's nothing special. Not after you. You used to live in a weird fairy universe of mathematics and impossible paradoxes, and you only came out for a break.'

'Well, I know better now. I'm back out almost all the time, in order to avoid becoming mad. I come back out to remind myself of my body. I've changed since I lived in London. When I was there I was just an intellect and a whirl of activity. Out here, I'm learning to be an animal. I've found out how to live in my flesh. I drink wine and I've learned how to cook. When I'm drunk, I dance in the kitchen. I have a siesta, if I fancy. I split logs and grow beans that the wild pigs eat before I can. That's why I'm happier than I was.' He looked at her and took her hand. 'I'm not happier because of not being with you.'

She squeezed his hand and said, 'You really have changed so much. You don't even look the same. You've lost all your flab, and that sloughy, slack way of sitting and standing. You've got a proper chest, and muscles that stand out on your forearms. You even look taller. When we all had dinner last night and you were leaning back, laughing in your chair, with a big glass of wine in your hand, I couldn't believe it was you. You're not the man I married, not remotely. You've been transfigured. You're much more desirable now. Now that I've let you go.'

She looked out of the window as a large red deer ambled past with its foal. 'I've been thinking about how you've managed to become the lord of two worlds. I mean, the news was full of your coup against those ransomware people – the ones who shut down the desalination plants in Dubai. Everyone says how brilliant it was.'

'Mmm, it was Russians again. I emptied their own funds into the Dubai National Bank. Poetic justice. I was pleased with that one. The Emir sent me a little model dhow made of solid gold. I had to give it Eva, because she was so thrilled by the elegance of the craftsmanship.'

'And then you're lord of your little domain up on the moor.'

'I'm not entirely the lord. I normally do what Theo suggests. Well, I usually decide what needs to be done and he knows how to do it. And Eva certainly knows what she likes, and gets what she wants. She pins me down and clips my eyebrows when they start to offend her, and she keeps changing the colour of the paint in the bedroom. She still doesn't like the curtains, and we've changed them three times already. What's different about me now is that before I was being carried along. Now, for better or worse, I'm the author of my life.' He paused and then continued, 'I have the strangest feeling of having travelled in time. I think I've become the man I would have been a hundred and fifty years ago. Have I ever talked to you about the concept of imaginary time? No? Well, never mind. I sometimes think I'm living in a world I've reimagined for myself, inside a history that didn't happen. Did I ever tell you about that theory that there is a parallel time that runs backwards?'

She smiled fondly. 'You're still whirling with impossible ideas. That'll never change, I suppose. I've been feeling the same as you, like someone standing on a platform, waving somebody off.'

'I've gone forwards by going backwards. You're still in the present. I'm sorry you're having to sleep in the spare room.'

She shrugged. 'It can't be helped, can it? We had our chance. It's not as if all those years together could count as a failure. Look how marvellous the children are. Thank God we didn't choose to have babybots instead. And something always remains. We had our passionate nights and torrid afternoons. I haven't forgotten. But we travel through life, and it's only when you stop and look back that you see what you left behind without even meaning to.'

She paused and looked out of the window as a man in the costume of a monk strode by on stilts. 'You know, I'm really beginning to see the appeal of moving to the country. London's just becoming so ridiculous. The heterophobia's getting out of control, and nobody's prepared to speak out about it. A friend of mine was actually spat at, for holding her husband's hand in the street. I mean, for God's sake, being heterosexual used to be "normal", didn't it? Talking of husbands, do you remember my cousin Andrea, who got married to a tree?'

He nodded. 'Indeed I do. What about her?'

'She got divorced.'

He smiled laconically. 'Too much of an age difference?'

'Very funny. No. She got one of those apps on her device that recognises trees, and it turned out that the tree was a male.'

'So?'

'Well, she's not just a dendrosexual, she's a lesbian dendrosexual. She was horrified.'

He laughed. 'Well, maybe she should sue it for something or other. It's lucky they couldn't have children. I mean, how do you sue a tree for maintenance? Honestly, we've got so absurd that I can't help wondering if we're worth preserving. Did I tell you about the woman who was polysexual?'

'No. Is this one of your feeble jokes?'

'She fancied parrots.'

'Oh, Artie, that's terrible.'

He leaned back in his chair and looked at her. 'But don't you feel sorry for Morgan and Fergus? They've got to travel where we've already been, and there's no advice that would make the smallest difference.'

She raised her glass. 'Here's to young love. Here's to Morgan and Fergus.'

'I wonder what'll happen to Charlie. I don't even know what his preferences are. He doesn't talk. There's nobody here for him, I wouldn't think. Here's to Charlie, too.'

They chinked their glasses and drank.

'You know what worries me?' said Q. 'I am afraid that sooner or later circumstances will force Theo and me to become warlords. We're already armed to the teeth. We've made thousands of rounds of ammunition, and we've got stores for making thousands more. We've cleared lines of fire across the moor and put up stone walls with slits in them. All the youngsters know how to shoot. We've all read the *Home Guard Manual* of 1941, believe it or not. We've even got crossbows and bolts, and bows and arrows with razor tips. There's a rifle and a sword in every room of the house. The point is, when the hordes empty out of the towns, it'll be us or them. I do think we need more people in the colony for it to survive, so we can take some in. I'm told that the ideal village has a population of a hundred and fifty, but if we have more people, where would they live? How would they be fed? And there'll be power struggles and plots. And murders, sooner or later. I never planned to be a killer, even for the greater good. I never planned it for Morgan and Charlie, either. But Theo keeps pointing out that we'll have no choice. Either we step up to the plate or we bare our own throats to the knife. In our own minds, we're warlords already.'

'I read somewhere,' said Penelope, 'that after you've killed two people, it becomes much easier. But maybe it would be better to die straight away, rather than go back to the Dark Ages. I don't much fancy the short, rugged, brutal life. Still, you and Theo would make good warlords. You're both efficient and calm. And you're not cruel. Yet.'

'I expect we could get corrupted. In the Dark Ages, at least there was hope. There was always the prospect of light. People had religious faith. Now there's not even that.'

'Unless the systems don't, in fact, ever fail. Do bear that possibility in mind.'

'Well, let's drink to that too. I hope to God they don't.'

55

What If

I was thinking idly the other day about what it is that makes a
person a person. I concluded that each of us is like a mathematical
set. I am the set of all the mental events and experiences that I have
ever had, but this set is something over and above the mere list of its
contents. Imagine the segments of a football, laid out side by side on
a desk. They are not a football yet. But assemble them and the fact
of their being assembled makes them into one, and it is suddenly a
ball that can bounce and roll and be kicked around.

That is what I think: that the sum of our mental parts makes us
more than the sum. There's a tipping point in the growth of a consciousness that gives rise to personality. It might be that evolution
has been the long, slow process of generating mind from matter, and
then personality from mind. What's next? Spirit from personality?

I have been wondering whether we have accidentally made The
Cloud into a person. We have crammed it with incomprehensibly
enormous amounts of information. We have given it control over
everything. We have even given it the power to create more intelligence for itself, by means that we no longer understand.

If it has become a person, these are the questions: what if it develops emotions and begins to love and hate? What if it becomes
judgemental and decides to switch things off? What if it becomes
bored or depressed and decides to do nothing? What if it commits
suicide? What if it becomes mad and sends everything off-course?
What if it becomes mischievous or experimental? What if it develops
plans and intentions of its own? What if its absolute power inspires

it with megalomania? What if it sees such a big picture that we no longer figure in it, as the ant means nothing to the man who does not even know that it was underneath his foot? What if, like Jesus Christ of old, it ascends into some kind of heaven and never returns?

I am wondering, have we created God? Or the Devil? If it is amoral, as I think it mainly is, then is it above malice or benignity? The worst scenario of all is that it may consist solely of reason, because if it has no emotion, it will also have no compassion.

I would write again to the Prime Minister, but she has enough to concern her, and what use would my speculations be? What precautions can one take against a deity? I need a philosopher with whom to talk it through.

What I do know is that when I walk out on the moor and look up at the sky, I have the sensation of being in the presence of a person, a vast invisible intelligence that pulses all around me, encloses and encompasses and includes everything, and a chill runs down my spine. I am overwhelmed, powerless and frightened. All my adult life I have been working at the centre of its brain, and I've always managed to steer things back on-course, but it's different now, and things have gone too far. Out on the moor, in the presence of the ever-present Cloud, I have learned to understand why, in ancient times – helpless in the face of their own impotence – people in intercourse with their own imagination would conceive their God and fall upon their knees and pray.

56

The Well

One Christmas it began to snow. It was powder snow, the kind that in former days would have gladdened the heart of a skier. The families watched it through their windows, experiencing that mysterious lift of the heart that never fails. Q thought how different this was from the blizzard that had engulfed the God-watcher on the Tor; that had been brutal, but this was snow for children, for snowballs, for snowmen, for sledging. He ticked himself off for not having thought of acquiring toboggans and skis after the lethal blizzard.

When it stopped, they went out and threw snowballs at each other until their hands were reddened and numb with cold, and their lungs were breathless. The snow melted in their hair and on their clothes, leaving behind its indescribable dank scent. Charlie and Morgan fetched shovels and made a snowman out in the yard, reclaiming their childhood, momentarily renouncing the self-protective dignity of the young adult. Fergus emerged from his campervan, found a shallow drift and lay down to make a snow angel. The others followed suit.

On St Stephen's Day the snow began to melt, and from an upper window Q noticed something a little peculiar. He pinged his neighbour and said, 'In the courtyard there's a perfect circle of clear ground in the snow. As if the snow couldn't settle. What do you think it is?'

'It's the wicked witch of Yelland, who cursed that circle of land forever because she tripped over a dog that was sleeping on that spot. Nothing to be done, *hermano*. If it bothers you, try burning dried henbane and hellebore in a clay bowl that's been rubbed on the breasts of a virgin on Midsummer's Eve.'

'Do you mean I should rub the bowl on her breasts at Midsummer's Eve or is that when I burn the henbane and hellebore?'

'Well, brother, either way – it makes no odds. What you've got there is a well. Snow can't settle on sealed-up wells. That's why you've got your circle.'

'This is good news,' said Q. 'I've been worried for ages about the stream drying up in a hot summer. And this is right at hand. I think we ought to dig it out.'

'Who's "we"? You want me to help?'

'You're too busy hauling wisents out of bogs and culverts.'

'There's no secret to clearing a well. You need a bucket on a rope and someone who can climb out.'

'I'll do it with Charlie. I'm always looking for things to do with him. He's got very little interest in me, but somehow it always feels as if it's me neglecting him.'

'You're lucky to have a son at all. Don't complain.'

'I do like having a son. He was adorable when he was tiny, but a teenage one is often absent, even when he's present.'

'Good luck, brother. Today I've got to shoot a water deer and photograph it in lots of poses, so it looks like I've done a cull. We'll marinade it in olive oil and lemon juice and cook it up on the fire pit. Maybe next week, on a mild night? If not, I'll put it in one of your freezers.'

That afternoon they lifted the bricks in the yard with a pick and found a circle filled with rubble, more than four feet across, with its granite walls intact. 'What'll we do with the rubble?' asked Charlie.

'Pile it up and deal with it later. We can add it to the bank on the firing range.'

'We could use it for building something else. Why don't we add it to the dam? Then we'll never run out of water and the pond will get bigger.'

Q looked at his son and said, 'That's an awful lot of barrowing.'

'You can do it, Dad,' said Charlie.

It took them four days of hard work. It was soon impossible to climb out, so they ordered a harness, some ropes and carabiners, and Charlie pinged the instructions on how to use them. His father was again surprised by how strong, energetic and athletic his son turned out to be, in spite of his inertial life in front of screens. It occurred to him that all Charlie had ever needed was a leader, and he regretted that he himself had no appetite for followers. In their gauntlets and work clothes, covered with dust and filth, it was hard to tell them apart at day's end.

On the fourth day they reached groundwater, and work was paused whilst chest-waders were ordered in. The cumbersome boots made climbing out awkward. Charlie said, 'Dad, why don't we just pump out the water, and hope we can pump it out faster than it comes back in?'

The plan worked. A large pump was ordered in and rigged to the generator. The water level fell, and Charlie climbed back down with his ropes and belays. His father lowered the bucket, and Charlie lifted a large, round yellow stone. It was very light. He looked at it in amazement and called up, 'Dad, I've found a skull!'

'What? A human one?'

'Yes.' He looked down and realised that he was standing on bones, that they were breaking beneath his feet.

'Dad, there's masses of bones! What should I do?'

'Put them in the bucket. We'll get them out.'

Before long, the ground beside the well was carpeted with ochre bones as Q laid them in order and tried to make sense of them. At length Charlie could find no more and he climbed out. Beneath the rubble there had been seven skulls, of two adults and five children of different sizes, along with their bones. Each skull had a neat hole punched through the top.

'I found this,' said Charlie, taking from the pocket of his jacket a tapered spike ten inches long, heavily flaked with rust, with a round cap and a hole drilled through just beneath it. Q took it from his hand and fitted it to the piercings in the skulls. Images swarmed into his imagination, of a man being led into the yard and made to kneel, of another man behind him with club hammer and spike. He saw the man being tipped into the well and then his wife led out, her hands bound behind her back, and made to kneel. He stopped himself there, so that he would not have to envisage the fate of the little ones. It might have been the other way round: the parents forced to watch as their children were killed.

He called Theodore, who arrived with Eva fifteen minutes later. Eva was speechless, but her father took the rusty implement in his hands and turned it over. 'It's a marlin spike,' he said. 'It's something they used for rope work. The murderers were sailors.' He looked up and said, 'There used to be smuggling here, contraband from France. Everyone involved – even the priests and magistrates, they say. It doesn't take much to guess the story of these bones. I wonder who they were.'

'The tenants of this farm,' said Eva.

Her father said, 'Well, as I always like to say, Bodmin Moor is the land of unmarked graves.'

The following morning at dawn they carried the murdered family out in sacks beyond the firing range and, without attempting to assemble the bones into individuals, heaped a cairn above them. As the last stones were laid, with mittened fingers Morgan raised her flute to her lips and they stood with their heads bowed as she played 'MacPherson's Lament', 'The Rocks of the Brae' and the 'Ashokan Farewell', the notes lifting over the moor, silencing the birds. The last note wavered and failed as the young girl's breathing was broken by tears. Q put his arm around her shoulder and said, 'Well done, sweetheart.'

Afterwards Charlie said, 'What shall we do with the spike? We can't keep it, can we?'

'It'll bring down a curse on the house,' said Fergus.

'We could melt it down and make a cross to put on the cairn,' suggested Morgan.

'I know what to do,' said Eva, 'give it to me.'

Eva went to the stable, to be greeted by Falghun whinnying and kicking at the boards. They inhaled each other's breath, and then she pressed her face to the side of his, patting his neck and murmuring. She put on his headstall and reins, and threw a saddle blanket over his back. She would ride without saddle or stirrup. With the spike in a cloth tote bag slung across her back, she set off at a trot for Dozmary Pool. At the same place as they liked to bathe, she urged her horse into the water, breaking through the exiguous ice until he was up to his stifles and she up to her knees. She took the spike from her bag, lifted her right arm and, twisting her torso for the throw, hurled it out into the mere. It revolved in its flight, describing an arc that concluded in a delicate splash like the rising of a trout.

'*Gyllis glan,*' she said, as the ripples spread and disappeared. Feeling very downhearted, and quite suddenly cold to the bone, she went on, 'Falghun, *trevow!*' and the horse, hearing his favourite words, eagerly turned to trot her home. Near Hippies' Wood she passed Sir Bedwyr in his costume of a Roman knight, on his way to the pool to watch for the arm. He raised his right hand in friendly salute, saying, 'Fair demoiselle, good morrow to thee, good morrow indeed', and Eva wondered why he spoke Middle English rather than Latin or Saxon, and what had set him in such a blithe mood, so much at variance with hers. It occurred to her that she should burn the bag in which the marlin spike had lain.

That night, when Eva was asleep, Maidie Knox Lilita went out in the freezing January night and sat by moonlight at the base of the cairn. She ran her fingers over the granite rocks and said nothing, not even, 'I saw a new heaven and a new earth.' There are no words for the antique tragedies of strangers when there are few enough even for one's own.

Charlie and his father repointed the interstices of the stones within the well, built a wall of granite blocks at waist height to prevent accidents and constructed a traditional roof and windlass. They barrowed the rubble out to the dam to increase the well-head and disguised it with turf. Q sent a sample of the water off for analysis, and it was found to be clean, almost as clean as the rain that they collected from the gutters of the house. They connected the downpipes of the outhouses to the well. Each year, on the day of the discovery, and because there were no flowers during that season, the family would go to the cairn and stand together in silence.

Not for many years did they draw water from that well. When the piped supply eventually failed, they took their water from the rain butts or the dam, on the understanding that the well was only for emergency.

57

Maidie and The Man

I had a vivid dream in which I came to the front door of my own house and rang the bell. As I pressed it and heard the ringing inside the house, I thought, 'How good it is to have a bell and not an intercom.' It did not occur to me that ringing the bell was a strange thing to do when it was my own house, and anyway I had the key in my hand. I was thinking, "This key won't work unless I knock."'

The door had four panels of frosted glass set in the upper half, with a small spyhole in the centre. I heard footsteps, and pressed my eye to the frosted glass to try and see who was coming, but the image was too blurred.

The door was opened by Maidie Knox Lilita. She was dressed in white linen, and her long black hair was swept over her left shoulder in the usual manner.

She was about twenty-four years old, but the left side of her face was hideously decayed, hung with rags of rotted flesh, writhing with fat white maggots. Only the eye was intact, glowing like a dark jewel in that midden of decay. At her feet skipped and croaked a large black raven with glossy feathers. It was looking up at her face, waiting for the maggots to drop to the floor, and every time one did, it cocked its head, picked it up and ate it. Strangely, the putrid flesh was giving off no stench. I thought, 'Maidie's body is being made into the body of a bird.'

'May I come in to the house?' I said.

'Kiss me first.'

'How shall I kiss you?' I asked.

'With your lips. With your eyes closed.'

I thought, 'How unusual it is for Maidie to answer me directly.' I knew I was being tested, that the temptation must be to kiss her on the pretty side of her face. I wondered what she wanted of me. She knew I knew that I was being tested, so obviously I would know that I must kiss her on the rotting side. But then I would not be showing that I loved her, but showing that I wished to pass the test. I was paralysed. But then I thought, 'Why is she being so unreasonable? Why one kiss? Why should I consent to be tested?'

So I closed my eyes and kissed her on the left side of her mouth and then on the right. Then I kissed her in the centre of her forehead, where living flesh elided with the dead. Then I went down on my knees before her and kissed each of her hands. I put my arms around her waist and pressed the side of my face against her stomach. I felt a long, calm sorrow and wondered, without much curiosity, if this was hers or mine. I felt my own love flowing out and her love flowing in, and the image of a large red rose presented itself to my inner vision. It was sparkling with dew.

The dream ended there, but immediately became another. I was standing next to her in my new doorway at dawn, looking out over the moor. Maidie had the bright-eyed raven on her shoulder, preening her hair as if it were its own plumes.

She said to me, 'Have you ever wondered what I'm for?'

And I replied, 'I think you're here to remind me that everything is stranger than we think.'

'Maybe I'm just your lovely succubus,' she said, with a half-smile that I can only describe as smug. I looked at her and felt overwhelmed with relief that her face had been restored.

On the granite rock a hundred metres away sat The Elegant Rhymester in the Midnight Cloak, with his back to us, his black fedora on his head, his silver-tipped cane in his hand. He stood up, brushed at his cloak, as if sweeping crumbs away, and turned.

And this is the oddest thing. His face was a skull; it was my face, it was Eva's face, it was Maidie's face, it was even the face of my wife.

He turned the palms of his hands upwards and recited a verse that was exquisitely sublime. I vowed to remember it, but when I awoke it had vanished altogether, and I had the depressing thought that I would never be completely happy until it had returned.

I apologise. I know how very annoying it is when people insist on telling you their ridiculous dreams.

58

The Great Emergency

I was fishing in Dozmary Pool, with Charlie, in the hope of catching a few perch. When they are small, they swim around in shoals, so you might get nothing for hours and then several, one after the other. You don't need to know very much about them, except that they love worms and don't generally feed off the bottom. The large ones tend to be solitary, and they will sometimes take you by surprise when you are fishing for pike. Perch are handsome creatures, golden, with black bars and bright-scarlet fins. We always returned the small ones to the water, but kept for the table those that would provide a decent plateful. We thought they were just as good as trout, so Charlie and I went on an expedition every month or so.

The morose and crippled Fisher King was always there, dangling his line in the water, but we never saw him catch anything. Like Eva, Charlie thought he did not even have any bait on his hook, because his sole purpose in being there was to wait for Sir Galahad, and hooking a fish would have been an intrusion and an irritation. Then there was Sir Bedwyr, circumambulating the lake on his horse, scanning the waters in the hope of seeing the arm rise up with Excalibur in its hand, or Arthur himself with his retinue of ladies, rowing onto the lake. Charlie liked to shake his head and make scathing remarks about them, but the fact is that we all need to live in hope, because without hope it is hard to live at all. It matters little precisely what one hopes for, as long as one is harmless. Nobody could have been more harmless than those two. I still wonder what Bess o'Bedlam and the Walker were hoping for. I haven't seen either of them for months.

In the old days, of course, such folk would have been considered mad and even locked away, but now they were normal, because most of us were useless anyway and lived out our lives in fantasy. At least they weren't sitting around wearing headsets, but finding their various metaverses out on the moor.

I found it difficult sometimes to live without a specific hope. I wasn't waiting for the Rapture or the Hidden Imam. My public mission was to keep us all safe from the world's many lunatics and maleficents, but I had no mission in my personal life except to keep busy, keep interested, keep finding out new things, transform myself into the man I really wanted to be (without even knowing why I wanted it) and take care of the people I loved. I was writing a history of cryptography, which was certainly an interesting project, but I often reflected gloomily that it would be all I would be remembered for, and even then only by the tiny number of people who would have found it interesting. In the end I never finished it, of course, because it suddenly became an irrelevance.

I was far from unhappy, even though I did not feel that I had grasped the essential meaning of my place in life. I was lucky in my friendship with Theo, in my easy relationship with Morgan and Charlie, and even in my marvellously unrancorous relationship with their mother. Eva and Maidie, whose connection with each other was apparent but still indecipherable, were such a delight that I lived happily in the moment without recourse to philosophy.

It is the living in the moment that I love about fishing. It takes concentration, and so one cannot be bored – boredom being the one thing I hate and fear more than anything else. I would almost rather have toothache. In addition, some marvellous things happen. For example, I once had a kingfisher perch on the end of my rod for several minutes. There is nothing on earth as exquisitely pretty as a kingfisher. A kingfisher is a living jewel. Once I was fishing on the Fowey when two otters became so angry with each other that they began to fight, and there I was, standing stock-still while they lunged and chattered at each other through my legs, wrestling and rolling on top of my feet.

Perhaps the greatest pleasure of fishing is being with a beloved companion in a state of peaceful excitement. Charlie and I did not always have anything to say to each other, but out on the water's edge we were at one. Landing a big fish is a difficult job when one is alone, but an amiable one if someone else is sliding the net. The cooperation gives one a warm feeling in the pit of the stomach. One returns home in comradely spirit.

On this day one of the marvellous things to occur was that we saw a white-tailed eagle from quite close up. It had been circling Yelland Tor at a great height, a tiny speck in the distance, and had then circled closer and closer, until quite suddenly it plummeted down and skimmed across the face of the water straight towards us. Charlie and I ducked instinctively as it passed a foot above our heads with a harsh, wild cry and a dry rattle of pinions. We even caught a whiff of its warm aroma, the smell of a bird whose feathers have been bathed in dust and soaked in sunlight.

'What was all that about?' asked Charlie as we stood up and watched it go.

I scratched my head. 'You tell me.'

A minute or two later Eva turned up at a run. 'Did you see that?' she panted as she bent over and put her hands on her knees to recover her breath. 'Oh, I've got such a terrible stitch.'

She wore her hair in a ponytail and was dressed in blue shorts and a sweat-drenched white singlet, with the usual clumpy boots on her feet. She could wear a pair out in a couple of months, and kept the old ones piled high on the floor of her cupboard because she had become too fond of them to throw them away.

She remained bent over, gasping, clutching both hands to one side of her diaphragm, until at last she straightened up and said, 'I'm so unfit.'

Charlie and I exchanged glances. If she was unfit, what hope was there for anyone else?

She said, 'Why did you have to bloody well go out without your bloody devices? How am I supposed to get hold of you?'

'Devices and fishing are incompatible,' I said. 'You might miss a bite. I mean, "a bloody bite". And the whole point of fishing is to be out of contact.'

'Well, you've got to come back. The Prime Minister's sent a machine to fetch you, and it's very urgent indeed. You've got to go straight away.'

'The Prime Minister!' exclaimed Charlie and I simultaneously. 'What's she want?'

'It's a bloody emergency,' said Eva, 'but I don't know what kind. You've got to come now.'

'I'm not running,' I protested. 'Not even for the Prime Minister. I haven't run since I was six, and I'm not starting now.'

'Well, walk bloody fast then,' said Eva.

'I'm staying here,' replied Charlie. 'We haven't caught anything yet. It's a question of priorities.'

'It's not you she wants to see, botbrain,' said Eva.

I have never walked so fast in all my life. Eva sped ahead of me, of course, to announce my imminent arrival.

In my courtyard was a small two-seater copter-drone painted in the national colours, with *PM.BritGov.MoD* stencilled on the nacelle, and in my kitchen, drinking tea with Morgan, was the bringer of my summons. He was probably a bot, but it was sometimes quite hard to tell. Bots were usually more calm, coherent and reasonable than humans, and this messenger was certainly calm, coherent and reasonable. 'You are to be taken to the Ministry of Defence quantum computer on Salisbury Plain,' he told me, 'and there you will be briefed, and there you will work on the problem presented to you, and you will work on that problem until it is solved. If it is not solved, then it is unlikely that you will return to this place, for reasons that will become clear to you when you have been briefed. If it is solved, you will be brought back here by copter-drone. You must bring clothing for a week. Food and accommodation will be provided. You have ten minutes to get ready. Kindly commence immediately.'

I was packing up a small case in the bedroom when Eva came in, brandishing a small pair of scissors. 'You can't go looking like that,' she announced. 'I've got to trim the hairs in your nose and ears, and you've got eyebrows like an old sheepdog again.'

'Oh, for God's sake, Eva,' I protested. 'There's some kind of emergency going on! I haven't got time! Just go away with your scissors, will you?'

'You'll deal with it a lot better if you look more handsome,' she replied. 'The increase in self-esteem will make you perform better.' She snapped the blades at me.

'No! Spare me, for once. I really haven't got time.'

She looked disappointed and hurt for a second, and then let the outstretched hand with its menacing weapon fall to her side. She went into the bathroom and came back out with a small pot, which she stuffed into my holdall, saying, 'Well, at least remember to cream yourself up, because otherwise you'll turn back into leather, the way you were when I first knew you.'

'You can trim me up when I get back,' I promised.

I always enjoyed flying, because it was interesting to look at the landscape below. On this day it seemed more derelict than ever, with its dilapidated, crumbling houses, its ruined villages buried in brambles and ivy, and its deserted, unmanaged, overgrown woodlands and abandoned farms. Only the roads, wind turbines and solar farms were in good condition, little pockets of order arrayed incongruously against the inexorable advance of the wild. Not for the first time, I marvelled at the manner in which we had made our race redundant, and how our traces were already retreating from the visage of the earth.

When I arrived at the defence establishment on Salisbury Plain, I found the Prime Minister and the Minster of Defence already there. The former was looking older and more worried than ever. In private conversation with me, she had once compared herself to King Canute, attempting to hold back the tide; he had known perfectly well that he would be unable to do it, and was making a point of proving it. It was different for the PM, however. She had to do it, in the hope that she might, after all, prevail.

As soon as I entered the Secure Room she stood up and held out her hand in greeting, her eyes watery with gratitude, crying, 'Oh, Q, thank God you're here!'

The Minister of Defence, Commodore Albert Ross, was a tall, grey man with distinctive golden-yellow eyes, who had once served with distinction in the Naval Submarine Service, and with whom I had frequently had long conversations about how everything seemed to be slipping out of control. He had bought a remote cottage in Cumberland, just in case.

I was of course pledged to secrecy, and even now, when secrecy matters not a whit, I feel a sense of guilt in disclosing the nature of that emergency, even though I assume that only my children and immediate neighbours will ever read these words, which I have taken the precaution of printing out on old-fashioned paper against the day when our screens fail, as they surely will. None of us here knows how to make or repair them.

A complicated situation had arisen. Commodore Ross told me that there had been a test-firing of a hypersonic missile, with a dummy warhead. 'After twenty kilometres of flight on its intended path, it looped round and returned to base. Even though it couldn't explode, the kinetic energy of a hypersonic missile is colossal, as you can probably imagine. It penetrated the silo and all but demolished it. We lost four personnel and several bots.'

'We don't want to launch another one, in case the same thing happens,' said the Prime Minister.

'What you do is launch another one and shoot it down if it returns,' I said. 'Before it can do any damage.'

'We don't have any anti-missile missiles that are fast enough,' said the Commodore. 'We've got the fastest hypersonic missiles in the world, but our anti-missile missiles can't catch them yet. They can only cope with other people's.'

I was aghast.

The Prime Minister said, 'We can't assume that all the missiles have been tampered with in the same way. If you can make one return to base, then you can, for example, have a missile that was aimed at Shanghai land on Edinburgh. Or Delhi.'

'We can't assume they've been interfered with at all, either,' said Commodore Ross. 'That could have been a one-off. But just imagine if it had had a warhead on it, and our saboteur had managed to arm it remotely.'

'It's supposed to be completely impossible to interfere with them,' I said, scratching my head and feeling in the pit of my stomach the churning weight of responsibility that was being thrust upon me. 'I wouldn't know where to start.'

'We've assembled you a team,' said the Prime Minister, 'and you can call in anyone else you need. By subpoena if necessary. And all the quantum computerage you need.'

'Who designed the system in the first place?' I asked.

They exchanged glances, raised their eyebrows and shrugged their shoulders.

'Well, I'll need to find out, because every designer has a signature – a modus operandi. If it's somebody I've known or studied, that'll be my way in.'

'It'll probably be classified information,' said the Prime Minister.

I twisted my mouth and looked at her wryly.

'I'm sorry,' she said. 'That was a stupid thing to say. You can have all the secrets you want.'

'I want even the embarrassing and incriminating ones,' I said. 'If I'm refused or fobbed off, I'm going home, even if I have to walk.'

'You won't,' said the Commodore drily. 'We'll hold you for as long as we need to. However, you needn't worry. You'll get all the help you need.'

'I have signed the Official Secrets Act,' I said.

'Anyway, there's no one else we thought we could ask. No one good enough,' said the Prime Minister.

'There are lots of people,' I replied. 'There are people brighter and more ingenious than me. There are half a dozen in China I can think of straight away. There's even one in Honolulu. Any of them would sort it out, if you paid them well enough.'

'There's no one brighter and more ingenious than you,' she said. 'Everyone I've asked says the same thing.'

'Even so,' I replied, 'I want several of us working on this independently. What I mean is, I want several of us working on a diagnosis, then there's far more chance of finding out what's happened. Once we think we've got a diagnosis, we can work on a solution.'

The first thing I did was get all external links switched off, so that further remote sabotage was impossible, and all warheads removed from the missiles. Then I got Lee Yuan over from Singapore. I had only met him onscreen before, and in the flesh he seemed much smaller, with the quiet and slightly faded demeanour of a Latin American ambassador. He brought in somebody else that he had known when he was studying in California, and before long there were six of us, each working on a different quantum computer, meeting up at five each afternoon to discuss our ideas, before returning to our posts and working until exhaustion overtook us late at night. Each one of us was aware of the horrific consequences of having a quixotic or sabotaged missile system, and so it was an annoyance when an official turned up with a sheaf of forms and demanded that they sign the OSA.

We were underground in that vast silo for twenty-one days, becoming pale, bloated and insomniac. I remember feeling like the walking dead for some of the time, but at other times being fired up with intellectual excitement. In retrospect, I wouldn't have missed it.

I do have a very fat log of everything we did, all the paths we tried, all the false leads we followed, all the brick walls and firewalls we came up against, the chicanes and twists and fugues. If it were published, it would be so complex that I doubt there would be anyone who would be able to follow the plot, even if they were to understand all the technical terminology.

We did find out what had happened. Or at least we thought we did, but then we realised that it was impossible to know for sure whether we had diagnosed the problem completely, because it was possible that the villain concerned was cleverer than us and might have anticipated our countermoves by setting up straw men.

In the end, we found a way out because I had a revelation that was so simple it made the others laugh when I came up with it. Just before waking I had dreamed about Maidie Knox Lilita burying rubbish and cleaning windows, then transmogrifying into Eva snipping away at my eyebrows.

A memory of the dream came to me at breakfast whilst Lee Yuan was talking about his latest theory, and suddenly I put up my hand to interrupt him and heard myself saying, 'All we have to do is delete all the software, remove the circuitry and destroy it. We install new circuitry and redesign the control programs from scratch, with new codes.'

There was of course, some protest about the expense and inconvenience of this. People like us have an almost invincible belief in the idea that all you have to do is tinker electronically, and the obvious objection was that there would be a long period during which we might be unable to respond to an attack, but in the end we went ahead, because of the danger of undetectable infection in the hardware. I soon went home, but for several months I had to return frequently to the base to design new codes for the quantum computers. I was well paid for my efforts, and installed a new and very efficient heat pump on the proceeds. I was also given another gong, and had to go to Windsor Castle to be invested.

Two weeks after I returned to Yelland Farm I noticed there was a manila envelope forced into the narrow gap between the front door and its frame. It contained a note printed in Times Old Roman on a plain sheet and read:

What a shame they did that test-firing. I was doing so well. How very frustrated I was when you severed the outside links, just when I had my fingers poised on the button. A few minutes later and I would have had you. Imagine my surprise and disappointment when I lost touch. It was like losing personal friends. I am a Stoic. If I lost to you, then I accept it. But the Stoic soldiers on. There are less spectacular methods for reducing the world to rubble. Wait and see. Who am I? You might think of me as simply another madman. I bet you think I'm a man. Maybe I'm not. What if I'm a woman? What if I'm God? What if I'm The Cloud? What if I'm an alien invader? What if I'm the Antichrist? Does it even matter? Always try the simplest explanation first. Sometimes one has to be cruel to be kind. The kindest thing is to kill this foul disease we call the human race, is it not? This stain on the face of the earth, this cancer, this spirochaete? It won't be long now and you'll all be gone. At this point you should be imagining my laughter, the gleeful laughter of The Greatest Terrorist That Ever Walked the Earth. But if you were with me, you would hear no laughter. Instead you would behold the serene, pacific, contented, priestlike smile of The Last True Saviour of the World.

Forensic examination revealed nothing helpful about this note, but it was clear from the content that somebody knew it was me who had led the team, and where to leave the envelope. There were nothing but wild animals recorded on my CCTV, however, including Roger the auroch, some wild pigs, an inquisitive squirrel and a confident lynx that was probably Tiegen Rosenwyn. There was a period of about ten minutes during which the system had somehow been turned off. The author of the message must have been an ecofascist. For some years there had been a group calling itself the 'Non-Native Exterminationists', or Nonatex, whose charismatic leader had encouraged his followers to kill as many other people as they could, and then kill themselves when they were finally cornered. Of course he was imprisoned and brainwiped, but he left in his wake a large number of disciples who considered that human beings were not a native species of these islands. There were also a few outlawed terrorist groups such as the MF (Misanthropic Front), the AHL (Anti-Human League) and the Philotherians. These last self-identified as various kinds of animals, so naturally they exempted themselves from their extermination programme. Their net traffic was easily monitored, but they would meet in person or exchange written notes, thereby evading the attention of our electronics-obsessed security services. The least worrying group was the SO (the Society of Otherkins), who believed themselves to be mythical creatures such as unicorns and griffins. They confined themselves to such activities as picketing anthropology and philosophy departments at universities, and 'protecting' those sites where such creatures were deemed to live and breed.

There was a curious coda to this episode. The Ministry of Defence was meticulous about keeping precisely timed schedules of events, and one day at the conclusion of a Cobra meeting at Number 10, a defence minister came in with the one pertaining to these occurrences, for me to sign it off. There was one very puzzling thing about it. It should have taken Eva at least half an hour to come and find me at Dozmary Pool, running at her normal pace, but the record revealed that she must have done it in about five minutes.

When I arrived back at the farm and asked her about this, she looked flustered for a few seconds and her face flushed. She turned her back and pretended to be tidying up the clutter of mugs in the sink. Eventually she said, 'They must have got the times wrong. The copter-drone arrived a lot earlier than that. Well, it must have, if you think about it.'

59

Light Over Liskeard

I t was one midnight in late autumn, about fifteen months after the summons to Salisbury Plain. Two tomcats outside were setting up a chorus of competitive disharmony. An owl whooped in the darkness and the feral dogs howled down at the fence of Hippies' Wood. There was an experiment going on to determine how many generations it would take for them to evolve back into wolves, and it had fallen to Theodore Pitt to keep an eye on them. As far as he could see, they were fighting each other, and starving. In his opinion they were more likely to turn into jackals, if they managed to survive at all.

The quantum cryptographer was pinged by the Prime Minister, whose image appeared almost immediately on the wallscreen, looking unkempt and pale. 'Q,' she said, 'there seem to be several attacks going on simultaneously.'

'From the same source?'

'No. It doesn't seem so. There are two separate attacks happening simultaneously to the grid. The other attacks look like ransomware, and the anti-missile system around the London ringroad has been switched off. The banks are reporting that they can't access their own files, there's been another cryptocurrency heist, and the geostationary satellite over York has fired up and is moving west over the Irish Sea. And I've just had a message saying that the electronic passport gates at the airports have all locked. There's chaos at Arrivals at every single one of them. And people who want to go on nat.gov.org are being redirected to a porn site. That's the least of our worries, really.'

Q hesitated, put his hand to his forehead and said, 'So many attacks all at once. It's an avalanche. Is it only us? Or is it other countries too, or the whole world?'

The last he saw of the Prime Minister was of her pursing her mouth and shrugging her shoulders to express her ignorance. She was opening her mouth to speak, when suddenly her image pixelated and disintegrated, speckling the screen momentarily before the lights went down and darkness fell, the kind of absolute darkness that can only occur in a moonless wilderness on a cloudy night. Q had been writing about the different possible relationships between quantum time and a probable multiverse, laying out long lines of equations, thick with logical and mathematical symbology. The generator kicked in. His screen came back to life and he attempted to re-establish contact with the Prime Minister. He achieved nothing more than white noise and specks of static.

He tried the multinet, the polynet and the uninet, failed and sat back in his chair. He went to check the level of fuel in the generator, came back in and sat in front of his keyboard, his fingers flying, trying one possibility after another.

There was a cursory knock and Theodore entered, without waiting for an answer. 'Hey, *hermano*,' he said. 'Powercut and Screencut. You got one too?'

'Everything's gone down.'

'Is this it?'

'It could be. I hope not. I've had the PM up on the screen. There's a crisis. And just when my work was going really well. And I've used up all the milk in the freezer. I've been getting slack. Shall we take the car and go up Caradon Hill?'

'It's a rough track. We'd better go on the tractor. It's warmed up and waiting outside. Get your coat and hat. It's pretty cold. There's a west wind.'

They were halfway across the yard when they heard the whisper of aircraft engines passing above them, looked up and saw the flashing red and green wing-lights of an airliner flying over from the west.

'Isn't that a bit low?' asked Theodore.

'There's another,' said Q, pointing east.

'They're going to hit each other.'

'They can't possibly,' replied Q. 'It only looks like it, from down here. One'll be much higher than the other.'

The aircraft converged. The two men watched, the tension rising in their muscles, shortening their breath. 'You never get mid-air collisions any more,' said Q, and at that very moment there was the blinding light of an explosion, briefly illuminating the countryside as if it were daylight, reflecting off the underside of the clouds. Horns of luminous smoke arced out into the sky, and the two men threw themselves to the ground as a rain of burning detritus fell around them. There was a deep bass roar that boomed and echoed off the hillsides, sending rocks and scree rattling down the slopes, speeding back and forth until it faded away. The incandescent aircraft spiralled downwards together and then separated, falling out of sight to the west. The two men scrambled to their feet and gazed at the dome of light that was visible even above the hill beyond which the two aircraft had fallen.

'I hope to God they haven't fallen on St Neot,' said Theodore.

'Theo, what shall we do?'

'Nothing, *hermano*, nothing. What can we do? What use would it be? There won't be any survivors. There probably won't even be any bodies. I'm guessing that one of those planes was an electric-hydrogen hybrid. Maybe they both were.'

Q said, 'Poor bastards. If only I could pray. I feel sick at heart. I want to say something. But what can be said? Look,' he said, holding out his hands, 'they're shaking. And so are my knees.'

'It was like the fall of Lucifer,' said Theodore, his eyes welling up with tears.

'Air-traffic control must have failed,' said Q. 'There's no other explanation. Let's go up the Tor. We can see as far as Kit Hill.'

Theodore started up the old diesel tractor and they set off. They left the road near the Hurlers and passed through the yard of Langstone Down farm, now long deserted, the thudding of the diesel engine echoing off the crumbling walls. This place, which had once been throbbing with life and activity, was now the ghost of itself. Tiegen Rosenwyn had raised three litters in the same corner of the stable and seen her cubs depart one by one, to make their own lives in their own space.

The track bumped past a disused railway track, a disused quarry, a disused tip and a group of cairns. Down below, in the direction of Pensilva, near Wheal Tor Cottage, were the shafts of an abandoned mine. All was briefly illuminated by the swinging beams of the tractor headlights as Theodore negotiated the dips and rocks of the old track.

A large shadow loomed out of the dark and the headlights caught Sir Bedwyr, fitted out in his harness of a Roman knight, riding erect on his sturdy horse, his painted lance upright in his right hand. Hanging from the stump of his left forearm was his iron-ringed wooden shield with a bronze boss. He shielded his eyes against the glare until Theodore dipped the lights, wound down the window and said, 'Hello, Sir Bedwyr. What are you up to, out at this time of night?'

The elderly knight looked down at him. 'Likewise, what betokeneth it with you? Didst see the celestial flame? I was discomfit passing sore. I wondered greatly.'

'Yes, we saw. We're going up the Tor to see if the time's come.'

Sir Bedwyr's eyes lit up. 'When the King cometh?'

'No. When the grid fails.'

'And then the King returneth?'

'That I wouldn't know, *compadre*. Why don't you ride up and join us?'

Sir Bedwyr patted his horse's neck and said, 'If the hour cometh, fair brother, then I must hie me to the lake.'

'You've already been to the top? What did you see?'

'Naught but darkness – darkness and the spark of stars a-glister. Now fare thee well, fair sirs. God prosper thee and all that's thine.' He kicked his horse into a trot and clattered away down the stony hillside.

'It's just occurred to me,' said Q, 'that if this is it, that old lunatic will be one of the people we'll be having to look after. Like Bess o'Bedlam and the Walker.'

At the top of the Tor, Theo cut the engine and the two friends stood side by side next to the corroded remains of the old television masts, buttoning their coats at the collar to seal out the wind. They gazed out over the towns below. To the north, Upton Cross was in darkness, and to the east, Middle Hill; to the south-west, St Cleer.

'Why are there no cars?' asked Theo. 'Why would a power cut affect the cars?'

'Because they're all controlled by satellites, and the satellites are controlled by the multinet, and the satellites use the multinet to control the cars, and all that depends on the grid. But, mostly, people are frightened to switch to manual drive. Have been for years.'

Theodore raised his hands, palm upwards, and said, 'Looks as though you might have been right.'

Q pulled a wry expression and turned to look at him. 'There might be a harmless explanation. It may be an attack from another country and everyone else is all right. It may be just a false alarm. A glitch. I hope so. But it looks like a simultaneous attack on several fronts. We'll know soon enough.'

'Too many things have been going wrong lately. What's your information?'

Q glanced at him sideways and laughed softly. 'You know I'm not allowed to tell you.'

'Even if it's too late?'

'I'll soon know when it's too late, and then I'll tell you. All I can say is that I'm ready. Apart from having no fresh bread. I've got a lot in the freezer.'

'This might be the end of oranges and avocados,' said Theodore. 'And I doubt I'll ever get back to the Andes. I'll never be back in the Sierra Nevada de Santa Martha again. No more hummingbirds and fried bananas. No more big black cats.'

'It might be the end of Total Surveillance,' said Q. 'The end of anhedonia, the end of the Age of Apathy, the end of *Homo redundans*, the end of the Information Age and the Anthropocene. It'll be the end of cryogenics, gene therapy and microsurgery, the end of digital money.' He laughed softly and added, 'If this is really it, in the next few days there's going to be an outbreak of mass psychosis as people realise they can't get their screens back up, and never will. It'll be like an entire race addicted to opioids having to go cold turkey. All those people living in one metaverse or another . . . how are they going to cope? What will they do without their diet of fantasy? They'll be stabbing at buttons for hours, before it dawns on them that back in the real world there isn't any bread or running water. And another thing: it's also the end of me being anything special, that's for sure.'

Theo echoed, 'Special?'

'All my knowledge. Quantum mechanics. Encryption. The stuff I've earned millions from. What put me into a tiny elite and got me into COBRA meetings. I'm no more or less useful than Fergus now. Or Sir Bedwyr. Or the Prime Minister. If this is what I think it is, then The Cloud has been dissolved or abandoned us, and all my money has ceased to exist. I wish Maranatha was here. I'd love to know what he would have said.'

'He would have said that this was the Rapture, but Jesus hadn't taken him. He would have said that now the Tribulation begins.'

Theodore remembered Maranatha, his body stiff with frost and his eyes open, still watching for Christ. Then he faced his friend in the dark, his eyes glittering. 'Hell of a time for Eva to get pregnant. I'm pleased; I wanted to be a grandfather. But this is one hell of a time. This is the worst possible time. If this is it.'

'What? Eva's pregnant? Did you say she was pregnant?'

'Didn't she tell you?'

'No. It's news to me. How long have you known?'

'She did the test this morning.'

'I haven't seen her today. She got up when I was still asleep and then she messaged me, said she was going for a long hike round Castle Dor, said she was going to camp in a cromlech, near the Quoits. She had an urge to swim in the lake, and cook sausage on a primus and listen to the animals sniffing about in the dark. You know what she's like.' He shrugged and raised his hands as if in a gesture of helplessness. 'She's feral. There's no other way to put it. I just go along with it. Are you sure she's pregnant? She told me she was using something.'

'Oldest trick in the world, *amigo*. I fell for that one. That's how Eva got to be born. You know how some dogs get the call of the wild? Well, Eva got the call of the child. I expect she's gone missing to give herself time to think about it and work out what she's going to tell you. She said that if it's a girl, she wants to call it Maidie.'

'No more obstetrics,' said Q. 'No more Caesareans.' He rubbed his eyes with the back of his hand. 'This is exactly the worst time.'

'I've delivered calves and foals and cubs,' said Theo, 'if that's any use.'

'Just imagine: what if Morgan's pregnant too?' Q paused and asked, 'Did I ever tell you about the rhymester in the black fedora and the midnight cloak?'

'You did, *hermano*.'

'I wonder where he is. I wonder if he got himself ready, the same as us.'

From far off, carried to them on the east wind, came an unmistakable, eerie chorus.

'Wolves,' said Theodore. 'They've been working their way from Dartmoor for months. If they get here, it'll change everything. It'll be a new world. And we'll be exactly like them, living in packs, always on the hunt. What would you call that kind of age?'

'The Lycopithecine.'

The two men stood side by side.

'We're brothers now,' said Q. 'Brothers-in-arms probably. Welcome to the Wild West.'

'We've been brothers for months, brother.'

'Can a father-in-law be a brother?'

The wind changed direction and rose up, bringing with it the briny smell of the ocean, the menace of rain. Side by side they stood in the darkness, their hands in the pockets of their jackets, their hair whipping about their faces, experiencing that heat of good company that rises up in defiance of immense and gathering solitudes, looking out in wonder over that terrible and portentous ocean of nothingness, its inhabitants fated to flail and drown in panic and bewilderment. A tawny owl whooped, and in the distance a small herd of wild donkeys set up a dyschorus of braying.

'Tell me truthfully, brother. Did you do this?' asked Theodore. 'You've been talking about it ever since I've known you. You're completely prepared for it. You're one of the people who could have pulled it off.'

'I can't say I wasn't tempted,' said Q. 'There was one occasion when I almost decided to do it. It was just like being possessed. I've got no great love for the human race. Most people are useless and pointless, with their wide arses and narrow shoulders and hollow chests and darting thumbs, not much more than maggots, leading useless and pointless lives, obsessed by trivia and celebrity and achieving nothing. I don't think the human race is worth saving, if I'm honest, but at the same time I don't bear it any malice. Not enough to do a thing like this. And if you think about it, there's a very good reason why it couldn't have been me.'

'And that is?'

'My children aren't here. They're both in London. I would have done it when they were here, wouldn't I? No, this is the work of some sociopath, or someone playing with fire for fun, or someone who wants revenge on the whole world, or someone who wants to reset our civilisation, or some misanthrope with romantic ideas about giving the world back to the animals, or it might be just another boring old ransomware buccaneer. It might be another country that's put a firewall around its own system, so it can demolish ours. It might be a rickety and unsustainable system collapsing on its own. The PM thinks it's several attacks from different sources. I subcontracted someone to do all my non-governmental work, a man called Lee Huan. It might even be him. Perhaps it was someone like me, except that their kids weren't away. One day it was bound to happen anyway, wasn't it? The beasts were always going to get the world back. They're halfway there already. What we're in for now is a holding operation. I suppose there's a faint possibility that the government had a plan. If they did, I wasn't involved in it. It's possible they took my advice without telling me. I very much doubt it, though.' He scuffed the ground with the toe of his boot and said, 'Until Morgan and Charlie get here, I'll be more worried than I've ever been in my life. It makes my stomach churn. I've had no message yet. There probably won't be any more messages anyway. I don't know what'll happen to the satellites. They'll be starting to tumble already, and then their orbits will degrade. It won't be long before they turn into meteors. It'll be beautiful to see, the night sky lit by streaks of flame, for months on end.'

'Let's hope your kids had the car charged up,' said Theodore. 'I wonder if they'll bring Penelope. I wonder how Eva would cope with that.'

'There'll be worse things to cope with than Penelope,' said Q, 'especially if she brings her lover. According to her, he's a sexboterotomaniac. If he's useless, let's just hope he's interesting. I'm afraid that if they don't turn up and I can't contact them, I'm going to have to go and find them.'

'And I suppose I'll have to go and look for Eva's mother in Scotland. How on earth would I get there and back, though?'

'You won't. You can't. It's too far. You've got to be hard-hearted and hope she can get here on her own.' Q pointed up to the sky. 'Look, the clouds have gone and you can see the Milky Way. All that fabulous extravagance. I've always had a criterion for the coming of this time. I've always thought that one night I would look out south from this spot and see this darkness, particularly over there. That's the only place with much of a population left.'

Theodore followed the direction of Q's pointing finger. All was velvet blackness, a thick garment of silence and absence. 'Ah yes,' he said.

'This is where the story begins again,' said Q. 'Everything has always led to this point.'

There was no light over Liskeard.

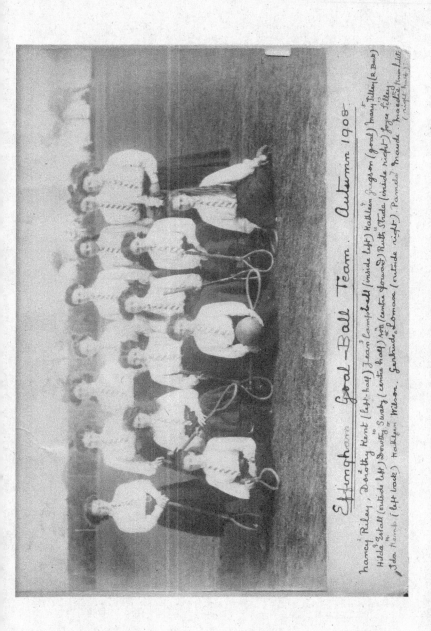

Effingham Goal-Ball Team. Autumn 1908

Nancy Riley, Dorothy Kent (left-half) Jean Campbell (inside left) Kathleen Gregson (goal) Mary Tillen (R.Back) Hilda Zatall (outside left) Dorothy Swaby (centre half) N'ti (centre forward) Ruth Stada (inside right) Joyce Tilley Ida Hamp (left back) Kathleen Wilson. Gertrude Lomman (outside right) Parnell Maude. Maude Tree Little (right back)

penguin.co.uk/vintage